BLANK SLATE: BOOK 2

DAMAGED
GOODS

JENNIFER BARDSLEY

Month9Books

DAMAGED GOODS by Jennifer Bardsley
All rights reserved. Published in the United States of America by Month9Books, LLC.
No part of this book may be used or reproduced in any manner whatsoever without written permission of the publisher, except in the case of brief quotations embodied in critical articles and reviews.

Hardcover ISBN: 978-1-942664-95-6
Paperback ISBN: 978-1-945107-80-1
ePub ISBN: 978-1-945107-48-1
Mobipocket ISBN: 978-1-945107-53-5

Published by Month9Books, Raleigh, NC 27609
Cover design by Beetiful Book Covers
Printed in Canada

Month9Books

To Bryce and Brenna, with all my heart.

BLANK SLATE: BOOK 2

DAMAGED GOODS

Chapter One

All I smell is leather. Seth's arms are around my back, his hands tangled in my long brown hair. My lips devour his, hungry for contact. Beyond us a seagull cries and soars above the waves of Santa Cruz beach.

If I kiss Seth hard enough, my scars fade into oblivion. Barbelo Nemo and his mind control tricks. My childhood spent in seclusion at Tabula Rasa, hidden from the Internet. I slide my fingers underneath Seth's jacket against the stickiness of his shirt. I begin to undo a button.

"Whoa, Blanca." Seth pulls my hands away. "We're not the only people in the parking lot."

I look to the left and right of the rest stop. Strangers are everywhere. "Since when did you care about what other people think?"

"Since I started dating a Vestal."

I pull back and look out at the cliffs. "I'm not a Vestal anymore. You know that." I feel the antique chip-watch on my wrist. Seth's dad, Cal, gave it to me as a present after my platinum cuff was removed. Once a Vestal is de-cuffed, they are expelled from the Brethren.

"So those tourists snapping our picture don't bother you?" Seth motions to a small crowd a few cars over.

I look to where he points, and the flash of thumb-cameras blinds me. Vestals must never have their pictures taken by random people. That privilege belongs to the companies that purchase them and market a Vestal's privacy one advertisement at a time. I reach by instinct, to protect my face from the public. "I'm fine with it," I lie, pulling my hands down. "But we better leave now or we'll be late to the restaurant."

"My dad can wait a few minutes." Seth scoops me into his arms.

"Blanca!" one of the spectators calls. "And Veritas Rex! Is that really you?"

Seth holds up his hand and wiggles his finger-chips. "The one and only!" Then he dips me back for a kiss.

I stiffen like cardboard. "Stop it," I mumble, trying not to squirm. All I can think about is the cameras, my face flashed worldwide, and weirdoes slobbering over my private moment with Seth. "We've got to go or we'll be late."

Seth kisses my nose. "I didn't know you were so punctual."

"Yes." I pull myself out of his grasp. "Cal's waiting." The sooner I put my helmet on and get back on my motorcycle, the better.

"Blanca," a man calls as we ride away. "I love you! I've watched you all year!"

Underneath my jacket, I shiver. The fame that surrounds me is chilling.

A few miles of pavement put me in a better mood. The day is radiant, perfect for riding our bikes from Silicon Valley over to the coast and back. It's our favorite weekend ritual. Seth cruises next to me on his motorcycle with the lion-headed cobra painted on the side, and I zoom along beside him in head-to-toe white.

The speed rushing over me tastes of freedom. When we shift into high gear, I can forget—for a moment—that three months ago I was a captive at the Plemora compound in Nevada. The memory of my mother's face exploding gets sucked away.

But not for long.

●●●●●●●●●

The restaurant Cal picked is smothered in shadows. Candles in glass jars at each table are the only source of a hazy glow. As I walk by, other patrons stare at me.

Their whispers don't surprise me. Seeing a Vestal in public is unheard of, and I'm the most famous Vestal in history, with the exception of Barbelo, my birth father.

But "father" isn't a word I use to describe my tormentor. I don't think of Ms. Lydia as my mother either, not usually. The closest thing I have to a real parent is Cal McNeal, who paid thirty-two million dollars to purchase me from Tabula Rasa, the school Barbelo founded fifty-one years ago with the ostensible purpose of shielding students

3

from the Internet. Barbelo's real objective was to create a network of Vestals in key positions. Spies all over the world who were devoted to him.

Cal waits for us at the table, a smile on his tan face. His hair is long around the ears. I need to remind him to trim it. Cal wears his usual tweed jacket with soft brown patches on the elbows. He stands up when we reach the table and hugs us both. "Enjoy your ride, you two?"

"From the mountains to the beach." Seth slides into the booth. He pulls off his jacket and exposes forearms covered with ink. Seth also has tattoos on his face, the most prominent of which is the lion-headed cobra. That snake was the first thing about Seth I noticed. A year ago, he snuck into Tabula Rasa, took my picture days before graduation, and posted it on *Veritas Rex*. Seth is a viral blogger who does anything to snag a story even if it involves breaking the law.

My own skin is pure white. I've been a consummate rule follower my entire life, with a few notable exceptions. Remaining unmarred by ink or technology tops the Vestal code. It's a hard habit to break.

Cal passes me the bread basket. "So, Blanca, I heard from my friend at Stanford today, and I've got good news."

"Yes?" I take a deep whiff of the yeasty aroma and push the basket over to Seth without taking a piece.

Cal spreads a thick slab of butter on his slice. "I told the dean about your special circumstance. That you've been out of school for a year but graduated top of your class."

Seth chokes on his water. "Top of her class? You mean she was auctioned off to the highest bidder at the Vestal Harvest."

"Exactly," Cal says. "Blanca, you're Tabula Rasa's version of a valedictorian. I told the dean that you had a classical education from a different era and that you were being tutored in science and technology so that you'd catch up in STEM by matriculation."

Eagerness glides over me. Six months ago, when Cal suggested college, I thought he was joking. I dismissed the idea without consideration. But since I returned from Nevada I've made attending college one of my primary goals.

It's not that I don't love being the face of McNeal Solar. Every time I see a billboard featuring me, I get tingles. But representing McNeal Solar and actually understanding how solar power works are two different things. I don't want to be a token bobblehead. I want to be a real engineer who designs power systems and imagines new inventions.

Cal wants to help me achieve that dream. Seth is so committed to *Veritas Rex* that there's no way he'll work for his dad's company. But maybe someday I'll join the McNeal Solar board of directors and people will respect my opinion. It'll be another way I can be Cal's daughter. I'll become his intellectual heir.

"What did the dean say?" My knees shake with excitement until I tense my muscles.

Cal puts down his butter knife. "He knows who you are, of course. He watched the news story unfold along with the rest of the world when you were kidnapped."

"And?" I toy with my napkin.

Cal smiles. "Given the special circumstances, he agreed to let you take a private entrance exam with a panel of professors ten weeks from now."

"Yay!" I lean across the booth and hug Cal tight, my face brushing the scratchy fabric of his blazer.

"Awesome, Dad," says Seth. "How the hell did you pull that off? I've never heard of Stanford admitting a student like that before."

"Well, that's because they've never had a Vestal apply. Plus, it helps that a dorm is named after your mother, Seth. Being a large donor has its perks."

Cal's wife, Sophia, was an anthropology professor at Stanford until she died of the Brain Cancer Epidemic when Seth was seventeen. It was decades before the world realized cell phones caused cancer. Sophia was one of many victims. Before she died, her life work had been researching Barbelo Nemo and the Vestal order he created.

"Mom would have been thrilled to have you as a student," Seth tells me. "She'd probably follow you around and take notes on your well-being."

"To your mother, then!" I lift up my water glass.

"To Mom," Seth answers.

Cal holds up his glass of wine. "To Sophia, a three-way toast."

"Smile, McNeals." A guy with greasy black hair and an ugly smirk holds up finger-chips in our faces. "What a touching moment." The flash pops.

I drop my glass, and water drowns the tablecloth.

"Veritas Rex and his Vestal girlfriend. Gotcha!" Another loser creeps up too. The fact that they're both frantically typing into the air makes me assume they're viral paparazzi, uploading us straight to the net.

"Get out of here," Seth growls, chucking bread at their faces.

A rounded man with a balding head rushes over. "Is there a problem?" He turns to the paparazzi. "I am the maître d' of this establishment, and I will notify the police unless you leave this instant."

Seth pelts them with more bread. The one with greasy hair catches a piece and crams some in his mouth. "Thanks, Rex," he mumbles through crumbs. "See you around."

Several waiters rush over to pick up bread and clear off our wet tablecloth. "I sincerely apologize, Ms. Blanca. I don't know how those Viruses got in." The maître d' uses the derogatory term for viral bloggers, the one that Headmaster Russell taught me at Tabula Rasa.

"It's not your fault. Viruses are hard to shake." I slide my foot underneath the table and brush my leg against Seth's.

"They must have seen your white outfit." The maître d' tugs his collar.

"It's okay." I nod. "I'm used to it." I wave off his offer of a meal on the house, but he insists.

Later, over cheeseburgers, Cal brings up my wardrobe again. "You know, you don't need to wear white anymore, unless you enjoy the attention."

"Of course I don't want the attention!"

"Then why not change things up a bit?" Cal asks. "Shop for new clothes. Try to blend in."

I look at Seth for support, but he nods in agreement with his father. "Fatima wears colors now," Seth adds, "and she's still a Vestal."

I picture my best friend, Fatima. The last time I saw her she wore a silky green dress from her fashion house and looked like a snake that had swallowed a watermelon. Six months pregnant, her figure still says "babe." Tomorrow night is Fatima and Beau's engagement party.

I, on the other hand, am the proverbial girl next door. Brown hair, green eyes, and clear skin. Back at Tabula Rasa, they said I had a face that could sell soap. "I don't want to be a Vestal. I'm a McNeal now. But wearing color seems wrong."

"It's not just the clothes." Seth's finger-chips buzz, and he flicks them off. "The only time you leave the house is with me or Dad."

"That's not true!" I insist. "I went to the soundstage last week to shoot a McNeal Solar ad."

"True," Cal admits. "But it's what a Vestal would do."

"What's that supposed to mean? Don't you want me as the face of McNeal Solar?" My stomach feels bubbly, like I ate too many French fries.

"Of course I do, sweetheart. I love your campaign for my company." Cal reaches out and pats my hand. "We're concerned about you though. We want you to get out there and make new friends."

I turn and glare at Seth. "This is about the other night, isn't it? You're still mad because I wouldn't go to that club with you, so you got your dad to take your side."

Seth stares at me hard. "It's not just the other night. It's all the time. Your world is so tiny that it's unhealthy."

"College is a big step," Cal says, "in terms of academics, forming new friendships, and learning to mingle."

"I meet lots of people! I've made a ton of friends online. Every time I write a new post for *The Lighthouse*, I get thousands of comments."

Seth looks at me with piercing brown eyes. "Blanca, you're new at this, but online friends are easier than people you meet face-to-face. It's a different type of interaction."

At that moment, a flash makes me jump. But it's not a Virus snatching my picture this time. It's a family in the corner taking a photograph of their kid. "Face-to-face can be scary," I say.

"Sometimes," Cal nods, "but not normally."

"Normal for me is different."

"Exactly our point," says Seth.

Cal leans forward in his seat. "We think it would be helpful if you could chat with someone to help you process all you've been through."

"You mean like a psychiatrist? You think I'm crazy?" I twist my chip-watch around and around my wrist where the cuff used to be.

Seth scoots closer and lowers his voice. "We don't think you're crazy. But some really shitty things have happened to you."

"You lost your mother," says Cal.

"Ms. Lydia wasn't my mother! I mean, she gave birth to me. That's it. What do I care what happened to her?"

"You must feel something," Cal says.

"I feel nothing."

"Then why are you talking so loud?" Seth asks.

I take a quick glance of the room and notice stares.

Our waiter rushes over. "Are you ready for dessert now?" he asks.

"Yes," Cal answers. "Please bring the menu."

"No, thank you." I squeeze my fists together, stress coursing through my body like lightening.

When the waiter leaves, Seth touches my elbow. "We've made an appointment for you."

"What?"

"With Dr. Meredith," Cal says. "A therapist."

"You want me to tell my private secrets to a total stranger?" I speak with a steadied calm while a storm builds inside me.

"She's not a stranger, Blanca. Seth and I started seeing Dr. Meredith when you were kidnapped."

My heartbeat is ragged. "You told her about me? You shared my private life with an outsider?"

"Of course not." Seth's dark hair sticks up in wild tufts on his head. "Dad and I had our own stuff to work out. You know I spent five years mistakenly thinking Dad cheated on my mom."

Cal flinches. "And you have your issues too, Blanca."

I swallow hard. I reach over and stroke my white leather jacket. Maybe I should get up and go. Ride back to McNeal Manor on my motorcycle. But that would mean going someplace by myself. The last time I rode off into the night, my good friend Ethan was killed and Ms. Lydia kidnapped me.

"Sometimes being an adult means doing things you don't want to do," says Cal.

"I'll drive you to your appointment next week, if that helps," Seth offers.

"No way," I say. "I don't need that type of care."

I can do this if I try hard enough.

I stand up and pick up my jacket. "Thank you for dinner," I snarl.

But as I turn to go, I walk smack into dark suits. The man is six feet three, every inch of him as sharp as his buzz-cut hair. The woman is my height, about five feet five, with silver stud earrings.

"Blanca Nemo?" The woman has a steady voice. Both of them hold up their palms to flash electronic badges. "Agents Plunkett and Marlow with the FBI. We need to bring you in for questioning."

"What the hell?" Seth leaps to his feet.

"Blanca?" Cal springs up. "What's this about?"

"I don't know." I shoot him a frightened look the agents can't see.

"Don't say anything without a lawyer. Okay, sweetheart?" Cal types at his chip-watch. "Hold tight until Nancy gets there."

"Come on, Ms. Nemo." The male agent grabs my arm. "Our car is outside."

"Ouch! Not so tight!"

"Her name's not Nemo," Seth shouts. "It's Blanca McNeal." He and Cal hurry after us into the night where a black sedan is waiting.

I turn to look at the McNeals one more time. Seth towers over Cal whose face is twisted with worry.

I smile wanly as the agents shove me into the backseat of the car. The irony kills. I'm going someplace without them after all.

Chapter Two

I force a full breath into my lungs. After my imprisonment in Nevada, small spaces grate on my nerves. The two large mirrors make the room seem bigger. But I've read enough of Cal's detective novels to assume these are actually one-way windows.

I feel like a butterfly, pinned down for display.

Agent Marlow sits in front of me, his gigantic frame overwhelming a plastic chair. His biceps look like they could crack walnuts. Agent Plunkett, by contrast, is petite. She has ladybugs tattooed on her left hand that walk across her knuckles. Her boyish hairstyle looks youthful, but she has wrinkles around her eyes.

"Let the record show," Agent Plunkett says as she clicks her finger-chips to record the interrogation, "that the subject refused to speak until her lawyer was present."

"You know," says Agent Marlow in a kind tone. "You're not in any trouble. You can answer a few of our questions. There's no need for a lawyer."

I look down at my wrist and don't respond. The first thing they did when they brought me into the brick FBI building was take away my chip-watch for "safekeeping."

"We won't access your accounts," said the agent who sealed off my watch in a special box. "This is standard protocol for being escorted into a federal building. Most people hauled in get the lead-lined mitts. We can't let their finger-chips make trouble."

Naked skin taunts me. First my cuff and now my watch.

"I know all about you," says Agent Plunkett. "Every last detail."

I look straight at her. I know all about Margie Plunkett too. I studied her in the class I took during junior year called Vestal Enemies. She's aged significantly compared to her picture in my textbook.

Agent Plunkett leans into the table. "I've monitored the Vestals for seventeen years. You were in diapers when I first started investigating Barbelo Nemo."

I cross my ankles and fold my hands. I straighten my spine like I'm being pulled from above. I smooth my expression so all evidence of emotion evaporates. If there's one lesson Ms. Corina taught me, it's that 60 percent of communication is nonverbal. No way am I going to let my body speak while I keep my lips closed.

Agent Plunkett raps her tattooed fingers on the table and stares back at me. "I have a lot of questions, Blanca. It's time to prove whose side you're actually on."

I answer by not moving one muscle. I could sit like this forever. Headmaster Russell, Ms. Corina, and the other teachers at Tabula Rasa would be proud. Barbelo too, of course, if he was still alive.

The seconds tick away like hours. After an eon, I hear a rustle at the door. I turn to see the McNeal family lawyer, Nancy Robinson, enter in a flurry of worsted wool. Her hair is up in an elaborate French twist, and her face gleams with determination.

"I'm finally here." Nancy blusters into the room. "Traffic was awful." She reaches out her hand to shake with the agents. "Nancy Robinson. Pleased to meet you. Now let's get this travesty over with." She sits down in the chair next to me and clicks on her finger-chips. "We'll record this for our own evidence, of course, even though Blanca is here completely voluntarily."

"Yes, well. Let's get started." Agent Plunkett eyes me closely. "We are here to interview Blanca Nemo about the inner workings of the Vestal order."

"My name's not Nemo."

"Have you been adopted by Mr. Calum McNeal?" asks Agent Marlow. "I was unaware of this."

Nancy nods at me, so I answer. "No," I say. "Not officially."

If we made it official—supposing Cal wanted that—it would be tricky. Legally, Seth would become my brother. Hypothetical incest is more than I could handle at the moment.

"Blanca has the right to use any name she chooses," Nancy says. "Please honor it."

Agent Marlow continues. "Are Barbelo Nemo and Lydia Xavier

your birth parents?"

"Lydia Xavier?" I ask, before Nancy can stop me. "Where did you hear that name?" I'm angry with myself as soon as the words leave my mouth. I know better than to reveal unnecessary information. But I've never heard Ms. Lydia's last name before.

"We don't reveal our sources," snaps Agent Plunkett. "Answer the question."

"No, I think not," interjects Nancy. "There's no need for Blanca to cooperate if you're going to be rude. She's not under arrest. And her question is a good one. We've been trying for months to discover Lydia's last name. I need it for probate court. We're working under the assumption that Blanca is Lydia's legal heir."

Agent Marlow's lips twitch. "I'm sorry, but we can't expose our sources. This is an ongoing investigation into the alleged criminal activity of the Vestal order. We thought, given the posts Blanca's made on *The Lighthouse*, that she would be as committed as we were to achieving justice for everyone who was wronged."

"I told you, Marlow," Agent Plunkett says in her harsh, raspy voice, "she'd be as tight-lipped as the rest of them. Never trust a lunatic in white."

"I'm not a lunatic!"

"That was uncalled for." Nancy's voice is shrill.

"Prove it." Agent Plunkett holds out her hand and flashes me a picture. "Do you recognize this person?" She points to a tall Asian man close to Seth's age—twenty-three. He's naked from the waist up and kicks a punching bag. Sweat drips off chiseled muscles.

Do I recognize him? Of course I do. That's my friend Keung. He's looks older than I remember and more handsome than ever.

"No," I say. "I don't know who that is."

Agent Plunkett stares at me sharply. Then she flashes more pictures across her palm. "This person? Or this one?"

I shake my head but keep the rest of my body perfectly still. I see no benefit in telling them anything.

"What about him?" Agent Marlow shows me another picture.

"Sorry. No idea."

"Damn it, Nemo!" Agent Plunkett slams her hand on the table. "I know you're lying."

Despite my training, I startle. I jerk back in my chair so hard that the plastic rattles on the linoleum. Then I take a deep breath and focus on my heartbeat.

Nancy's gaze turns steely. "That was uncalled for. You have no reason whatsoever to question her integrity. Let me remind you that Blanca spent her childhood in seclusion and has a recent history of being abducted, attacked, and almost murdered."

"All the more reason for her to come forth with information rather than obstructing justice," says Agent Plunkett.

"No," Nancy replies. "All the more reason for Blanca to be cautious. If she doesn't tell you something for fear of her safety, that's not obstructing justice. What will you do, put her in witness protection? She's been in hiding her whole life."

"Whoa." Agent Marlow lifts up his hands to stop the verbal assault. "Nobody is accusing Blanca of obstructing justice. Let's take a moment to calm down and get back on track."

"Ask me something else." My words are soft and quick. "Ask me a different question."

Nancy raises her tattooed eyebrows at me. Then she turns back to Agents Plunkett and Marlow. "You heard the girl. Try asking Blanca something in a different way."

"In a different way?" Agent Marlow repeats. "Okay, Blanca. How about this, what can you tell us about the Guardians?"

This, I can do. I know exactly what to say because the textbook answer is engrained in my brain. "Founded in 2028," I begin, "the Guardian order was created in Beijing as a rival to the Vestals. Tabula Rasa was sixteen years old at that point and celebrating its first Harvest of graduates."

"Where your mother was purchased by Barbelo Nemo, your father," Agent Plunkett interjects.

"I don't consider either of those people to be my parents." I sit up a little straighter and don't say another word.

For a full minute, there is only silence, all four of us staring at each other in a quiet contest of wills.

"Please, Blanca," Agent Marlow finally says, his deep voice rumbling. "Please continue. Agent Plunkett won't interrupt again." He glares at her.

Nancy nods at me, so I move on to the next memorized line. "Tabula Rasa was gaining international fame as the last bastion of privacy. As the world became aware that lack of a virtual footprint was a commodity, a Chinese businesswoman named Wu Park rushed to copy our success. In the years that followed, the Vestal system Barbelo Nemo established at Tabula Rasa became so popular that it was copied in other countries as well. The Keiner school in Berlin for example and the Nadie school in Mexico. As parents began to realize there was financial value in their children's privacy, more and more families begged for placement."

"You said 'ours,'" says Agent Plunkett.

"What?"

"You said '*our* success.'" She places her hands on the table, and the ladybug tattoos make me squirm.

"No, I didn't."

Or did I? I can't remember for sure.

"Ms. Nemo," Agent Plunkett is expressionless, "do you still consider yourself to be a Vestal?"

"I'm no longer a Vestal, and my name isn't Nemo. It's McNeal. I told you."

"We want to believe you," says Agent Marlow. "But we can't."

"It's hard to trust a liar." Agent Plunkett sneers.

"A liar?" Nancy exclaims. "Blanca, do not under any circumstance say another word. You are done helping these people without a court order."

"That can be easy to arrange," Agent Marlow says simply.

Agent Plunkett flicks her fingers and pulls up one more picture. It's grainy and hard to decipher, like the photograph was shot in the mist.

But my white pants are easy to spot. I'm standing on tiptoes leaning up to kiss Seth. We snuggle in front of the doorway of his apartment building.

"So what? Lots of people photograph me every day."

Agent Plunkett smiles like a panther about to eat fresh meat. "Look in the corner."

So I do. And what I see stuns me.

Keung is in the picture too. Watching us.

"Blanca," Nancy says, "I highly advise you to not answer any more questions."

I nod my head in agreement and rub my blank wrist.

If there's one thing that Keung inspires, it's silence.

●●●●●●●●●●

Goose bumps race down my back as my skin touches the evening air. The night is moonless, the stars hidden by the city's ugly glow. My leather jacket hugs me but offers no protection from the chill. When I see Cal and Seth waiting for me outside, I sprint toward them.

Seth reaches me first and swings me around in his arms. Cal says a quick good-bye to Nancy, and then leads us to the limo. Our driver, Alan, waits at the front of the parking lot and holds the back door open.

"What happened to my bike?" I ask.

"Don't worry," says Cal. "It's home in one piece."

I sink back into the middle seat of the limo and squeeze my eyes shut. I don't open them again until we're driving to the manor at top speed. Cal and Seth each take one of my hands.

"It's okay now." Cal gives my hand a gentle squeeze; then he releases it.

"What did they want?" Seth pulls me in close so that my head rests against his shoulder.

"They asked me about the Guardians."

"The Chinese Vestals?" Seth asks.

"They're not Vestals." I jerk my head away and shift positions. "Guardians are entirely different."

"How are they different? Lock up your kids in a cyber-safe school for eighteen years and then auction them off to the highest bidder." Seth scratches the back of his neck. "It sounds exactly the same to me."

The irritation that crawls up my throat surprises me. I bite back bile. "It's not the same. Vestals harvest ten people a year—all carefully screened for image, IQ, and likeability. The Guardians churn out hundreds. They have so many graduates of questionable quality that they can't land big contracts. A few lucky ones get placed as spokespeople for multimillion dollar firms, but the rest are assigned to miniscule government positions. It's like a twisted version of the ancient Confucian exam."

"The Con-fu-fu what?" asks Seth.

I turn to look at him. "You don't know who Confucius is?"

"Should I?"

"He was an ancient Chinese philosopher," says Cal. "Starting in the Han dynasty, men who were interested in becoming government bureaucrats either had to know somebody who could offer a recommendation or pass the imperial examinations, which were based on Confucian classics."

I nod my head in agreement. "It's similar to what the Guardians do now. Graduate the program and get a job. Except with the Guardians, the government can dispose of them at will. Since their families have forsaken them, they have no recourse except to do what their bosses say. It's nothing like the Vestals."

"That's exactly like the Vestals," Seth says.

"Vestals don't work for the government!" Sometimes it feels like Seth doesn't listen to me.

"So the FBI is interested in the Guardians?" asks Cal.

"Yes," I say. "Now you know everything."

Well, almost everything. I don't tell them about Keung.

Or the likely reason he's following me.

●●●●◉●●●●

Tonight in the safety of my room, I can't make my mind go quiet. I wash my face and brush my teeth. I change into soft white pajamas. Then I lie facedown on the velvet coverlet of my bed and press my face into the pillow. Agent Plunkett, the viral paparazzi, Cal and Seth betraying me to their therapist—I can't turn any of it off.

And that picture of Keung watching Seth and me kiss. Is that the only time Keung has followed us?

I push onto my elbows and stretch up into Cobra. Yoga always helps me relax. Then I decide to go for it and have a real workout. I cross the room to my window which looks out into an internal courtyard of McNeal Manor. Last year when I was having some problems and locked myself in my room for an entire month, Cal had workers install a ladder outside my window. Later on, when Ms. Lydia and Cal started dating, she had shutters put up on the outside of the first-story windows. So now I can climb down into the garden and get some exercise whenever I want without anyone seeing me.

The metal rungs of the ladder burn icy cold on my bare feet. The sandstone pavers feel scratchy, but the courtyard is bathed in starlight. In the corner is a redwood box where I keep my yoga mat. I roll it out in the center of the courtyard and step onto rubber.

Instead of Salute to the Sun, I salute the dark. When I slide into Downward Dog, the blood rushes to my head.

I focus on Keung. The first time I saw Keung I was fifteen, a few days away from my sixteenth birthday. Not that it mattered. Birthdays were never celebrated at Tabula Rasa. We didn't know parties existed.

Keung was eighteen years old, tall and lean. He was in the gymnasium jumping rope. His Guardian friends were kicking the air and practicing martial arts.

Fatima was with me. As soon as the Beijing boys saw her, they did a double take. She filled out her gym shirt in a way that made everyone stare.

"Come on," I told her. "We'll be late for calisthenics." I fiddled with the end of my braid and turned away.

But Fatima was always bolder than me. "Hi, guys!" She stood up on tiptoes and waved, showing off her impressive cleavage. "Welcome to Tabula Rasa."

"Fatima," Ms. Lara, the PE teacher, bellowed. "You come here this second! You know you're not supposed to talk to them."

Fatima giggled, and we rushed to join our classmates. When I turned back to look, the Guardians were watching.

Chapter Three

· · · · · · · · · · ● · ● · · · · · · · · ·

My best friend's apartment rings with rage. The plush white carpet can't absorb the noise. Fatima's Vestal-mom is six feet tall and wears razor-sharp stilettos. Pilar's long black hair swishes down her back in a raven river. Through the skintight satin of her white dress, I see nipples. But most of all, I hear her voice, because Pilar shouts at the top of her lungs. Ever since I stepped foot in Fatima's home, my ears have bled.

"A Virus?" Pilar shrieks at Fatima. "You want to invite a Virus into our home?"

"Not a Virus, Mami. Seth McNeal." Fatima cuts me a glance and raises her shoulders as if to apologize for her mother's histrionics.

"But what if he takes our picture? What if he uploads us straight

24

to the Net?" Pilar slices perfectly manicured fingers through the air.

"He's not going to do that, Mami. Besides, how could he? Our whole apartment is lined with lead. We live in a cloister, remember? Seth's finger-chips won't work."

"Seth would never betray you," I add. "He's not like that."

Pilar sits down on the bench of her grand piano and crosses her impossibly long legs. She's not Fatima's birth mom. They've only been a Vestal family for a year, after their fashion house purchased Fatima's contract at the Tabula Rasa Harvest. But they are exceptionally close. "Don't be ridiculous," Pilar says. "Veritas Rex was the one who took your picture before you were Harvested, Blanca. He stole your privacy and then broadcast it to the world!"

"Yes." A chill passes over me as I remember the humiliation. "But that was a long time ago. Seth has changed."

"He helped rescue me. Remember, Mami? Mr. McNeal arranged it, but Seth was the one who brought me to the safe house."

"Yes, *mijiha*." Pilar reaches out and places her hand on Fatima's belly. "And I'll be forever grateful. Who knows what would have happened to my little grandbaby? All the more reason to be careful. Do you want your child to be exposed to the world before it's been born?"

"Seth would never!" I feel my face go hot.

Pilar shakes her head. "Blanca, I worry. This isn't the life your mother wanted for you at all. I feel like I'm failing Ms. Lydia by not speaking up or offering you more guidance."

"Ms. Lydia wasn't my mother."

"Blanca," Fatima says softly.

"She wasn't." I look straight at Pilar. "She never loved me the way you love Fatima."

"You don't know that." Pilar's full lips pout. "Ms. Lydia was a good woman. The best Vestal ever. It would kill her to know you chose a Virus over your Brethren."

I shake my head vigorously. "No. You've got it all wrong. The Brethren would have killed me if it weren't for a Virus."

"So can Seth come?" Fatima pleads.

Pilar doesn't answer. She turns toward the piano and plays Chopin. A cacophony of notes swirls around us, sucking the heat out of the conversation.

"Mami!" Fatima toddles over to the piano on dangerously high heels.

Pilar attacks the keys harder, not budging an inch as Fatima struggles to sit next to her on the bench. She wraps her arms around her mother and presses her nose against Pilar's cheek.

"Please?" Fatima pleads. "Beau's brothers are okay with Seth coming."

I turn away and look across the suite. Images of Beau's wasted frame in our Plemora prison fill my memory. I squeeze my eyes tight and try to make Nevada go away. But the picture of Beau striking Barbelo's neck with a garden hoe is stuck forever in my psyche.

"Fatima is like a sister to me." I speak loudly so I can be heard over the music. "She's my best friend. But I'm done arguing." I walk over to the piano and slam my fist on the keys, making a dreadful noise. "The McNeals are my family now, and I won't go anywhere they aren't wanted. If it weren't for Seth, Beau would be dead. If you care at all about the father of your grandchild, you will see that."

Pilar grabs my wrist, her fingernails digging sharp into the skin. "Don't you dare question my devotion to my family."

"Then trust me." I look deep into Pilar's hazel eyes. "Seth is not your enemy."

Pilar lets go of my wrist and brushes nonexistent wrinkles off her lap. She takes a deep breath that pushes her chest up against the boning of her bodice. Finally, she looks at Fatima and smiles. Brilliant white teeth take up her whole face. Even in her forties, Pilar is every inch the supermodel. "How about a compromise? Seth can come, but he needs to wear lead-lined gloves over his finger-chips."

"But this place is cloistered," I protest.

"And he's a Virus," Pilar answers. "An expert hacker."

"Where would you get lead-lined gloves?" Fatima asks. "I've never heard of those."

"Your father has some." Pilar points back to the bedrooms. "Alberto has a pair that lock."

Fatima shifts her weight to one foot. "What do you think, Blanca? Will that be okay?"

"I guess," I answer.

Hoping it's the truth.

●●●●●●●●●

27

"Absolutely not!" Seth exclaims when I hold up the gloves. We're in the back seat of the limo parked in the garage underneath Fatima's building. If my powers of persuasion fail me, we'll be late for the engagement party.

"It's only for tonight. A few hours." I bite my lip.

"Lead-lined gloves?" Seth stares at my offering. "Locked to my wrist?" He glowers at his father. "Why doesn't Dad need to wear them? He's not a Vestal."

Cal wiggles his fingers. "No finger-chips. Remember? They were surgically removed before Blanca moved to the manor."

"Which I've been begging you to do too," I say to Seth. "If you used a chip-watch, this wouldn't be necessary."

"I'm not wearing an antique." Seth uncrosses his legs and sprawls in the backseat.

I tilt my knees toward Seth and lock our feet together. "This is just for one night."

"But I thought they lived in a cloister," Seth says. "My finger-chips won't work up there anyway."

"They're taking no chances," I say. "You know how Vestals are."

"Exactly. So why would I want to hang out with them?"

"I can't believe you said that!" I pull away.

Seth reaches for my hands. "Blanca, that came out wrong. Of course I want to be with you and your friends, but I don't want to make nice with people who hate me." He picks the gloves up and waves them around. "To people who think I'm the enemy."

"Fine," I say. "Be that way."

"Seth," Cal tries, "it's a few hours."

"Don't bother, Cal. I don't want him to come anyway." I climb over Seth's lap out of the car as fast as I can. Alan doesn't have the chance to open the door for me.

"Blanca!" Seth calls. "Come back."

I walk resolutely toward the elevator and pound the button. I feel the white fabric of my full skirt swish behind me. The door slides open right when Cal approaches.

"Going up?" He smiles half-heartedly.

As soon as the doors close behind us, I sob.

Fatima and Beau's companies have gone all out. There's a child-sized four-wheel drive truck exactly like Beau drives in his latest commercial set up in the entry way of the apartment. It's loaded down with designer clothes from Fatima's fashion house, with outfits in every size from infant to teen.

"Smile," a photographer says as soon as we step out of the elevator. I blot my eyes to hide the tears.

"Oh," I say. "Hi." The photographer is the director of my McNeal Solar commercials. Jeremy was one of the first Vestal-rejects I met in the real world. Unlike most Rejects, Jeremy left Tabula Rasa of his own accord a few months before his senior year, despite the fact he had a good chance of being Harvested.

"How's it going, Blanca?" Jeremy sports three nose rings and unidentifiable neck tattoos. His curly brown hair is neatly combed and matches his brown shirt.

"Fine." I smooth my hairstyle. "Are you on photographer duty tonight?"

"Yeah. Me and some others."

Vestal photo shoots are always packed with Rejects. Ms. Lydia thought they were the best choice because they were familiar with Tabula Rasa and understood the Vestal mindset—although they weren't good enough to be part of the Brethren.

"Would you mind posing for a picture?" Jeremy holds up his camera. "Beau and Fatima's companies are using this for their next ad campaigns."

Cal wrinkles his forehead and steps away. But I grab his arm and pull him back into the frame. "*Now* who's afraid of having their picture taken?" I tease.

"Thanks," says Jeremy. He takes a few shots. "See you around."

I wave a quick good-bye and then lead Cal through the lobby to an enormous table piled with gifts.

"I thought this was an engagement party," Cal whispers. He puts the present I picked out, a cut crystal vase wrapped in ivory paper, into a sea of stuffed animals and booties.

"I guess people are bringing baby gifts too," I say. "I didn't realize. This is all new for us."

It's new because Vestals don't normally have babies. Back at Tabula Rasa, all girls—including me—were sterilized at age fourteen. It was one of Barbelo's sicko decrees. After Ms. Lydia became pregnant with me, Barbelo decided no Vestal should become a mother ever again. It was easier for him to control childless minions. Until last year, I didn't understand how despicable this was. I was so committed to being a Vestal that I willingly gave up everything, including my future children. Now, I try not to think of it. Luckily for Fatima, her operation didn't work.

Cal and I are about to head into the party when the elevator doors open again. My heart leaps when Seth walks in with his hands in the lead gloves.

"Smile!" Jeremy says, and then cowers as Seth lunges at him.

"Don't you dare," Seth growls. Then he stuffs his hands in his pockets. "I suppose you want the key to these mitts, Blanca."

"Not necessary." I wink. "I trust you."

"Well I don't." Cal grins and holds out his hand. "Why don't you give it to me?"

"Funny, old man." Seth pulls a hand out of his pocket and slams the key down in Cal's palm so hard his dad winces. "I knew you always wanted to lock me up."

"Maybe once or twice." Cal winks. "Are you two ready?"

Seth holds out his elbow to me. "Sure."

I link my arms with both of them and get ready to party.

●●●●●●●●●

Fatima's apartment has been transformed into a dazzling club. Thousands of white lights twinkle across the ceiling and outline every window. It's like stepping into a glowing cage of brilliance. Most of the furniture is gone, and white-clad Vestals dance on a temporary parquet floor. Electronic house music beats rhythmically, and my toes tap with anticipation.

Unfortunately, the first people we encounter are my old boyfriend, Trevor, and his girlfriend, Sarah.

I know she's Sarah. Cal and Seth know she's Sarah—because I've told them—but the rest of the world thinks Sarah is actually Trevor's mom and that her name is Lilith.

The tragedy is that the real Lilith is my aunt, my only remaining blood relation. But many years ago, Barbelo made Lilith disappear and replaced her with Sarah. The real Lilith could be buried in a pit somewhere. That's probably part of what twisted Ms. Lydia—never knowing what happened to her sister.

Sarah's been going gray since ninth grade. Now she's making women all across the world believe that she's Lilith and that the wrinkle cream she advertises will make them look as young as her. The public is completely duped since as a Vestal, Sarah doesn't have any virtual fingerprint to betray her. The only pictures of Sarah in existence make her look exactly like Lilith but with silky smooth skin. Nobody knows that Sarah and Trevor swap spit whenever the cameras turn away, even though supposedly they are mother and son.

Trevor and Sarah's Vestal-cest wouldn't have mattered to me except last year Ms. Lydia made Trevor be my boyfriend. He's the only person I've ever met with skin as nice as mine. No wonder Ms. Lydia paired us together. One perfect date after another was caught on film for the whole world to see. The problem was, Trevor was a sloppy kisser, and every time I was with him I thought of Seth.

"Hi, Blanca." Sarah wears a white pantsuit with padded shoulders that makes her look a million years old. "I didn't know *you* would be invited."

"Why wouldn't she be invited?" Seth's voice booms over the music. "She's Fatima's best friend."

Sarah eyes Seth across the narrow rim of her champagne glass. "I don't talk to Viruses."

"Uh, I do." Trevor gives Seth a curt nod. "How's it going?"

Seth eyes Trevor up and down. This is the first time they've met in person, although Seth has seen Trevor hundreds of times on billboards sticking his tongue in my mouth.

"Fine." Seth grunts.

"Er … uh … Lilith," Cal says to Sarah, "it's so nice to see you and your son Trevor again. Is your husband Richard here?"

Sarah nods across the dance floor where her token husband talks with Alberto, Fatima's Vestal-dad, a tall man with golden brown skin and silvery gray hair.

"Wonderful," Cal says. "I'll go and say hello."

As soon as Cal leaves, Trevor says, "Look, Blanca. I want to say again how sorry I am we used you as cover for our Vestal-cest."

"That's okay," I say. "I'm over it."

"It sucks that your relationship can't be public," Seth offers.

At this, Sarah turns around. "You won't say anything, will you?"

"Of course not," I blurt. "Seth has known for months and hasn't revealed your secret. You should be thanking him instead of being rude."

Sarah looks down into her glass. "Whatever."

"It's been difficult," Trevor says. "People would freak out if they thought I was kissing my mom." He puts his arm around Sarah's shoulder. "Isn't that so, Mommy?"

"Ugh!" Sarah shrugs his arm off. "I told you to stop calling me that."

Seth smirks.

"Do you know what happened to the real Lilith?" I ask Sarah. "My aunt? Ms. Lydia's sister?"

"Sorry." Sarah shakes her head. "I have no idea."

"Speaking of family, if your last name is McNeal now, doesn't that make you two brother and sister?" Trevor points his finger at me and Seth.

I grin mischievously. "Don't think about it too hard." Then I reach up on my toes and kiss Seth full on the mouth.

"Blanca!" I hear somebody squeal. "You're here!"

I look over and see Fatima run over with quick, tiny steps. Her red dress is so tight she can barely move her legs. Beau is behind her wearing a white suit. Like the rest of the Vestals, they wear gold cuffs on their left wrists. Ms. Lydia and I were the only Vestals I know who wore platinum. We were top picks.

Fatima gives me two quick air kisses so we don't mess up our makeup. Then Beau brings me in for a bear hug. Without each other's help, we never would have escaped from Nevada alive.

"Congratulations on your engagement," Seth says.

"Hey, man. We're glad you could come." Beau reaches out to shake Seth's hand.

Seth pulls his hands out of his pockets to show his lead-lined gloves, and then stuffs them away again.

"Dude!" Beau exclaims. "Who made you wear those? That blows."

Seth glances at me sideways.

"It wasn't my fault!" I look across the room to Pilar. She wears a skintight strapless dress and sky-high heels that make her tower over Cal, who is beside her. Pilar flips her hair back, exposing a naked shoulder.

Is it my imagination or are they both leaning together? Cal laughs at something Pilar says. Then he whispers in her ear. At that exact moment, Jeremy walks up to them and holds out his camera. Pilar jumps away like Cal is poison.

"So did you hear?" Fatima asks.

"What?" I jerk my head back toward our conversation.

Fatima pulls me a few steps away from Seth and lowers her voice. I can barely understand her over the loud music. "The Harvest might not happen. With Headmaster Russell in prison, Ms. Corina doesn't know what she's doing."

"Headmaster Corina," I correct, although I can't bring myself to think of her like that. "And maybe it's all for the best. Maybe this class of Tabula Rasa graduates will get a say about their lives instead of being auctioned off to the highest bidder."

Fatima wrinkles her perfectly arched eyebrows at me. "How can you say that?" She waves her hands around at the apartment packed with Vestals in white. "Without new blood, this whole thing falls apart."

"You sound like a vampire."

Fatima crosses her arms across her chest. "You know what I mean."

"Yes, I do. But that doesn't mean it's okay."

"None of this is okay," says Beau, causing Fatima and me to turn around.

"Honey," says Fatima.

"I thought this was supposed to be *our* party," Beau says. "Our private celebration."

"It is!" Fatima argues.

"Then why all these photographers?" Beau asks. "Jeremy and the rest of the Rejects?"

"What do you mean? There're only three or four." Fatima looks over to where Trevor poses with Alberto and Pilar on the dance floor. "This is good PR for everyone."

"But I don't want more PR!" Beau's face is blotchy.

Seth takes a step closer to me, his hands still stuffed in his pockets.

"After Nevada I thought we would leave this behind." Beau turns to look at me. "Like Blanca did."

"You know we couldn't do that." Fatima glances sideways to make sure nobody outside our little group can hear. "How would we get jobs? What would we do? How could we take care of our baby by ourselves?"

"We'd figure it out," Beau insists.

"I'd help you," I rush to say. "You could come live at the manor with Cal and me. I'm sure he'd say yes." I look at Seth, who shrugs.

"But this is so much easier," Fatima protests. "It's only some pictures. We're set for life."

"At the expense of what?" Beau places his hand on Fatima's belly. "Our family?"

"The happy couple!" A photographer invades our circle. "Let's get a picture with you two and Blanca." The Reject does a double take when he sees Seth. "And Veritas Rex. What an opportunity!"

"Forget about it," Seth grumbles. "I'm going to find my dad."

I pose for the photograph and rush to follow him.

I spot the McNeals on the far side of the room talking to Trevor's father, Richard, and two tall burly guys who must be Beau's brothers, Ryan and Zach. I recognize them from their truck commercials but have never officially met. They were a lot older than me when we were at Tabula Rasa together.

I swerve around party guests and make my way through the crowd. Some of the Vestals say hello, but most eye me with suspicion. I reach Seth when the lights flicker and the whole room goes quiet. I turn to see Agents Plunkett and Marlow at the entrance to the room, holding up FBI badges.

"Ladies and gentlemen," Agent Marlow's deep voice blasts, "Headmaster Russell has escaped from the federal penitentiary. We hope someone here knows his whereabouts."

The crowd parts as Alberto stalks across the room. "What is

the meaning of this? You're interrupting my daughter's engagement party." Alberto walks straight up to the agents and inspects their badges.

"I'm sorry, sir," says Agent Plunkett. "Your cooperation will be noted. Your companies requested you answer our questions."

In the madness that follows, I don't feel a hand enter my space. I don't spot the unknown messenger who stuffs a torn page from the Vestal Code of Ethics into the side pocket of my dress.

It's only later, back at home, that I find the mysterious note in my bedroom. I step out of my white dress. As I lay it out on the velvet ottoman, I see the crumpled paper stick out of the pocket.

`Keep yourself private, and everything will`
`be all right.`

The words are underlined in red.

Chapter Four

My lace bra feels scratchy, especially compared to the soft angora of my white sweater. I cross my leather boots at the ankles and pull my feet under the chair. I relax my shoulders and smooth my expression of anything that might tell what I'm feeling. It's been over a week since Fatima and Beau's engagement party, and the authorities still haven't located Headmaster Russell. But I don't show one ounce of fear. Dr. Meredith's office is chilly, and I resist the urge to rub my hands against my arms to warm myself up. The slip of paper in my pocket reminds me to be careful.

Keep yourself private, and everything will be all right.

"Are you cold, Blanca?" Dr. Meredith looks at me across her coffee table. She has curly red hair tied back with a tortoise shell clip. "Would you like me to adjust the thermostat?"

I smile blandly, observing Dr. Meredith as much as she observes me. She keeps fiddling with her pearl necklace at the nape of her neck.

"I'm fine." I fold my hands in my lap and straighten my spine like Ms. Corina taught me back at Tabula Rasa. *You're placid, Blanca. Perfectly placid,* she'd say.

Dr. Meredith's office is lined with wall-to-wall bookshelves. The occasional houseplant creates trailing lines of green leaves. There are more places to conceal a camera here than I can count. Dr. Meredith could be hiding anything.

"Would you like a glass of water or a cup of tea?" Dr. Meredith asks.

"No, thank you." She's trying to put me off guard by offering me a favor—making me feel indebted to her. But I'm smarter than that.

"I'm really happy you're here, Blanca. I've been looking forward to meeting you for a long time. I want you to know that this is a safe place."

I don't believe that for a second. This woman's life work is prying into people's secrets. Cal and Seth might be charmed, but I'm not fooled. Dr. Meredith is devious. I know because she keeps saying my name over and over again. That's Mind Control 101.

All you need to do is make somebody feel important, Barbelo Nemo wrote. *A little appreciation goes a long way. People love to talk about themselves. Speak their name softly, melodically. Say their name whenever possible.*

"I'm perfectly comfortable." Without taking my eyes off Dr.

Meredith, I look behind her toward the windows. That's where I would hide the camera.

"Blanca," she continues, "I want you to see this room as your sanctuary. You can tell me anything you want here and I will keep it entirely confidential."

What a liar. Only Vestals understand confidence. Dr. Meredith will probably upload all her notes the moment I leave.

I know what I have to do to get out of this office unscathed. I plan to tell Dr. Meredith exactly what she wants to hear.

"It sounds like you are a good listener, Dr. Meredith."

She doesn't know who she's dealing with.

"I am pleased to hear you say that." Dr. Meredith smiles. "Your ... friends, Cal and Seth, they've referred you to me because they believe you have trust issues. What do you think about that?"

I nod my head in complete agreement. "Yes. You're correct. Cal and Seth both believe I have trust issues."

"Would you like to talk more about that?"

"Yes, I would be happy to talk more about that."

Dr. Meredith stares at me with raised eyebrows. Finally, after a long silence, she prods. "What would you like to say?"

"About Seth and Cal believing I have trust issues?" *Clarifying questions are my friends.*

"No, I mean ... " Dr. Meredith shifts in her seat. "Do *you* think you have trust issues?"

"Dr. Meredith, I am an excellent judge of character. That's why I so appreciate you fitting me in your schedule. I know you must be incredibly busy." *A little appreciation goes a long way.*

"I always make room for clients." Dr. Meredith sits back in her seat and eyes me closely. "Let's talk about your mother."

"How conventional." I sit back in my chair too.

Dr. Meredith grimaces. "I understand from the news reports that you witnessed your father murder her in Nevada."

In spite of myself, I picture Ms. Lydia's head exploding for the millionth time.

"Well?" Dr. Meredith probes.

"The news reports were correct." I stretch up my spine.

"And how do you feel you are coping?"

Follow your Vestal training. Keep yourself private, and everything will be all right.

"I have a very hard road, Dr. Meredith. In so many ways, it's difficult being me. But I know that I can do it. I have everything I need to achieve happiness."

Dr. Meredith smiles. "Thank you for sharing, Blanca. You're doing good work today."

I smile back broadly. The Vestal blessing always works.

Tell people what they want to hear.

My lean body glistens in the afternoon sun, taut in a white spandex catsuit. My brown hair falls, a silky rope down my front, and caresses my breasts. One hand holds the orange extension cord, with the other placed smartly on my hip, my fingertips brushing my pelvis. I look at the camera with green eyes and a knowing smile. Behind me, a spinning globe glows with fire. The headline reads: MCNEAL SOLAR HEATS THINGS UP.

No matter how often I see myself on a billboard, I still feel electrified. On the ride home from Dr. Meredith's office, I stare out the window and try to spot every one. But most of all, I look for other Vestal billboards, because seeing my friends offers comfort. Fatima modeling the latest designer purse. Trevor selling body spray. His dad Richard showing off razors.

Then we pass a newsboard and my stomach lurches. HUNT FOR RUSSELL, it says. ABUSER ON THE RUN.

I look down at my chip-watch and wonder if the authorities have released new information. Since the limo is cloistered, I can't access the Internet.

"Alan," I say, sliding open the privacy divider, "would you please stop the car for a moment so I can check my messages?"

"Sure thing, Miss Blanca. Oh, and I almost forgot. Somebody delivered this for you while you were gone." With one firm hand on the wheel, Alan passes a small envelope to me in the backseat.

I see the red and blue markings of the USPS and shudder. Nobody uses the postal service but government officials and VIPs anymore. It's the primary way Vestals deliver important information.

"Thank you, Alan." I carefully slice open the seal. Inside is a piece of thick cardstock. In the middle of the paper, written in beautiful calligraphy, is another direction from the Vestal Code of Ethics. As soon as I see it, my skin goes clammy.

`Vestals avenge all wrongs, especially when`
`our honor is at stake.`

The limo lurches to a stop.

"What's wrong?" My voice shakes.

Alan looks back at me. "You asked me to stop the car. Are you okay?"

"What? Yes. Of course." I try to clear my thoughts as Alan parks. When he opens the door for me, I step out onto the sidewalk and look out across a busy intersection. "I'll only be a moment."

"Whatever you say, Miss Blanca." Alan heads back to the driver's seat.

As soon as the door is shut, I activate my chip-watch. "Call Seth." I speak clearly, but Seth doesn't pick up. "Veritas Rex!" I try again. The lion-headed cobra springs up in silvery gray. The big bold headline reads: YOU CAN RUN, RUSSELL, BUT YOU CAN'T HIDE.

What is Seth getting himself into? How can he not understand who he's dealing with?

My worries are interrupted by a call from Cal. His small image stands in the great hall of McNeal Manor. "Blanca," he says, "I thought you'd be back from Dr. Meredith's by now. Where are you?"

"Nowhere. Alan stopped the car for a moment so I could check my messages."

"Oh." On the tiny image, I see Cal's forehead furrow. "Do you think you're safe out and about with Headmaster Russell on the loose?"

No! my insides scream. "Yes," I say. "I'm sure I'll be fine."

"Okay, sweetheart. Whatever you think. I know you make good decisions. But listen, your tutor will be here any minute."

"I'm on my way."

I click off the chip-watch. The sooner I'm home, the better.

● ● ● ● ● ● ● ● ●

Cal waits in the library with Irene Page. She's an intern at McNeal Solar who tutors me several times a week. Calculus, physics, chemistry; I have a lot to catch up on before I can pass the qualifying interview at Stanford.

"How'd it go with Dr. Meredith?" Cal asks.

I glare at him. No way do I want Irene to know I see a therapist.

"Sorry." Cal flinches. "We can talk about it later."

Or never, as far as I'm concerned. I glance at Irene and try to discover what she's thinking. She's Asian American with short black hair and a wispy figure. Irene usually doesn't wear any makeup, but today her lips are covered in gloss. Her torso faces me, but the rest of her body points away.

Interesting. That's how people welcome you when they don't mean it.

I walk a few feet closer, and Irene steps back.

"Yes, Cal. We'll talk later," I say. "Irene and I better get started."

Irene forces a smile. "Blanca and I have a lot to cover."

"Excellent." Cal kisses me on the cheek. "Well, I'll see you tomorrow then. Tonight you're going to Seth's house for dinner, right?"

"Yes. He's making lasagna."

Irene colors when she hears Seth's name. Normally she is an exacting teacher, but whenever Seth appears, she turns into pudding.

"Will you be okay on your own?" I ask Cal.

"Of course," he says smoothly. "In fact, I have a date." Cal grins at both of us and then closes the door behind him.

"A date?" I ask Irene. "With who?"

"Mr. McNeal's personal life is none of my business." Irene spreads out tablets and clicks up screens. "But your Stanford interview in two months is."

"Do you think I'll be prepared?"

"Perhaps." Irene pulls a strand of black hair behind her ear. "But maybe you should set your sights lower."

"Oh." I'm not sure how to respond.

"There're lots of colleges that would be a better fit for you."

I squeeze my toes inside my boots. "Yes. You're probably right." My ego floods with discouragement after hearing my own tutor doesn't think I can do this.

"I don't believe in sugarcoating things. There's no point." Irene slides over the tablet with my calculus lesson. "Let's begin."

The hours move like molasses. The library windows look into my private courtyard, but the shutters are closed. Daylight offers no reprieve. It's Irene, artificial light, and me.

When numbers flash through my brain so fast that there's no room for words, Seth arrives. He wears jeans and a black T-shirt, and smells like shampoo. His dark hair, usually so wild, is slicked back neatly.

"School's out for the day, ladies." Seth throws himself down on the green leather couch and puts his boots up on the armrest. He grins at Irene. "How's your favorite pupil doing?"

"Gorgeous. I mean—beautiful. Blanca is doing great."

"Of course she is." Seth leans over and looks straight at Irene. "How could Blanca be anything less than spectacular with you as her teacher?"

Irene turns beet red.

I glare at Seth, and he smiles wickedly.

"Be a love, Blanca." Seth holds out his hand. "Help me off the couch and take me home."

● ● ● ● ● ● ● ● ●

The technology in Seth's apartment creeps me out, even after all these months. At least the place doesn't smell anymore. Ever since we started dating, Seth hired a regular maid, so dirty socks no longer contaminate the floor.

He waves his finger-chips and turns off the tech screens before we cross the threshold, but I know they're still there. Seth can watch ten different things while brushing his teeth. He has special servers for hacking into places he doesn't belong.

But as crazy as it sounds, Seth's apartment offers privacy. It's not that I dislike living at McNeal Manor, but with Cal around, PDA with Seth is awkward.

As soon as the door closes behind us, I leap into Seth's arms and wrap my legs around his waist. His hands grab a firm hold of my butt and pull me tight. We lose each other in kisses, the delicious feeling of not knowing where one of us ends and the other begins. My heart pounds as I slide my hands around Seth's neck, clinging to his shoulders with both arms. Seth takes a few steps back, and we tumble over onto the couch.

"Blanca," Seth moans, his hands creeping up my sweater. His touch feels hot against my bare skin.

"Yes," I gasp. My breaths are ragged. I roll onto my back and feel the pressure of Seth's whole body leaning into mine.

We've officially been together for three months.

I'm nineteen years old now.

Maybe this is the moment.

I kiss Seth down his neck and help pull off his shirt. His collage of tattoos melts into me like liquid ink. When I see the one that says "Tiffany," I think about scratching it away.

"Blanca. Wait. I have to—"

At that precise moment, I hear a loud electronic beep. It shocks me back into clarity.

"What the hell is that?" I push him away and scramble off the couch. "I thought you turned everything off!"

"I did," he says, reaching for me. I swat his hands away and he groans. "It's the oven timer. The lasagna's ready."

"Oh. I thought—" But I don't finish my sentence. The beeping calls again.

Seth frowns. "I sincerely hope Dr. Meredith helps you deal with your trust issues." He pulls his shirt back on and goes to the kitchen.

"I don't have trust issues," I declare, following him. I take a seat at the table in the corner of the room. Seth's kitchen has tall windows that look out into Silicon Valley. When I stare through the glass, my chest aches. I see an advertisement for the tech company my friend Ethan modeled for. The last time I saw Ethan, he introduced me to the Internet. I thought he could help me find Ms. Lydia, who was missing.

Instead, Ms. Lydia found Ethan—and killed him for corrupting himself with finger-chips.

"Saying you don't have trust issues doesn't make it true." Seth opens the oven and reaches inside. "Damn! That's hot."

"Are you okay?" I look over to see Seth sucking his finger.

"I'm fine. Only I've never made lasagna before. I'm not much of a cook."

I don't cook either, but at least I know enough not to reach into a hot stove with bare hands. I walk over to the counter and deftly reach for oven mitts. "Here. These might help."

"Thanks. Dinner will be ready in a second."

I wander back to my place at the table by the window. I squint out the glass and stare down at the sidewalk. I don't think Keung is spying on us, but I can't be sure.

A few minutes later, Seth brings over two plates of gooey, red lasagna with Caesar salad on the side. It looks like more calories than I would have eaten all week at Tabula Rasa where our diet was prudently limited to fish, vegetables, and the occasional gluten-free carbohydrate.

I've only had lasagna once before, when I turned nineteen last month. The McNeals took me out to an Italian restaurant.

"Wow, Seth. This looks delicious."

He smiles. "You are worth the effort." He hands me my silverware, and we take the first few bites, enjoying the meal in silence. The herb and cheese flavors explode in my mouth. Ms. Lydia would be horrified at the decadence.

"Have you heard the news?" Seth asks.

"About Headmaster Russell? Have they found him?"

"No, about the Defectos. They're organizing themselves."

"What are you talking about? Who are the Defectos?"

Seth wipes his mouth with a napkin. "I thought you knew. That guy at Fatima's party. Jeremy? The one taking the pictures?"

"You mean the Rejects?"

"The Rejects! Who calls them that? Vestals?"

I reluctantly nod.

"Well, that's not what they call themselves." Seth flicks his hand and types something with his finger-chips. A picture pulls up above his palm. "Here. Look at this."

I hold Seth's hand steady so I can stare at the screen.

DEFECTOS WANT HARVEST STOPPED, the headline says. Seth scrolls down so I can read more.

HUMAN RIGHTS INFRINGEMENTS! VESTAL ORDER MUST BE DISBANDED.

"So?" Seth asks after a moment. "What do you think?"

"Probably a lot of what they say is true." It's tough for me to admit that. I've been trained my entire life to think of Rejects as unworthy of anything but scorn. But I'm not a Vestal now, and I need to analyze things for myself. I reach my hand into my pocket and feel the two messages I received. The ones with the Vestal Code of Ethics on them. I've meant to tell Seth about the first one for days.

But right when I'm about to reveal all, Seth stabs his fork into his lasagna and accidentally splatters marinara sauce. It goes flying across his plate and splashes my white sweater.

"Uh-oh. I better clean this off before it stains." Eating messy food is one of the most difficult parts of my white wardrobe.

"Why wear a shirt at all? Clothing is overrated." Seth raises his eyebrows. "Especially on you."

And I consider it. I could strip off my sweater and show my lace bra. Peel off my jeans and wear nothing but boots and panties. Forget dinner and every last thing that happened today. Lead Seth into his bedroom.

It's not like I could get pregnant. Tabula Rasa took care of that five years ago. There will never be a tiny baby with my clear skin and Seth's unruly hair. Seth will never stand next to me, like Beau with Fatima, intent on protecting his family. Add that future to the list of everything my parents stole from me.

But they can't stop me from living.

Seth and I have been together for three months now. What am I waiting for?

I don't know. A sign maybe? I'm still new at this making good decisions thing.

"Blanca. Hello? You look like you were lost in space." Seth hands me a napkin.

"Oh, sorry. I better blot this with water."

When I get to the bathroom, I stare at myself in the mirror. My virginal white reflection overtakes the whole room.

And it taunts me.

Chapter Five

When I was in Nevada, trapped at the compound Barbelo named Plemora, breakfast was another test. Was I worthy of my birth father's trust? Would I blindly do whatever he suggested? Survival meant convincing him I was utterly brainwashed. At the table in the atrium together, we'd eat steamed tilapia and fresh figs. Sometimes Ms. Lydia would join us. But never once did I enjoy a bite.

Breakfast with Cal is different. The dining room at McNeal Manor is formal, with wallpaper, wainscoting, and tall brocaded chairs. But the atmosphere is cozy because of Cal's company. The latest news stories project from our chip-watches, and we read companionably over omelets.

Cal pushes buttered toast in my direction. "Have a bit more."

"There were three egg whites in my omelet. I'm full."

"That's protein, not starch." Cal puts the toast on my empty plate.

"I had lasagna last night."

Cal sighs. "Blanca, you can eat whatever you want now. You know that."

"I know."

"So why not eat a few more bites?"

"Because I'm not hungry."

It's not like I have an eating disorder or anything. I'm a perfectly fine weight. But after so many years of being a Vestal and having every last morsel of food chosen for me, it's tough figuring things out on my own.

"Maybe you should discuss your fear of carbohydrates with Dr. Meredith."

"No, thank you." I take the offered toast and shove it in my mouth. Dry crumbs make me gag.

"Are you okay? Have some juice. That's better." Cal clicks on his chip-watch and pulls up the news. "It looks like Russell is still missing."

I fiddle with my napkin. "Yes. I'll stay close to home until he's found."

"I don't want you to live in fear, Blanca."

"I know."

"You'll be perfectly fine driving around with Alan."

"Yes, Cal."

He gawps at me. "Well, don't parrot everything I say. We've been over that too."

"Ye—" I start to say, but then I stop myself.

Cal leans on his armrest and rests his head on his hand. "I don't know what to do with you."

A stab of fear hits my heart. The last person I want to disappoint is Cal.

"I'll try to be better." I let myself sound earnest, although it betrays exactly what I feel.

"You don't have to be anything but yourself."

"Well, this is me." I hold out my hands. "There's a lot of junk inside me that will probably be there forever."

"Maybe you should see Dr. Meredith twice a week. Maybe once a week isn't enough."

"No! I don't want to see her at all."

"But, Blanca—"

At that exact moment a maid enters holding a silver tray. She excuses herself for the interruption and leaves it on the table.

I notice the red and white markings of the USPS immediately.

"It's for you." Cal raises his eyebrows and holds out the letter. "Were you expecting something?"

"No." Not exactly. The other two messages are in the pocket of my white jeans.

Cal watches as I slice open the letter with my knife. Inside are several pieces of ecru paper with the Tabula Rasa letterhead.

Dear Blanca,

I can never hope to understand the path you have taken. For Tabula Rasa's star pupil to throw her privacy away so recklessly disturbs me.

I do not know what you think you heard or saw at Plemora or what nonsense that Virus has filled your brain with, but I hope there is still a part of you that is loyal to your alma mater.

Now is a dark time for us, Blanca. The Harvest is three weeks away and we do not have enough bidders. Headmaster Russell and Ms. Lydia used to arrange that sort of thing. This is not my area of expertise!

Plus, due to all the bad press you have heaped upon us, some parents have pulled their children from school. We only have 500 students left! Imagine how traumatic it is for these young people to be so close to their goal of becoming real Vestals only to be yanked away from their dream.

I call upon you to right this wrong. Do a blog post or go online or whatever it is Viruses like you do. But let the world know the value of your Brethren. Bring the bidders back!

You took a vow, Blanca. You promised to give your highest self to our cause.

You still have an important role to play.
Please come to Tabula Rasa at once.
Headmaster Corina

I hand the letter over to Cal who crumples it as soon as he reads it. "Garbage. Absolute rubbish. None of that vitriol is true."

I stare down at my piece of toast. "She called me a Virus."

"You're not a Virus. You know that. Besides, even if you were, Viruses aren't all bad. Look at Seth. He does important work, and I'm incredibly proud of him."

"Ms. Corina is correct, though. I took a vow. I promised to protect my fellow Vestals."

Cal holds up both of his hands. "You never have to help them again. We're talking about people who almost destroyed you."

"But they didn't. I'm right here! And it wasn't the graduates. It was Headmaster Russell. And ... Barbelo and Ms. Lydia. It's not the students' fault. I can't turn my back on the only community I've known for years."

"Let their parents help them."

"They won't help. Their parents gave them away."

"What if Russell is behind this? Have you thought of that? This letter could be a trap."

"Wouldn't that be obvious?" I hold up the envelope. "If the FBI came looking for me, you'd have the evidence."

"By then it might be too late. Tabula Rasa isn't a safe place. You don't know what Corina really wants."

"She wants my help. It says so here."

"And since when are Vestals trustworthy?"

Vestals are always trustworthy, something deep inside me whispers. *Vestals are the only people I can trust.* But I know that's not true anymore. It was probably never true to begin with.

"So are you telling me I can't go?"

Cal grimaces. "No, I'm not. The hardest part of being a parent is letting your child grow up and decide for herself. I'm only giving you advice. I don't think you should set foot in Tabula Rasa again."

I look at Cal square in the eyes. "Ten Tabula Rasa graduates need my help."

Cal returns my fierce gaze. "They need help, but does it have to be from you?"

"Who else?" I throw down my napkin and stand up.

"Blanca!"

"Cal, do you trust me?"

I watch as Cal's face tightens.

"Yes, sweetheart. I trust you."

"Good," I say. "I'll see you tonight."

●●●●●●●●●

I can't believe I am doing this. Every fiber of my being tells me this is wrong. The sun feels hot on my white leather jacket as I weave through Silicon Valley traffic on my motorcycle. I intensely hope Seth got my message.

I pray he understands.

Windows roll down and hands flash at every intersection. "Hey, Blanca!" fans call, as I fly by. "We love you!" I've turned my chip-watch off for the moment, so I can't be scanned, but it doesn't make much difference. The public still spots me. The whole world knows me as Blanca, the only de-cuffed Vestal alive. The only one who drives a motorcycle.

I hope they have no idea where I'm headed or that it's the last place on Earth I want to be. At least I have a friend waiting for me when I get there.

I tighten my grip on the handlebars and zoom through the blinding sunshine.

Chapter Six

Nancy's fingers are short and stubby, but she can type air so fast her fingers blur. My feet bounce up and down. Nancy works quickly but not fast enough to keep the damp of the stone bench from penetrating the legs of my pants. Any minute now, we'll head into the FBI building where I'll give a statement. My heart races with anticipation. I'm still not sure this is the best decision. I fold my arms tight against my chest and squeeze hard.

I want to help the Vestal graduates, I do. But first, I have to help myself. I need to do something my lawyer has bugged me about for months.

"Almost done, Blanca. I'm glad you agreed to this. What changed your mind?"

"I want to take charge of my own life." I look down at the wrist where my cuff used to be. "I'm tired of manipulation."

Nancy gives one final click of her finger-chips. "There. This might not work, but it's worth a try. If any of the property was acquired through illegal activity, your chances are nil." She twists toward me. "Are you ready?"

"Yes." I run my fingers through my hair to fluff it. "Thank you for coming with me on such short notice."

"You bet." Nancy stands tall in her wool crêpe pantsuit. The color is as steely as her expression. "I won't let them take advantage."

We only wait in the lobby for a few minutes before Agent Marlow shows up and escorts us through security. "This is a surprise," he says. He's so tall that when we ride in the elevator, his hair grazes the ceiling. He leads us down the hallway, and I hustle to match his strides.

The room we enter feels cold and uninviting. I smell stale donuts. It's the interrogation area from last week. Agent Plunkett waits for us with her ladybug tattoos.

"Blanca Nemo." Her fingers rap the table. "I didn't expect to see you again so soon."

I give her my most brilliant smile. For this to work, I need every Vestal skill I've got. I extend my pale hand. "Agent Plunkett, thank you for seeing me this morning. I can only imagine how incredibly busy you must be."

Her handshake is firm, and she looks me straight in the eyes. "Why don't we take a seat?" Agent Plunkett indicates the plastic chairs by the table.

I sit down on the edge and neatly cross my ankles. I place my hands on the table so they can see I have nothing to hide.

Now if only I can convince these agents of my integrity.

Nancy nods at me. "It's okay, Blanca. Go ahead."

"Agent Plunkett and Agent Marlow," I say with as much earnestness as I can muster, "I wasn't as forthcoming as I could have been the other day. Your interest caught me by surprise."

Agent Plunkett sits ups straight. "Interest." Her voice is cool. "That's one way to put it."

I lean forward, like I'm sharing a secret. "I bet you have a file as big on Barbelo Nemo as he had on you."

"And what exactly do you know about Nemo's files?" Agent Marlow rumbles.

"A lot." I nod toward Agent Plunkett. "Margie Plunkett, fifty-two years old and divorced. You've investigated the Vestals for seventeen years after your nephew was rejected from Tabula Rasa at age seven. Your interest in the Vestals caught Barbelo's attention.

"You have two daughters, one in tenth grade and the other in college. As a rookie, you almost lost your badge after kissing your commanding officer's husband at a Christmas party. Your husband was in the other room helping serve food. Your boss caught and suspended you. You're lucky you didn't lose your badge."

Agent Plunkett shrugs. "Office gossip. Anyone can make stuff up."

But I'm not done yet.

I carefully control my expression to prevent my glee from showing. I look straight at Agent Plunkett. "Since then you've had three long-term affairs. One with a man you met at your gym, one with a father on your daughter's softball team, and a three-year relationship with your former partner."

Agent Marlow raises his bushy eyebrows.

"That's slander," Agent Plunkett snarls.

"Not if it's true." My tone is neutral.

"Plunkett isn't on trial here," says Agent Marlow.

"And neither is Blanca," Nancy interjects. "She came here voluntarily."

"So why are you here? To show off your ability to prattle filth?" Agent Plunkett cracks her knuckles.

"Plunkett," Agent Marlow says, "be nice." But the way his body inclines toward her shows me this is an act, like good cop, bad cop. He agrees with her.

I turn toward Agent Marlow. "I'm sorry, but I don't know anything about you. I'm not sure if you were on Barbelo's radar. I hope you're not insulted by that."

"Of course not." Agent Marlow folds his arms. "Why would I be?"

I shrug. "Only important people make it to the Vestal files."

Agent Marlow presses his lips tight.

I look back at Agent Plunkett. "I thought you were interested in what I know. I'm here to cooperate."

"And to show you this." Nancy flicks on her finger-chips and holds out her palm. "I have filed a motion on Blanca's behalf for the immediate return of all her parents' property."

"What?" Agent Marlow scratches his jaw.

"We don't bargain for information," says Agent Plunkett.

"We're not here to bargain." Nancy's voice is crisp. "As the only known offspring of Barbelo Nemo, and without evidence of a will, Blanca is sole heir to all his property. The Plemora compound in Nevada, all contents held inside—including his files—all assets both foreign and domestic, and quite possibly, Tabula Rasa itself. My people are still looking into it."

"And Ms. Lydia's things too." I try not to shift in my seat.

"Yes," Nancy continues. "Blanca is also Lydia Xavier's heir. Yet you have withheld key information that we need for probate, such as Lydia's maiden name. Or perhaps you have encountered a will?"

Nerves course through me like high voltage. This is the moment. This is why I have come. But if I act too eager, I'll ruin everything.

Agent Plunkett stares at me like she's scanning every inch of my soul. Then she shakes her head.

The tiniest release of pressure escapes my spine. I surge forward with my mission.

"You discovered Ms. Lydia's last name in Barbelo Nemo's private files," I say. "He kept them in his study in Plemora where I was held captive. One day, when I was supposed to be cleaning his office, I sat down and read them all. Well, not all of them. I only got from A to P. I never saw the file for Lydia Xavier."

There is silence for a moment.

"Well?" I look back and forth between the two agents. "You have this file, don't you?"

Agent Marlow glances at Agent Plunkett, and a few seconds later, he nods. "Yes," Agent Marlow answers. "We do."

"I would like that file back," I say sweetly. "It belongs to me."

Agent Plunkett leans casually on her armrest. "Those documents are part of an ongoing criminal investigation. You can file as many motions as you want, but you'll never get them back."

"We at least need copies for probate," says Nancy.

"I'm not sure that can happen," says Agent Plunkett.

"That's too bad," I say. "I really thought you were the type of person who could think bigger." I turn toward Agent Marlow. "I came here to cooperate, remember? Because I know that you didn't find any files on the Guardians."

Agent Plunkett sits up straighter.

"Well?" I ask looking back at her.

She tugs her blazer. "The information regarding the Guardians was not as complete as we would have liked."

"You mean it was nonexistent. Just like there wasn't an actual file on Agent Plunkett, was there?"

"Yes," says Agent Marlow. "That is correct." Agent Plunkett glares at him.

"I'm sure you both know," I say, "that memorization is the very foundation of Tabula Rasa. '*Vestals are a collective power. We are united by secrecy and code,*'" I quote. "I have lots of things I might say about the Guardians. But only to my friends."

"We could subpoena you," says Agent Plunkett. "Make you testify in court."

"You could." I lean back in my chair. "And maybe you'd find out that my memory has faded."

"Give us the file." Nancy is blunt. "And Blanca will talk."

The two federal agents eye each other, as if sending telepathic signals. Agent Plunkett raps her fingers on the table and flashes her ladybug tattoos.

Finally, Agent Marlow speaks. "We need to clear this with our superiors first. But we'll see what we can do."

●●●●●●●●●

The sun hits me like a blinding lightning bolt. The morning chill has worn off, replaced by Silicon Valley heat. Despite the warmth outside, I shiver. I pull the zipper up my leather jacket and click on my chip-watch.

"You did great," Nancy tells me as we walk to the parking lot. "You were amazing in there."

"Then why am I shaking?"

"Because you're human. And because Agent Plunkett could make grapes shrivel. Marlow isn't bad, but I thought Plunkett would burst a blood vessel when you said that about her personal life."

"It felt wrong sharing her secrets in front of Agent Marlow."

"Why?" asks Nancy. "The home-wrecker deserves it. A little shame could do her good."

"But it's her private information," I protest. "And I was supposed to be winning her over."

"Sometimes the best way to gain a person's favor is by showing them you mean business."

"You're probably right," I admit. "But it felt despicable."

We're standing in front of Nancy's car now, a silver sedan with a red interior. "Sometimes the ends justify the means," Nancy says as she searches for her keys.

"Who are you? Machiavelli?"

"Who's that?" asks Nancy.

"Never mind." Sometimes it's hard to remember that not everyone studied as much history as me. "Say, what did you mean about owning Tabula Rasa?"

Nancy unlocks her door. "It's a definite possibility. I have people at the courthouse searching through old hard drives as we speak."

"But I don't want to own Tabula Rasa."

"No," agrees Nancy. "You don't. It would mean a host of legal problems. You'd need your own army of lawyers to deal with angry alumni." Nancy glances back at the imposing FBI building behind us. "But we should talk more later. These walls might have eyes."

"Now you sound as paranoid as me."

Nancy smiles and climbs into her car. "Sometimes a little paranoia is a good thing. It means you care about your safety."

I take a step back and watch her drive away. Own Tabula Rasa? If I really do own Tabula Rasa, then I'll clean it up from the inside out.

I head over to my motorcycle and think about justice. The sun finally warms me up. But when I get to my bike, I get the chills all over again.

There, taped to my seat, is another piece of paper.

```
The holiest night is coming. We are a sacred
fire that will not burn out. We alone stand
together.
```

I crumple the paper loudly between both hands. The last time I heard those words was at my sealing, a few days after the Harvest. They're what Ms. Lydia said to me before she trapped my wrist in platinum.

Ms. Lydia is dead. I've relived her face exploding in front of me a million times. She can't possibly be behind this. But what about Ms. Corina?

No. It's not *Ms. Corina* anymore; it's *Headmaster*. She's in charge of all Tabula Rasa. Maybe she's cagier than I know and this is a creative way to bully me into helping with the graduation Harvest.

Well, I'm done being bullied. She can't make me support a system I no longer condone.

It's time to change the practice of Harvesting Vestals once and for all.

As soon as I climb on my bike, I gun the engine.

Chapter Seven

· · · · · · · · · ● · · · · · · · ·

When I see Seth waiting, I turn into a hot, sticky bundle of mess. He sits astride his motorcycle, scanning the road for me. His jacket is tossed on the ground, and his clean white T-shirt shows off muscles and tattoos. When Seth spots me, he smiles broadly, and the lion-headed cobra on the side of his face jumps to life.

"How did it go?" he asks as I engage the kickstand.

I take off my helmet and rake fingers through my hair. The fresh air hits my lungs and makes me gasp. I don't realize I'm shaking until I throw myself in Seth's arms and feel him wrap around me in a protective embrace.

"That well, huh?" Seth hugs me tight.

"It was okay." My voice is muffled by deltoid. "Nancy and I made our point."

"Well, that was a big step." Seth strokes my hair. "We could go home now. Call it a day. You don't need to do this unless you want to. My dad will have an ulcer when he finds out."

If I'm not careful, my nose will drip straight onto Seth's shirt. I pull back and reach into my jacket pocket for a tissue. Above me, I hear movement.

Somebody is watching.

"How long have they been up there?" I don't turn to look.

"The whole time," Seth says. "Ever since I arrived. I can't tell if they're students or teachers."

"Teachers," I answer immediately. "Students aren't allowed near windows."

The two of us have parked our motorcycles across the street from Tabula Rasa. I don't need to spin around and see it to know exactly what the edifice looks like. Twenty stories high with a stone-walled facade, my alma mater is half prison, half castle. When I was a young girl in history class and saw a picture of the Tower of London for the first time, I immediately noticed the resemblance. I had never been outside the compound, but I had seen the Tabula Rasa profile on our school seal.

Lux in tenbris lucet. The light that shines in the darkness. That was our school motto.

For the first eighteen years of my life, I thought Vestals were the answer. I thought we were a beacon of light in a dark world that had forgotten what was important. I believed when people looked at me, they wouldn't only see a girl in white, but a reminder that people were more important than technology. I thought I had dedicated my life to a holy purpose.

Now I realize I was a brainwashed indentured servant.

I can't allow that to happen to another class of graduates.

"Did you bring the camera?" I ask Seth. "Not your finger-chips, but the best equipment you've got? I want this to be crystal clear."

Seth reaches into his saddlebag. "Don't worry. I got your message." He pulls out an enormous lens. "What's your plan exactly?"

I unzip my jacket and throw it on my bike. I'm wearing a tank top underneath and bare arms feel good in the heat. "I don't have a plan. I'm going on instinct."

Damn it. I should have brought makeup. I bite my lips to make them darker and pinch both cheeks.

"Hey," Seth protests. "Don't hurt yourself."

"I'm fine." I bend over at the waist and shake out my hair.

"Can I take a picture of this?" Seth slides his hand down the back pocket of my jeans.

"Not funny." But I stand up and twist toward him. Then I crush our lips together. I slide my hands behind Seth's neck and play with his tongue, kissing him until we're both out of breath.

Let the teachers watch and seethe.

"Are you ready?" I finally pull away.

"What?" Seth stammers. "Oh, yeah."

"I need you to upload this straight to *Veritas Rex* and *The Lighthouse*."

Seth smirks. "You're going to have to give me your password."

"Only for a couple of hours. Don't get too excited." I take a step closer and whisper it into his ear. "Demiurge32."

Seth raises his eyebrows. "Like a lion-headed cobra from mythology?"

I grin. Then I notice Seth's gaze lift. "Uh, Blanca," he says. "We've got a visitor."

"What?" I turn to look and see Ms. Corina walk toward us. She wears ecru flannel trousers, a silk blouse, and her golden Vestal cuff.

"Blanca!" she exclaims in her sickly sweet voice. "I'm so glad you came. I was worried you didn't get my message." She squints at Seth, as if she doesn't want to acknowledge his existence. "But what's this Virus doing here?"

I take a deep breath. "I'm sorry, Headmaster. I'm not here to help you. Or actually, I am, but you won't see it that way. I think you'll be happier if you go back inside."

"What do you mean you won't help us? Blanca, the graduates need you. Everything is falling to pieces without Headmaster Russell. I—" Ms. Corina waves her hands around like she's searching for words. Then she fiddles with the collar of her blouse. "Didn't you get my message?"

"Yes," I answer. "All of them."

"What do you mean all of them?" she and Seth ask at the same time.

"There's no time to talk about that right now." In my clearest voice I say, "Seth, please turn on your camera."

"No, wait!" Ms. Corina holds delicate fingers in front of her face like spiderwebs. "You were sealed for life. I don't care what anyone else has told you." Ms. Corina peeks her eyes out and indicates Seth. "You know you can't trust a Virus. You're one of us, Blanca. Forever. *Please*."

I look from Ms. Corina to Seth and see a red light on the camera blink.

"I raised you," Ms. Corina whimpers. "I watched over you every minute."

"Supervised me!" I snap. "You supervised me. You didn't raise me. There's a difference!" I think about Cal and Sophia and all the love and attention they poured into Seth's upbringing.

"I made sure you brushed your teeth. I tucked you in at night." Ms. Corina's voice is weepy.

"You didn't tuck me in. You paced up and down the aisles of a hundred metal bunk beds. That's not the same thing."

"I did my best." Ms. Corina sniffs loudly behind her tiny hands. "I watched over you. I kept you safe, like your mother wanted me to!"

Ms. Corina pulls down her arms, and I see tears. It's like a sucker punch to my intentions. I feel my resolve waiver.

"She entrusted you to my care." Ms. Corina stares up at me with watery eyes. "When Ms. Lydia left, she put you in my arms. I'm sorry my best wasn't good enough, but please help me. Don't let the graduates suffer because somebody convinced you it was all a bad idea." She wipes away tears with a handkerchief.

That's when I remember. *Cry on cue. Stop crying. Tears are a tool.*

"I'm the one who knows the Harvest is a bad idea," I say plainly. "Nobody needs to convince me but myself." I turn to Seth. "Are you filming this? Is this live?"

He nods his head without moving the camera.

"Good." I face the lens squarely. "This is Blanca McNeal standing in front of Tabula Rasa. I have an important message for every person who is watching. Please share this across all social media networks."

"Blanca, no!" Ms. Corina cries out.

But I ignore her. "The Tabula Rasa Harvest is under precarious circumstances. Our nation is waking up to the fact that it is wrong to auction off Vestals to the highest bidder. A twenty-five-year contract imposed on a young person is morally abhorrent and against the founding principles of our country."

Behind the camera lens I see Seth smile.

"It doesn't matter what colors I wear. It doesn't matter if I have my cuff or a chip-watch." I hold up my wrist to the camera. "I will always love and support my Vestal Brethren. That's why it's imperative for me to advocate for their well-being.

"I still believe the Harvest can continue but in a different format. Instead of an auction, I propose a mutual selection process where Vestal graduates have a say in which company they join."

The next part I say straight from the heart.

"Tabula Rasa students still have valuable contributions to offer. They are the last examples of private living our country knows. But they deserve to make their own decisions. If they choose to commit themselves to a major corporation, fine. But if a Vestal graduate would rather be independent, then Tabula Rasa should offer a compensation package to help each individual begin life on his or her own."

I look straight at the camera, directly at Seth. "My adoptive father, Cal McNeal, paid thirty-two million dollars for my freedom. There should be plenty of money to help every graduate start a new life whatever way they choose.

"*Lux in tenbris lucet.* Vestals are the light that shines in the darkness. Please help me keep their flames burning for the whole world to see."

With a nod to Seth he cuts the feed.

And Ms. Corina tries to throttle me.

Immediately I shield my face, but not in time to protect my hair, which Ms. Corina attempts to rip out with her bare hands.

The hundreds of hours doing Kenpō with Ms. Lydia fail me. I can't bear to kick Ms. Corina in the knees like she deserves.

"How could you?" Ms. Corina screams.

Seth pulls her off me and her limbs flail wildly in the air. "Get on your bike, Blanca," Seth yells.

I thrust my helmet on as the Tabula Rasa security guards rush out. Seth throws Ms. Corina to the side and mounts his motorcycle too.

The last thing I hear as we drive off is Ms. Corina's histrionic sobs.

●●●●●●●●●

McNeal Manor's behemoth mahogany doors are designed to look stately and imposing, but they've never appeared as welcoming to me as they do now. As soon as my feet hit the doormat, I feel a sense of peace. Seth puts his arm around my waist, and we walk across the threshold into the great hall.

Tapestries hang on every wall, and ornately carved molding rims the ceiling. The enormous hearth is still today, and coolness emanates from the marble floor.

"You're home now, Blanca. And all that crazy Tabula Rasa shit can't touch you." Seth pulls me in for a kiss.

"Did somebody say Tabula Rasa?" calls a silky voice from the corner.

I pull myself from Seth and look across the room to a velvet sofa where two figures recline.

"Fatima!" I say. "And Beau!" I tug Seth's hand, and we sit on the opposing couch. "I didn't know you were coming."

"Neither did we." Fatima leans forward, her palms on her enormous belly. "A little lower," she says to Beau.

"Here?" Beau rubs her back with gentle hands, and Fatima moans with pain.

"Yes. There." Fatima looks at me with squinted eyes. "Blanca, don't ever get pregnant. It's nothing but misery."

My voice is quiet. "That won't be a problem." It makes me remember a question I've wondered for a long time. "Did your obstetrician figure out how *you* got pregnant?"

"You mean you don't know?" Beau wags a finger between Seth

and me. "But I thought ..."

I feel my face go hot.

Next to me, Seth's pulse beats extra loud against his skin.

"No. I mean, of course I know *how*," I say. "What I mean is why did the operation on Fatima when she was fourteen not work?"

"It was called a tubal ligation." Fatima settles back into the couch. "Two percent of them fail."

"And they can be reversed." Seth scoots closer, and his breath scorches my neck.

Seth has researched this? Is my sterilization a problem for him? I've never stopped to think about Seth someday wanting to be a father. That's not a future he could have with me.

"Why are you here anyway?" Without meaning for it to, my question comes across as rude.

"A last-minute dinner invitation." Fatima smiles when she mentions food. "But I think we're actually an excuse."

Seth puts his arm around my shoulder. "An excuse for what?"

"For Pilar to come visit Cal," says Beau. "Apparently their date last night went really well."

I feel Seth's arm jerk. "What?" he asks.

Fatima shrugs. "I have no clue where they are now. My mom asked for a tour, but I needed to get off my feet."

Beau looks up at the painted wood ceiling. "This place is gigantic."

Seth clicks on his finger-chips. "Locate Dad," he says. We all pause and wait a few seconds, but the silvery screen is blank. "That's funny. Either his chip-watch is turned off or he's—"

"In a place with a lead-lined room," Beau finishes.

"Ugh!" Fatima scrunches up her nose. "Hopefully not *your* room, Blanca."

"No, of course not. Ms. Lydia had Cal's rooms converted to a cloister when she ..."

But I can't finish the sentence. When what? When she seduced Cal to be near me? When Cal seduced her to milk information on the Vestal order? There are too many memories, and they all hurt.

Seth scowls at his finger-chips. "Since when does Pilar like my dad?"

"Ever since our engagement party." Fatima readjusts her couch cushions. "Alberto's thrilled."

"Huh?" Seth looks up.

Fatima squirms. "My dad's been trying to find my mom true love for years."

"Or lust." Beau grins.

Fatima lightly slaps Beau's shoulder.

"You mean Pilar and Alberto aren't ...?" I let my question dangle in the air.

"They're just friends," says Fatima. "It was a corporate match that never went anywhere."

"Cal's the perfect find." Beau wiggles his eyebrows. "He's discrete, knows all about what makes Vestals tick, *and* he doesn't have finger-chips."

"I can't believe you're talking about my dad like he's a man whore." Seth turns off his finger-chips with an angry flick of his wrist.

Beau chuckles. "Dude, we should all be so lucky."

I try to change the subject. "So we wait for dinner?"

Fatima and Beau both shrug.

"I don't want to crash their date." I wrinkle my nose.

"Can we please stop talking about my dad's love life?" says Seth. "Why don't we go out?"

"In public?" Fatima's jaw drops. "Are you crazy?"

But Beau pounds his fist in the air. "That would be awesome! We could wear disguises."

"No way." Fatima shakes her head so forcefully I'm afraid she'll hurt herself. "I'm lucky my company lets me come here as it is. They think McNeal Manor's a safe place."

"Why do you still care about what your company thinks?" I ask. "I thought you were the rebel who wore color?"

"The fashion house believes me wearing color is a great idea. They've begged Pilar to drop the white forever."

"Doesn't Pilar do whatever her purchasers tell her to?" I ask.

Fatima scoffs. "Don't be naïve. Nobody tells my mom what to do, especially this close to her contract completion."

"Why don't we go to my place?" Beau suggests. "Ryan and Zach are making fish tacos."

"But then Seth couldn't come," I say. "He'd never be allowed in Vestal quarters."

"What about the lead-lined gloves?" asks Fatima.

"No!" Seth declares. "Never again."

"We could swim," I suggest.

"You have a pool?" Fatima rubs her belly.

"I knew we should have gone on the tour," grumbles Beau. "Is it indoors?"

"Yeah," Seth says. "I'm not sure if there are security cameras out there or not."

"They're deactivated," I say. "At least that's what your dad told me."

"Swimming could be nice," Fatima says. "My doctor says that—"

"Blanca!" Cal rushes into the great hall. "And Seth. I didn't know you two were home."

Pilar is a few steps behind him in satin ballet flats. Even without the heels, she's several inches taller than Cal. "Your father showed me his collection of old-fashioned books in the library," she says. "It's stunning."

I look at Cal closely and see a gap in his shirt where he skipped a button.

"Where were you two?" Cal asks, his face flushed.

"I gave an impromptu press conference," I answer.

"What?" Fatima screeches.

"In front of Tabula Rasa," I admit. Seth and I explain what happened. "But what I still don't understand is how Ms. Corina left all those notes for me."

"What are you talking about? What notes?" Cal's voice is full of worry.

I pull out the crumpled paper from my motorcycle jacket. "This one was on my bike today," I say. "Outside of the FBI." I tell them about the other papers, the one that was slipped in my pocket at the engagement party and the letter that was delivered to Alan.

"Why didn't you tell me about this?" asks Cal.

"Or me?" demands Seth.

I look down at my hands and shrug. "I don't know."

But the truth is, maybe I do know. Because a little part of me felt pleased. It was nice knowing I was still important enough for the Vestals to take notice. Even if it was to control me.

"What if it was Headmaster Russell?" Pilar suggests. "He's a monster!" Her eyes spark with fire.

Fatima stares at Seth accusingly. "And you wanted us to go out."

"You can't live in fear forever," Seth mumbles.

But Seth doesn't know what he's talking about.

Chapter Eight

Again and again she circles her point. She wants me to cower in submission. She wants me to spill secrets and betray my innermost soul. With her curly red bun and corduroy skirt, she tries to look innocent. But I know better. This woman is not to be trusted. If Seth weren't waiting for me in the limo with Alan, I would bolt out of Dr. Meredith's office immediately and never come back.

"How does Headmaster Russell's escape make you feel, Blanca?" Dr. Meredith writes notes about me with her finger-chips.

I decide to use a Vestal strategy called Questions. I'll answer Dr. Meredith with questions until she gives up on interrogating me.

"How do you think I feel?" I reply.

Dr. Meredith eyes me with curiosity. "Scared. Worried. Perhaps anxious. Is that why you didn't tell Cal or Seth about the notes?"

"You know about the notes?"

"Yes." She holds her fingers still. "I do."

"Isn't what's said in a therapist's office confidential?" I ask.

Of course it isn't. I'm not stupid.

Dr. Meredith colors. "Sometimes in family therapy there are situations that overlap."

"And do you think that's appropriate?" I ask. "To betray one person's confidence to help another?"

"If the client gives me permission to share, it is completely acceptable." Dr. Meredith pulls a wisp of auburn hair behind her ear.

"But how can clients trust you knowing that stories revealed in these four walls might be shared?"

"Blanca, it's called 'doctor-patient confidentiality,' and it means that you can trust me."

I keep my face as neutral as possible so I don't betray anything I feel. "You really want me to believe that, don't you?"

"Yes, I do." Dr. Meredith clicks off her finger-chips. "Let's talk more about Russell."

"You know it's Headmaster Russell, correct?"

"That's what I said."

"Russell is his last name, not his first." Damn. I broke my streak of questions.

"Does it matter to you what I call him?"

"Does it matter to *you*?" I ask back.

"Well, he's the man who beat you as a child. Who whipped you when you were too little to fight back. Can you tell me about Discipline Hour?"

"Discipline Hour?"

You're weak, Blanca. You need atonement.

Me, kneeling before the pool of purity, the concrete scraping the thin cotton of my black pants.

"Yes. Discipline Hour. Describe it to me, Blanca."

"Where should I start?"

"Where would you like to start?"

Nowhere. I don't want to talk about any of it. What happened to me when I was little is none of this lady's business. I stare down at my wrist where my cuff used to be. "Would you like to hear that Vestal training was difficult?"

"That's a good beginning. Anything else?"

"Isn't it enough that I live in the real world with the McNeals now and everything is okay?"

"If everything is okay, then why do you keep spinning your watch around your left wrist?"

I freeze both hands immediately.

Dr. Meredith squints her eyes and examines me closely. "Let's talk about what happened to you when you were fourteen. When they forced you to undergo an operation that left you sterilized."

"Seth told me it can be reversed," I blurt out.

Forget this. The sooner this appointment is over, the better.

Dr. Meredith's eyebrows raise at my unprecedented reveal of information. "So have you and Seth talked about the possibility of having children someday?"

"*Should* we talk about it?" I ask.

"Is motherhood a role you would want?"

"Don't you think I should focus on college now?"

I'm only nineteen years old. No way should I have my whole life planned out at nineteen. That's something a Vestal would do. Dr. Meredith is the crazy one.

"But you and Seth are in a serious relationship," Dr. Meredith says. "Surely the topic of an unplanned pregnancy must have come up."

"Why would it come up? I'm sterilized, remember? And why are you so interested in what Seth and I do in the bedroom. Did Cal pay you to find out?"

"Of course not." Dr. Meredith sits back in her chair and looks at me across her long slanted nose. "It's interesting to me that you mentioned Cal just now. Do you expect Cal to meddle in your life?"

"No," I say definitively.

Unless he thought I was in danger. Then Cal would stick his nose where it didn't belong.

●●●●●●●●●

Seth should be here. The deal was he would escort me to and from Dr. Meredith's office. When I freaked out about my appointment this morning, Seth promised that he would wait for me. But when I step out into the piercing sunlight, Seth is nowhere to be found. All I see is Alan.

"Where's Seth?" I plant my feet on the pavement and don't budge.

Alan holds his hat in his hand and rumples the brim. "Something came up," he says. "Seth had a hot tip on *Veritas Rex* to follow. But don't worry, Ms. Blanca. I can take you home."

I'll take my fury out on Seth later. "Okay," I say to Alan. "I have a tutoring session with Irene in twenty minutes."

"We'll be there in no time, Miss Blanca." Alan holds open the door for me.

The plush interior of the backseat is a welcome relief, especially since the privacy divider is closed. I pour myself a glass of water from the crystal decanter and buckle my seat belt.

When the car rolls, I stare out the window and hunt for billboards. No matter how many times I see Vestal advertisements, I still smile. It's like being watched over by larger-than-life friends.

I'm so intent on looking for advertisements that it takes me a few minutes to notice that Alan's headed in the wrong direction.

"Alan," I rap on the divider, "we're going to the manor. Remember?"

But instead of turning the car around, Alan gets on the highway, headed south.

"Alan?" I slide open the panel in case he can't hear me.

The second I see what's in front of me I scream.

"Alan isn't here anymore," says Headmaster Russell.

His wicked laugh turns my blood to ice.

Chapter Nine

• • • • • • • • • ● • • • • • • • • •

D r. Meredith's office seems a million years ago. Her questions can't hurt me no matter how deep they probe. But the man in the driver's seat is real.

And he's terrifying.

"There's no need to scream, Blanca," says Headmaster Russell. "It's not like you to be so dramatic."

"Yes, Headmaster Russell. I mean no, Headmaster Russell. It isn't."

"Didn't you expect to see me?"

"No, sir. I didn't."

"But surely you knew I'd come."

"Yes, Headmaster Russell. Of course, Headmaster Russell." *Vestals avenge all wrongs especially when our honor is at stake.* "Where are you taking me, sir?" It's hard to keep fear from my voice.

"Not only you," says Headmaster Russell. "Your scumbag too." Keeping his left hand on the wheel, Headmaster Russell reaches over to the passenger's seat and pulls a blanket away.

Underneath is Seth, bound and gagged. His hands are locked into lead-lined mitts, and his wrists are fastened to a pipe bomb.

"Blaaaahh!" Seth yells before Headmaster Russell throws the blanket back down.

"What are you doing? Where are we going?" I've lost control of my tone. Headmaster Russell will sense my hysteria.

"You'll see soon enough. But first we need to deal with your boyfriend."

"No." My heartbeat pounds. "Let him go. Leave Seth out of this!"

"Oh, Blanca." Headmaster Russell's voice is soft. "You know I can't allow that. What do we say about Viruses? I know you remember."

"'You can't ever trust a Virus.'" The lie rolls off my tongue from the deep banks of my memory. "But Seth is more than a Virus. He's also my friend."

Headmaster Russell laughs. "Your 'friend'? Too bad for him. Your last friend didn't fare too well."

The words sting. But they also confuse me. Does he mean Ethan? Or Fatima? Or …

"Seth isn't a threat," I state. "He doesn't want anything to do with the Vestals. He doesn't care about power. He won't question your authority."

"Too late!" Headmaster Russell shouts. "That simpering idiot Corina is Headmaster now."

"She can barely hold things together," I say. "Tabula Rasa is falling apart." *If you want to control somebody instead of be controlled, tell that person what they want to hear.*

"I'm not surprised," growls Headmaster Russell. "All Corina is good for is fancy charm lessons."

"That's so true, Headmaster Russell." From the corner of my eye, I see Seth's blanket shift. "It would be better for everyone if you were back in charge." A hand. I see Seth's hand! There's a sliver of duct tape. "Maybe I could find a way to make that happen."

"You!" Headmaster Russell laughs derisively. "How could you fix things? You're the one who is responsible for all of it. Today I pay back old debts."

With a suddenness that jolts my pulse to staccato, the blanket moves, and Seth lurches toward the steering wheel. "Naaaaahh!" Seth yells through the gag.

The car veers left, headed straight for oncoming traffic. Headmaster Russell wrenches the steering wheel back, and the momentum tosses Seth's body like a rag doll. Headmaster Russell regains control of the car and then sprays Seth with a fine mist that clouds the passenger's seat.

Seth screams.

"Pepper spray," says Headmaster Russell. "It works every time."

Seth writhes in agony an arm's length away.

My nostrils burn as some of the vapor comes my direction. Panic clutches my insides. Fear saturates every pore. "What do you want?"

"To fix old mistakes."

"I want that too." The words rush out on instinct. "I'll do

whatever you want. But please don't hurt Seth."

"Virus," Headmaster Russell corrects. "He's a Virus, not a person. And Vestals don't concern themselves with scum."

"Yes, Headmaster Russell. Of course, Headmaster Russell."

My gaze lands on the crystal decanter of water. I reach out surreptitiously to grab it. A plan formulates in my mind.

I'll wait for an intersection. For the car to pause. Then, I'll clobber him.

I glance out the window to get my bearings. An old-fashioned sign decaying with age passes by. GILROY. GARLIC CAPITOL OF THE WORLD. Underneath is a faded picture of garlic, the paint peeling in the hot California sun.

"What's in Gilroy?" I ask.

"You'll see." Headmaster Russell pulls off the highway onto a quiet exit. We're surrounded by abandoned farmland. The dirt is cracked and dusty, forever parched by drought.

Now could be my chance. If we veer off the road, we won't hit anything but sage brush. I tighten my grip on the crystal.

But then a van pulls up next to us with a mother and children. I can't risk crashing into them.

"You were always such a good teacher," I say. *Make them feel important.* "The other day the FBI interviewed me and I was really scared. But I knew exactly what to say because of you."

"And what was that?" Headmaster Russell eyes me through the rearview mirror. His face is flushed red with heat.

"They wanted to know about the Guardians. So I recited verbatim from my textbook."

"That was stupid!" Headmaster Russell snaps.

My head jerks like I was slapped. "What do you mean?"

"You should have told them everything. The Guardians are the biggest threat to the Vestal order we know."

"Really? Why?"

"Enough questions!" Headmaster Russell slams the privacy divider shut.

I loosen my grip on the decanter and feel sick inside. Have I missed my chance?

I look out the window to rows of abandoned garlic fields. Occasionally I see a signs that say SAVE OUR AQUIFER or GARLIC NOT GOLF. It's hard to imagine that this area once contained rich farmland.

Ahead of us, in the distance, is a cluster of aging gray houses. The limo veers left into extensive farmland.

"We're almost there," says Headmaster Russell. He slides open the divider once more and smiles back at me in the rearview mirror. "Wait until you see what I've planned for your Virus."

Now's my moment! I can't wait any longer. I grab the crystal decanter and pound my arm through the opening to the front seat. But in my haste, I miss Headmaster Russell and shatter the windshield instead.

"What the?" shouts Headmaster Russell as glass bombards him from every angle. Shards scatter back to me, and I feel wetness. My whole body slams forward as the car lurches to a stop. I hear the screech of wheels. I barely pick myself up from the floor when I see

Headmaster Russell, his face gashed and oozing, lean back to attack me with the pepper spray.

"No!" I hold up my arms like a shield.

But the expected assault never comes.

Instead, somebody flings the car door open and hauls me out with strong arms.

When I look up, I see Keung.

And he smiles.

The row of perfect teeth gleams, but Keung's grin does nothing to soften the sharp, square edges of his jaw. Keung is a head taller than me and almost twice my size—in pure muscle. His black shirt bulges at the biceps, the cloth stretched across broad shoulders. The last time I saw Keung, I was sixteen and he was eighteen. Now, three years later, the pull of attraction is as strong as ever.

Guardians swarm all around us. Black cars are parked behind us, blocking the road. I hear rapid-fire Mandarin and Headmaster Russell screaming obscenities.

Keung sets me on the sidewalk with steady hands. "Are you okay?

I nod. "It's you!" I say like an idiot. Then I glance back to the limo. "Seth! He's tied to an explosive."

Keung barks an order to one of his companions, a tall skinny guy I don't recognize with a scar across his face, who releases Seth from the car.

I know Keung is here to rescue me. I've never been so sure of anything in my life. But I'm not positive that protection will extend to my boyfriend. "Please help Seth before it's too late," I blurt.

"Don't worry," answers Keung. "We'll take real good care of Seth."

Chapter Ten

I clench onto Keung, afraid that nerves will knock me over. The warm span of his hand steadies the small of my back. Keung was always good at taking care of people. He watched out for his friends and annihilated his enemies. I think that's why Fatima liked him so much. She was on a break with Beau when we first met him. Plus, the Tabula Rasa teachers told us to *stay away* from the Guardians. After that ultimatum, there was no stopping her. Fatima was obsessed with our new Chinese exchange students, and most especially Keung, who was not only the best looking but the ringleader of them all.

Some things never change.

I lived at Tabula Rasa my whole life, so I was used to seeing Guardians come and go. In many ways, they were similar to us Vestals. They were cut off from society and kept private and hidden.

Like us, their parents had given them up in the hopes that they would have a better life.

But the difference was scale. Instead of ten Vestal graduates each year, there were hundreds of Guardians. Enough to send a small handful to America to perfect their English and serve as cheap language tutors for Tabula Rasa students.

Of course, by cheap, Headmaster Russell meant free. He worked the Guardians harder than his minions. The only time I saw Keung or his friends relax was the two hours they spent in the gym each day practicing martial arts.

Suddenly, Fatima was very interested in PE.

But Fatima isn't here now, I'm not sure where here is, and there are some wounds that never heal, no matter how much time has passed.

The Guardian that holds Seth wields a gigantic knife.

I look up at Keung with pleading eyes. "Please don't let anything happen to Seth."

The skinny guy with the scar lifts up his blade. Another one stands inches away.

"Please!" I cry again.

"Relax, *tiānshǐ*" Keung murmurs. "You're safe now."

With several vigorous saws, the Guardian cuts the ties that bind Seth's hands and feet and rips the gag from his mouth. His companion removes the pipe bomb and cradles it like a newborn.

"Blanca?" Seth rubs his eyes with the lead-lined mitts. "Are you there? All I see is red."

I fly around the car and throw myself into his arms. The acrid stench of sweat greets me, but Seth has never smelled so good.

I look back at Keung. "Thank you," I say simply.

Keung raises his eyebrows and turns to his companions who are using Headmaster Russell as the target for roundhouse kicks. "Cho," Keung says with a voice laced in authority, "take Seth back to the car. This is a private matter."

Seth wraps his arms around me like a vice. "What do you mean private? What's going on? Who are you? I can't see shit because of the pepper spray." Seth holds up one of the mitts. "And the key! Where's the key to these things?"

"I don't have time for questions, Rex." Keung turns away.

"It'll be okay," I whisper to Seth. "Promise you'll do what they say."

"Do what who says?" asks Seth, too loudly.

I don't have the chance to explain.

The skinny Guardian with the scar wrests Seth away. "This way, Veritas Rex. You're coming with me."

My arms fall down like two limp noodles, my hands empty without anything to hold. I spin around to look at Keung. When I see his face and read the determination, I suddenly realize what will happen.

Because it has to happen.

Because this moment has been coming for years.

"What will you do to him?" I ask.

Keung takes a step closer to Headmaster Russell, who cowers in a heap on the sidewalk, and stares down at his matted hair. "What I've meant to do to him for a long time." Keung turns to the man holding the explosive. "How long until the bomb goes off?"

The Guardian shrugs. "The timer says five minutes. Maybe more, maybe less."

"That'll be perfect." Keung twists to look at me. "Maybe you should wait in the car with your boyfriend."

"No!" I surprise myself with the force of my voice. "Why not take off his cuff and leave him for the police?" I detest Headmaster Russell, but murdering him seems wrong.

Keung shakes his head. "I'm sorry, *tiānshǐ*, but you know I can't."

"But there are lots of ways to—"

"No," interrupts Keung. "There is only one path. And it's what he would do too in my position."

Two of the Guardians lift Headmaster Russell up. His nose is smashed, and his eye sockets seep blood.

The same blood that is splattered over my white shirt.

"Headmaster Russell," I whisper.

"*Tiānshǐ*, you need to wait in the car."

At first, I hesitate, but then I nod. Because I know that Keung speaks the truth. I don't have the stomach for what will happen next.

Keung's men escort me to a nondescript black sedan.

"What's going on?" Seth demands as I pile into the back seat.

"It'll be okay," I whisper. I reach over to fasten his seat belt. Through the back window I see the skinny man with the scar jam the limo into gear. Keung watches as the rest of them roll the vehicle away, down the road into the forgotten farmland. The car takes on momentum of its own and cruises into the horizon.

A few minutes later, I hear an explosion.

"What happened?" Seth thrashes in the seat, snapping his head toward the sound.

I reach for his lead-lined hands. "Nothing," I say.

Everything.

Chapter Eleven

My fingers knit together with Seth's, and our pulses beat as one. Faster and harder the blood pumps. Adrenaline clears my thinking. Keung saved my life.

"What happened?" Seth asks again. "What was that noise?"

"It was nothing." I don't blink. "How'd you get kidnapped?"

"I was checking my hits," Seth mumbles. "I didn't see him coming."

I picture Seth, so engrossed in his finger-chips he didn't notice his attacker until it was too late. *The people in front of you are what matters. Not your palm.* That's what Headmaster Russell would say—and he used Seth's tech-addiction to his advantage.

"It'll be okay, Seth. We're safe now."

I see movement out the left window, and suddenly the car door swings open.

"Get in the front seat." There is a determined bent to Keung's jaw. "I'm not your chauffeur."

I turn to look at Seth. His eyes are still watery, but the redness is fading. I wipe his tears away with my sleeve.

"Blanca!" Seth grabs my arm.

"I'll be fine."

Keung holds the door for me to climb out. He guides me all the way around to the front with his hand on my elbow. He closes my car door with a sharp whack and I settle into the upholstery. A few seconds later Keung sits next to me. We click our seat belts at the same time, and our hands touch. When he looks at me, Keung's eyes turn gentle, exactly like I remember them.

"The last time I rode in the front seat Ms. Lydia was abducting me to Nevada," I say.

"Don't worry, *tiānshǐ*. We're not going to Nevada." Keung smiles. "So is this guy your boyfriend?" Keung asks me in Mandarin.

I struggle to respond in a language I never truly mastered. "Yes, he is."

"What?" Seth calls from the backseat. "You speak Chinese?"

"No," Keung answers in English with a mocking tone. "She mangles it." He looks sideways at me and grins.

"It's because I had such an awful tutor." Despite my nerves—or maybe because of them—I giggle.

"I recall teaching you a trick or two," Keung says in Mandarin.

A flush creeps up my cheeks.

"Where are you taking us?" Seth demands.

My mind whirls. "What will happen? I saw—" but I don't finish my sentence.

"You saw nothing," answers Keung in Mandarin. "You were in the car, remember? And Rex back there was wiping his eyes the whole time."

The reality of what transpired hits me. "I'm not a witness to anything," I whisper. "You protected me." The foreign tongue comes out stilted, but the years of learning flow back.

"Always," Keung replies.

"So where are we going?" I ask in English so Seth can hear too.

"Somewhere you'll be safe. It's time for you to have another chat with Agents Plunkett and Marlow."

"The FBI!" I exclaim. "But—"

"Tell them the truth," Keung says. "Exactly what you saw."

"But I didn't see anything."

"Exactly," Keung answers.

"Hey guys," Seth says. "I think my eyes are clearing up." He leans forward from the back seat to look at Keung. "Holy shit it's you!"

"You know him?" I ask Seth.

"Of course I do. He's Timothy Wu, the Chinese representative to the Silicon Valley Tech Council."

"See, Blanca?" Keung wipes a smile from his face. "You can tell your friends at the FBI anything you want about me."

"He has diplomatic immunity," says Seth.

"What does that mean?"

"It means," answers Keung, "that I can do whatever the hell I want."

"Almost," growls Seth from the back seat.

●●●●⬤●●●●

The FBI building looms large in front of me. The trees sway in the wind, and the birds' musical notes sound surreal. But I am unaffected by the quiet afternoon and the calming presence of nature; my eyes are glued to Keung's car as it drives away from me. Anxiety tangles my heart. The fear doesn't come from worrying about what I have to do or figuring out what to say but from wondering if I'll ever see Keung again. I faced the thought of never seeing him once before and it crushed me.

"Blanca," Seth's urgent voice snaps me back into attention, "can you get these off?" He holds up his cloistered hands, the lead mitts still locked.

"I don't have the key."

Seth winces as he tries unsuccessfully to remove them. "We've got to call my dad. Does your chip-watch work?"

"Yes. It should." I click on my watch. "We should call Nancy too. I'm not going in there without a lawyer."

"Definitely. I've got my own lawyer for *Veritas Rex* too. Plus we need to find out what happened to Alan and make sure he's safe."

I furiously call for help as time flees away. Surely Agents Plunkett and Marlow know we're here. They're probably spying from one of the darkened windows above. When I'm done, I hand my watch over to Seth so he can call the lawyer he mentioned. Then I crumple in his arms and feel his heavy hands surround me.

"Oh, Blanca. What a freaking mess. I'm so sorry," murmurs Seth.

"It wasn't your fault," I whisper back. "And it's over now."

"No. It's not." Seth shakes his head. "And how do you know Timothy Wu? I didn't think you followed tech news."

"Who?" I ask. Then I remember that Seth means Keung.

"And since when did you speak Chinese?"

"Mandarin," I correct. "And I don't speak it very well."

I share how Keung and I met and make the story brief.

"He's a Guardian?" Seth asks.

"I told you Guardians filled government positions. Why are you so surprised?"

"No. I mean. I don't know." He pauses a moment before he continues. "So if it was some sort of Vestal/Guardian exchange program did Vestals go to Beijing too?"

The only way Headmaster Russell would have allowed students to escape his control was if there was something for Tabula Rasa to gain.

Or if Barbelo insisted.

"I'm not sure exactly. If they did, they never came back. Vestals have always dealt with the trafficking of secrets. So I really don't know. At the time I believed what they told me. The Guardians were there to perfect their English and to help us learn Mandarin."

"How long did you study?" Seth asks. "I didn't know you could speak another language."

"Five languages," I correct.

"Five?" Seth's eyes are wide with surprise.

102

"English, German, Spanish, Arabic, and Mandarin," I say. "I told you about this last year."

"No, you didn't!"

I shake my head. "Yes, I did! I told you that at Tabula Rasa we didn't learn any science or technology. We focused on the seven Liberal Arts."

"Yeah, like literature and poetry and stuff."

"No. Like grammar, logic, rhetoric, music, literature, history, and languages." It's hard to be patient.

"Okay, wow. So, Timothy was your tutor?"

"Yes," I answer. And I leave it at that.

Chapter Twelve

For a lawyer, Seth's attorney wears a lot of eyeliner. The dark, smoky lines make her emerald eyes appear catlike, which is fitting, because there's a feline essence about her whole person. The way her long body sits territorially in her chair or how her auburn hair is striped like a tiger. She carries herself in a way that says "hot" and "mess" both at the same time.

Even Agent Marlow falls under her spell. She gets him to remove Seth's mitts in two minutes flat.

But I can cast a spell too. Sexy lawyer might not be my thing, but girl next door is. And right now, covered in Headmaster Russell's blood, I've got damsel in distress going on too. I came here of my own volition to cooperate. Those are all the tools I need to make this work. I perch on the edge of my seat and lean into the table.

"Agents Plunkett and Marlow. Thank you so much for seeing us on such short notice. Seth and I raced here as fast as we could to tell you what happened."

I look at Nancy who sits prim in her boxy suit. She gives me an encouraging nod.

"I need to say, as a former Vestal, that I so respect what you are trying to do for our community. You seek truth and try to offer accountability for all the wrongs against us." *Controlling people is easier than you'd think.*

I smile pathetically.

On purpose.

"That's why when Seth and I encountered Headmaster Russell today, we immediately came to you to report what happened."

"What?" exclaims Agent Plunkett. "You saw Russell?"

My eyes are wet. I blot them bravely with my sleeve. *Cry on cue. Stop crying. Tears are a tool.*

"It's okay, Blanca. I'll go first." Seth wipes off my cheeks with gentle fingers. But his lawyer jumps in before he can speak.

"My client is here of his own accord," she says. Her husky voice sounds like a purr. "He is fully cooperating with your investigation."

I don't blink. Hopefully Seth remembers what to say.

Seth describes standing outside the limo checking his website and then being overtaken by Headmaster Russell.

I cringe when I hear the details of how Seth was tazed and gagged. No wonder Alan was forced to play along. One wrong move and Seth could have been killed.

But then Seth starts telling about Keung's rescue, which he was supposed to let me handle.

You can't ever trust a Virus. That's what Headmaster Russell always said. I interrupt Seth before he gets us in trouble. "Mr. Wu escorted us to his car," I say. "Then he drove us here."

Agents Plunkett and Marlow look at each other. Agent Plunkett jerks her thumb and Agent Marlow steps out of the room for a moment before rushing back.

"And where is he now?" asks Agent Plunkett.

"I don't know," I answer honesty.

"More importantly," says Agent Marlow in a low voice. "Where's Russell?"

This is the tricky part. I picture the last time I saw Headmaster Russell, when he looked like a human punching bag. "I didn't see what happened to him. I was in the car."

"What do you think happened to him?" asks Agent Marlow.

"There's no need for my client to speculate." Nancy jumps in. "She's told you what she knows."

"And you?" Agent Plunkett's voice is deep and grave when she addresses Seth. "Veritas Rex, is it? You didn't think to capture any of this online?"

"I still had the mitts on. They weren't removed until we were dumped here at the bureau."

I wince at the word "dumped." Seth should have said dropped off. Or accompanied.

"So neither of you knows what happened to Russell?" asks Agent Marlow.

"No, we don't," I reiterate. "That's why we came to you for help."

"My eyes were messed up," Seth says. "I couldn't see shit."

"Seth," says his lawyer, "it's time to take you to a doctor. We're done here." She stands up like liquid silk.

"But—" protests Agent Marlow.

Nancy rises too. "No, I agree with my colleague. Our clients have given you their statements. I'm sure you'll be very busy investigating further."

Agent Marlow jumps up. "But—"

"Can you tell us where Russell took you?" asks Agent Plunkett.

Can I? I think hard, trying to remember what Keung said about that piece of information. I'm not sure if he mentioned it at all. But it's only a matter of time before somebody discovers the wreck of the limo.

"Gilroy," I say. "I saw a sign that mentioned Gilroy."

"Did you see any street names?" asks Agent Marlow.

I shake my head.

"That's it?" Agent Plunkett asks. "One word? Gilroy is all you can give us?"

Agent Marlow presses on. "Distinctive houses? Landmarks? Anything?"

I picture the gray houses. "Sorry," I say. "I don't remember."

Agent Plunkett steps closer and peers into my face. "If you're not going to be more helpful than that, you can forget about acquiring your mother's file."

That was the worst thing she could have said to me because it only serves to harden my resolve.

I'll find out about Ms. Lydia no matter what. Agent Plunkett won't stop me. She'd be better off focusing on tracking that limo.

Cal paces the pavement. As soon as we step outside, he flies over and grabs us in a big hug. The night air feels chilly, but in Seth and Cal's arms, I feel protected from the cold.

"Blanca, Seth. Thank God you're both okay."

"Uh, Dad? I think you're crushing us," Seth says.

"Oh! Sorry." Cal releases us for a half a second and then hugs us again. "Oh my dear girl. If only it was easier to keep you safe."

"That's exactly what I was thinking," says Nancy. "Your daughter's legal fees will pay for my next vacation home."

"Hopefully a small one," Cal says. "Blanca's all done with dangerous situations." He looks at me with warm brown eyes. "Aren't you, sweetheart?"

I nod like I mean it.

"Tiffany?" Cal eyes the tall beauty standing next to Seth. "Well this is a surprise. You're about the last person I expected to see here tonight."

Tiffany? As in the name scribbled across Seth's abdomen in permanent ink?

I feel like something died in my throat and is choking me. What a fun way to meet the first woman my boyfriend slept with.

"Mr. McNeal." Tiffany extends her long, slim hand. "I'm the in-house legal counsel for *Veritas Rex* now." The sleeve of her blazer rises up and exposes a small tattoo on the inside of her wrist.

It's so tiny I have to squint. But there it is, in green and black—a lion-headed cobra.

"Tiffany graduated law school at Boalt Hall," Seth mumbles, looking at me. "Top of her class."

"That doesn't surprise me at all," says Cal. "You always were clever. But I didn't know that you and my son still had ..." Cal's forehead wrinkles as he struggles to find the words. "A professional relationship."

I glare at Seth, and he cowers.

Cal darts his gaze between us both. "Well, Seth and Blanca, let's get back home to the manor, shall we?"

"Wait," Tiffany says. "Seth, if I'm going to properly represent you, I need to know what the hell happened."

I dig my nails into my hand so hard that I almost pierce the skin.

"You can fill me in while I take you to the doctor to get your eyes checked," Tiffany says.

"Your eyes?" Cal jumps. "What's the matter with your eyes?"

"Pepper spray," answers Seth.

Which seems like justice right about now.

Chapter Thirteen

My blood pounds hot in my head. My lungs struggle for my body to catch up with my intentions. Running around my courtyard in circles pushes me to exhaustion. Sweat drips down my bra and trickles across my back. In the moonlight, my pale skin glistens.

What exactly are Seth and Tiffany doing at this very second? Are they at the doctor's? How long does it take to have a lawyer-client conversation?

I shouldn't think about any of that. This is the time to sweat.

An intense exercise regime was something Ms. Lydia insisted on. An hour of running, an hour of Kenpō, and then yoga every day like clockwork.

"You've got to be prepared for anything," Ms. Lydia used to say.

"The next photo shoot could happen any day."

I slow my pace to a jog before I walk it out. As it turns out, my next photo shoot is tomorrow. It's a big one too. Since McNeal Solar is sponsoring the next Vestal corporate banquet, other companies are loaning us Vestals to add extra star power to our commercial. I had been looking forward to it for weeks, but now all I can think about is Seth, Tiffany, and Gilroy.

My breathing is normal again as I lap the courtyard in a slow walk. I head to the redwood box and pull out my yoga mat. I unlace my shoes and step onto rubber stickiness with bare feet.

If Ms. Lydia were here now, what would she say? Would she have any motherly advice for me?

You can't ever trust a Virus. That's what Headmaster Russell would say. *And your last friend didn't fare too well.*

I squint my eyes and try to make Headmaster Russell's face go away. I picture my friends instead. I float back to the past.

"You've got minds like diamonds," Headmaster Russell told us. "We polish Tabula Rasa students to perfection but only the highest quality will reach graduation."

The thought of being sent home terrified me for seventeen years. Like most Tabula Rasa students, I didn't know who my parents were. I certainly didn't want to return to people who had sent me away.

So it didn't matter what the subject was— Vestal history, languages, or charm—I paid attention. I got good grades but wasn't a showoff. *The tallest nail gets wacked.*

Keung and the rest of the Guardians were black belts in Karate.

Fatima watched them practice every day, mainly to make Beau jealous.

She was annoyed when Headmaster Russell assigned Keung to be my personal language partner. Keung was supposed to teach me Mandarin, and I was to help him perfect his English accent.

I slide into Pigeon stretch and wince at the memory.

The language lab was filled with cubicles. Voices carried so you had to murmur. Ms. Alma paced the aisles, on the hunt for misconduct. But in the beginning, all Keung and I did was talk.

"How old are you?" he asked me that first session.

I wanted to say, "I turned sixteen a couple days ago," but I couldn't figure out the proper words. "Sixteen," I answered bluntly.

"And so sweet," Keung said. "I noticed you the first day I arrived."

I blushed at the compliment. It was a lot easier to understand Keung speaking than it was to formulate my responses.

"Most people look at my friend Fatima," I answered in stilted Mandarin.

"Most people look for the obvious. But I always search for angels." Keung took my hand and unfolded my palm. On my tingling skin he traced the characters for "angel."

Tiānshǐ.

Out here in the night on my yoga mat, that moment still feels fresh. I relax into Child's Pose and reflect on what happened next.

The weeks passed, and it became harder and harder not to tell Fatima. The silent touches … the feet brushed against each other … the feeling of Keung's hand on my knee when Ms. Alma wasn't looking. When I saw Keung, my body yearned to explode.

I spent every spare moment I had studying Mandarin. I wanted the hour I spent with Keung each day to be perfect. Still, I mangled simple phrases.

"You do better with gestures," Keung would say. Then he'd scan for teachers, and when the coast was clear, reach for my hand.

The first time he kissed me, I was afraid of being caught. But Keung's lips were soft against mine, and the wet feeling of our tongues excited me.

It was my first experience breaking the rules, and it made me feel alive.

After several weeks, stolen kisses were no longer enough. My whole body was coming to life, hungry for more.

So I went to Fatima for advice. By this point, Fatima had given up on flirting with Keung and the rest of the Guardians. She and Beau were back together and enjoying life as sterilized sixteen-year-olds.

At first, Fatima was shocked when I told her that Keung was interested in me.

"You?" she asked with disbelief. "And Keung?"

I tried not to be insulted.

But after a few moments, Fatima tapped her chin with her finger. "I can kind of see it," she admitted.

"Don't picture it too hard," I said. "The whole reason I told you is because I want a place where Keung and I can be private."

Fatima raised her eyebrows. "Oh! I see. Sure, Blanca. I know the perfect place."

I never should have asked for Fatima's help.

The cold outside penetrates me. The slick sweat from my run feels like ice. I stand up on my yoga mat and step into Warrior to get my blood moving again. I glide into Warrior Two and look up at the stars.

Keung and I had exactly fifteen minutes in the supply closet before either of us would be discovered. There were no token affections, no words of endearment. Just a hot mad rush of stripping off my black spandex suit. Of Keung tracing the curves of my sixteen-year-old frame. Of our two bodies entwined for quick thrusts of pleasure.

I didn't love Keung. He wasn't my boyfriend. But he was my release. My escape. The one time in my life I didn't follow the rules.

Which is what makes what happened next so difficult. I slide into Plank and brace myself for the memory.

The third time Keung and I met in the supply closet was the day he was caught. I left first. We thought if we exited at different times, it would look less suspicious. But somehow Headmaster Russell found out what happened. He just didn't know who Keung was seeing.

A couple of hours later, it was supposed to be dinner time. Instead of poached fish and asparagus, Headmaster Russell had every last one of us line up in the cafeteria at attention. He walked back and forth with the whip he used for Discipline Hour. Keung stood in front of us, his head held down.

"Someone has been meeting our Guardian friend for an illicit act that is strictly against the rules. Who is it?" Headmaster Russell fingered the whip, and a little girl whimpered. "Was it you?"

Headmaster Russell was grim. He walked up to the second grader and stared into her eyes.

"No, sir." She whimpered. Her blond hair looked shiny and thin.

"Are you sure?" Headmaster Russell cracked the whip. Some of her classmates wept.

"Please, sir," she said, "I don't know what you are talking about."

Ms. Corina rushed over and whispered in his ear.

Headmaster Russell stood back up to his full height and nodded his head. "Very well. Primary grades dismissed."

Then his violence began in earnest, and it was all directed against Keung.

"Tell me who it was," bellowed Headmaster Russell, lashing Keung's back.

"Never." Keung's shirt streamed blood.

"Who was it?" Headmaster Russell attacked harder and harder with the whip.

"*Tiānshǐ,*" Keung whimpered, "don't say a word. I endure this for you."

"*Tiānshǐ?*" Headmaster Russell screamed in broken Mandarin. "Who is that?"

"Don't speak," Keung cried. "I beg you to be quiet."

The words bubbled inside me like a volcano. Surely my tears would give me away. But I forced them down with determination. *Cry on cue. Stop crying. Tears are a weapon.* I couldn't risk betraying Keung.

The thrashing became more and more brutal. Usually with us

Tabula Rasa students, Headmaster Russell was careful not to leave a mark.

But he unleashed the full force of his temper on Keung. Headmaster Russell could send Keung back to Beijing in whatever condition he wanted.

"For you, *tiānshī*. For you." Those were the last words I heard Keung utter before he passed out on the floor.

Here on my yoga mat, my muscles can hold me no longer. I fall flat on the ground and bury my face in my arms.

My guilt overwhelms me. It presses me into the mat with the force of giants. Guilt for Keung's whipping. Guilt for withholding information about Keung from Seth earlier. Guilt for not thinking of Ms. Lydia as my mother.

Guilt for Headmaster Russell and whatever became of him in that garlic field.

I lay on that yoga mat forever, prostrate in front of the universe. As if I could atone for my sins.

The mantra Cal taught me embraces my soul. *I'm a survivor, I've got good instincts, and I can think for myself.*

But the truth is, I've done a lot of despicable things.

And surviving is not the same thing as living.

When I finally stand up, I am drained of all energy. I roll my yoga mat with limp arms and return it to the redwood box.

When I spin around to head back up the ladder to my room, my foot catches on a loose paving stone. The stone doesn't merely jut out, it looks different than the others, like it's a slightly different color. I bend over to inspect the imperfection. With cold hands, I reach down to lift the stone. Perhaps I'll find a colony of earthworms for my efforts.

But instead, I discover treasure: a white bag with the initials LX in gold thread.

I reach inside the bag with trembling fingers.

And find a silver key.

● ● ● ● ● ● ● ● ●

In the nakedness of the shower, I contemplate my prize, the soap suds slipping down me in clean white bubbles. The key feels sharp in my hand, but also small and fragile. How long has it been in the courtyard? Did Ms. Lydia want me to find it? It would be so easy to lose.

It was so easy to hide.

I know Ms. Lydia had secrets. But I don't know if she meant for me to discover them or not.

Suddenly there is a rap on my bathroom door. "Blanca?" Seth calls. "Can I come in?"

"Give me a minute!" I shut off the faucet and scramble for a towel. I hurriedly dry myself off, slip into my fluffy bathrobe, and pocket the key. When I open the door for Seth, I'm still damp.

"What are you doing here?"

"What do you mean?" asks Seth. "Of course I'd be here."

"You're all done with Tiffany then?" I march out of the bathroom into my dressing room.

"Blanca."

I open the middle drawer of my dresser and dig for flannel pajamas.

"Come here." Seth reaches for my shoulder. "Let me hold you. This day has been horrible."

I allow myself to be enveloped in his arms. Unlike me, Seth still hasn't showered. His taunt body reeks of sweat. It's probably making my clean hair stinky.

I press him away and turn back to my dresser. "Are your eyes okay?"

"Yeah. I'll be all right."

"You're lucky Tiffany was there to take you to the doctor. I'm not sure if Cal and I could have managed." I wrestle out the flannel and slam the drawer shut.

"Look," Seth crosses his arms, "I'm sorry you had to meet Tiffany that way. She's just my lawyer! We've been friends for years. She's really good with Internet piracy law. And with *Veritas Rex*, I need all the help I can get without somebody being all judgy about it." Seth talks so fast he babbles.

I pull on my pajama bottoms underneath my robe. "That's okay." My voice is curt. "You don't need to explain your private business to me."

"But it's not private. I don't want to have secrets from you."

I feel Ms. Lydia's key in my pocket. I'm not sure I can believe him. Everybody has secrets.

"So now it's your turn," says Seth.

"What?" I jerk my hand away from the key.

"How do you know Keung?"

"I told you. He was my language lab partner."

Seth takes a step closer and leans against the dresser with his elbow. We're mere inches apart. "Why'd he call you his angel?"

My shoulders jerk. "What do you mean?"

"His '*tiānshǐ*.' I looked it up."

"Oh." I adjust the collar of my bathrobe. "It's been a long day. Maybe we should talk about this tomorrow."

"I watched him kill a man for you. I lied about it to the FBI!"

"That's not true! You and I, we didn't see anything. We were in the back of the car almost the whole time. You didn't tell anything to Agents Plunkett and Marlow that wasn't true."

Seth reaches out and touches my shoulder. "But we didn't tell them everything, did we? We didn't tell them about what we think happened. Or about the explosion."

"That bomb would have gone off no matter what. We don't know who or what it hurt." I rush into my bedroom and pull the top of my pajamas over my head so fast that all Seth sees is a fleeting glance of my back as the flannel falls down.

He stands in the doorway and watches. "Why do you trust him? Why not give Keung over to the FBI and let him face the justice a vigilante like him deserves?"

"Because," I begin, still facing away from him. I can't quite say it, but I know the time has come.

I slowly turn around and walk over to Seth. I take my hand and slide it down his chest. Then, when it reaches his left side, I stop. Even with his shirt on I know exactly what the tattoos say underneath.

I trace the word "Tiffany."

Seth catches my wrist in a grip like iron. Then he releases me and turns away. "Oh," he says again.

"Seth—"

"No, I—" But Seth doesn't finish his sentence. He paces the room like his feet have springs.

"I never said I was a virgin." My voice is weak.

Seth runs his fingers through his hair, lifting it up like spikes.

"No. It's cool. It's just that … I thought we were waiting because … because … Shoot, Blanca. It's really late." Seth's words sputter out. He lifts his arm and smells an armpit. "Hell, I stink. I better go home and get cleaned up."

"Seth, wait." I rush toward him.

He leans down and kisses me on the cheek. "See you tomorrow. Okay? I'll pick you up from the photo shoot."

I nod and lean against the doorway. I watch him stalk down the hall and think about following him but choose exhaustion instead.

Sleep calls to me like a siren. I crash into bed and pull back the coverlet, stretching my legs into silky cotton sheets. But my cheek brushes something scratchy against my pillow. I lift my head up, annoyed at the intrusion, and discover a note written on ecru parchment.

Human beings want two things: relationships
and a feeling of importance. Vestals deserve
both.

Chapter Fourteen

• • • • • • • • • • ● • • • • • • • • •

The deep bass of the music pulses like blood. Partygoers in silk and spandex intertwine up and down the grand staircase. Their gleaming white outfits reflect in the light. Giant masks covered with feathers and sequins obscure every face. In this masquerade of Vestals, the only woman easy to spot is Fatima. Her pregnant figure totters on four-inch heels. Fatima's parents, Pilar and Alberto, stand next to her, supporting her elbows.

Suddenly the music cuts off.

Pilar removes her mask and shows off dangly gold earrings with the emblem of her fashion house. Fatima takes off her mask too and reveals smoky eyes wide with surprise.

Everywhere Vestals squirm and gasp until a sexy voice fills the soundstage.

I practiced that voice for days.

"On a night as important as this," I say, "don't let our competitors leave you hanging."

All eyes turn to see me perched at the top of the stairs. I wear satin pants, a lace halter, and stilettos. One hand wields an orange extension cord like a bull whip. With a silent prayer to the universe that I won't slip, I strut down the stairs straight to a handsome figure in white. It's Trevor, with his jaw dropped.

I plug the cord into the outlet next to him, brushing my arm against his silk shirt. "I rely on McNeal Solar Energy to heat things up," I say suggestively. Then I turn and look straight at the camera. "Don't you?" The music blares.

We've shot this scene twenty times since breakfast. This was a final take to make sure things were perfect.

Only for some reason, on this last try, Trevor does something stupid.

He scoops me around the waist and nuzzles my neck.

"Cut!" Jeremy yells. "What the hell was that?"

Trevor shrugs. "Improv. I thought I'd spice things up."

"We don't need your creative brilliance," snarls Jeremy. "Save it for soap carving. Stick to the plan."

"But the plan sucks!" argues Trevor. "The whole world thinks Blanca dumped me for a Virus."

"His name's Seth." I contemplate smacking Trevor with the extension cord. "And you're lucky that Seth hasn't said anything about you and—" But I stop myself in time.

"About what?" asks Jeremy.

"Nothing," Trevor and I both say together.

Fatima and Pilar climb down the stairs with small, pinched steps. Alberto strides behind them. "What's going on?" Fatima asks. "I can't breathe in this dress."

"It'll be okay, *mijiha*. Sit down while I deal with this bozo." Pilar glares at Jeremy. "I thought you were the director!"

"Without Ms. Lydia, you've lost all control," Alberto adds. He glances at me softly. "Your mother could multitask like nobody's business."

"I've got my team on it," insists Jeremy. "This will turn out great." He motions to his Reject stage crew. "Reset the scene and take it from the top."

A loud *pop* of burned-out lights startles us all.

"For crying out loud!" Jeremy scratches his neck along the tattoos. "Take ten, people."

"Come on, girls." Pilar tosses her hair. "Let's rest in the dressing room."

I take off my shoes and follow on bare feet. Fatima and Pilar don't bother. Their calves must be permanently stretched from their commitment to high heels.

Still, pregnancy is taking its toll on my best friend. As soon as we get to the dressing room, Fatima lies down on the cracked pleather couch and elevates her feet.

"Be careful not to mess up your hairdo." Pilar pulls Fatima's hair back and arranges it neatly.

"I know, Mami." Fatima closes her eyes like she's about to doze off. Maybe now's my chance.

"Pilar? That was really nice what Alberto said about Ms. Lydia back there."

Pilar gives me a patronizing smile. "Your mother was an excellent leader." She gestures to the door leading to the soundstage. "This place is a circus without her."

"Do you know, by any chance, where Ms. Lydia went after she was done working?"

Pilar blinks rapidly. "What do you mean?"

I put my hand in the tiny pocket of my pants that shelters the silver key. But I don't remove it. "Where did Ms. Lydia live?"

"Why would I know that?"

"You never asked her?"

"Of course not," Pilar answers. "Vestals don't pry into one another's private business." She narrows her eyes.

Her words might not have said it, but Pilar's tone is implicit. If I were still a real Vestal, I wouldn't poke around into Ms. Lydia's personal details.

"Look, if Ms. Lydia were alive I'd never ask. But ..." I let my words hang in the air. Then I glance at Fatima, who now snores on the couch. "If something happened to your daughter, wouldn't you want her to have a little comfort? Please, Pilar. I know nothing about Ms. Lydia. Everything I thought to be true was false. Can't you tell me a little bit about what she was really like?"

Pilar sighs deeply and then sits down in the chair in front of her mirror. "What do you want to know?"

The words come forth, small and desperate. "Did she ever talk about me?"

"No," Pilar answers. But briefly, ever so briefly, she nods her head yes.

That's the only bit of useful information she doesn't say. The rest of our conversation

is painfully futile. Pilar tells me Ms. Lydia always insisted on fresh crudités at every commercial shoot and that for special occasions she would stock the craft table with smoked salmon. But other than those tidbits of useless information, Pilar reveals nothing. So I go back to the soundstage and find out what's taking so long.

Some of the Vestals sit on the staircase and chat with friends. A few of them wave to me when I pass, but many turn away and block me from their conversations. I don't stop walking until I find Jeremy, engaged in a heated discussion with his Reject crew.

"Fix it," Jeremy says. "I don't care what you have to do." He rubs his hands through his curly brown hair.

Jeremy definitely has an adorable vibe going on. I can see why he made it all the way to his junior year without being eliminated. But I'll never understand why he dropped out so close to graduation.

"Oh. Hi, Blanca. I didn't see you there."

"Sorry," I say. "I didn't mean to sneak up on you. I was wondering if you needed any help."

"Nah, I think we'll be all set in a few minutes. Alberto's right. Things are still a little rough without your mom. It feels weird doing these shoots without her."

"It feels weird hearing you call Ms. Lydia my mom." I look up at Jeremy's face and see his eyes open wide. I could kick myself for the thoughtless release of private information.

"Hey, look," Jeremy says. "I want to tell you how much I admire you for that video you did in front of Tabula Rasa where you spoke up against the Harvest. That was really brave."

"Thank you." I cross my arms in front of me. The halter top I wear doesn't leave much to the imagination. I should have thrown on a sweater.

"But you didn't go far enough," Jeremy continues.

"What?" I freeze.

"Mutual selection is better than an auction but barely. Tabula Rasa needs to be shut down forever."

"Forever? That seems a bit drastic."

"Not when you consider how those kids are tortured."

"But they're not being tortured anymore. Headmaster Russell is gone." *Dead, probably.* "And Ms. Corina isn't like that. Don't you think Tabula Rasa still has a role to play as a school that focuses on important things?"

"What important things? Poetry?" Jeremy chuckles. "Look around this place. Does poetry make this happen? Could any of the Vestals shoot a commercial without the Defectos? Could they operate a camera or change a light bulb?"

"Maybe," I say. "With a little training."

Jeremy shakes his head. "They're useless. All Vestals are good for is looking pretty."

"That's not true!" I say it too loudly. Some of the Rejects hear and form a little crowd.

"It *is* true." Jeremy's face turns red. "Vestals aren't equipped for the real world."

"They don't have to be in the real world. That's the whole point!"

"I can't believe you're taking their side. I thought you were different."

"I *am* different." I hold up my forearm and show him my chip-watch. "But that doesn't mean I'll stand back and let you say bad things about the Brethren." With the corner of my eye, I see Trevor and Alberto walk up with a small group of Vestals.

This is getting out of control fast. I need to fix this. But how?

Get someone to agree with you by starting with a "Yes-Yes." Make them think that what you want, is what they want. And that it was their idea in the first place.

The old instructions whisper in my psyche.

When all else fails, smile.

"Jeremy." My voice is sweet. "Everything you've done with the Reje— I mean with the Defectos, I admire it so much. I hear you're organizing now?"

"Yes." Jeremy's back is stiff.

"That's amazing leadership on your part. And incredible foresight. Where'd you get the idea to do that?"

"From history," Jeremy says. "There used to be these things called unions."

"And the world has forgotten about unions, right?"

"Yeah. For the most part. I think some old people remember."

I nod my head in agreement. "And Vestals. Vestals remember because they study history."

Jeremy expels a quick burst of air in derision.

"Look. I totally agree with you, Jeremy. Dramatic change needs to happen at Tabula Rasa. But that doesn't mean Vestals are useless or what they stand for isn't essential."

"What *do* we stand for?" asks Trevor.

I spin around to look at him. His clear face has drained of color.

"Yes," says the Vestal next to Trevor. "What now that Barbelo Nemo is gone?"

"*You are a beacon in a dark world,*" I recite on instinct. "*You are examples of purity in a world that has forgotten what is important.*"

"Bullshit," says Jeremy.

"No. It's not." I look at the Rejects, clustered around their leader. "Defectos remember what's important too—one another! Not the people you know online but the friends who will show up for you when you really need help. That's what Vestals stand for too." I turn around slowly and look at all of them. "My father was messed up." Saying the word *father* cuts me like a knife, but I'm going for impact. "Headmaster Russell was a psychopath. But that doesn't mean that the whole concept of Tabula Rasa is evil. That doesn't mean we should shut it down. We need reform, not abandonment."

Alberto nods his head with me in agreement. Trevor has relaxed his fists and smiles at me with encouragement.

"And how would you reform it?" Jeremy sneers.

"I'd keep Tabula Rasa as a safe place where kids could learn. A school that wasn't only science, technology, engineering, and math but the humanities too. And maybe it wouldn't be a boarding school anymore. Maybe kids would go home and see their parents every night."

"So how's that different from a normal school?" a Reject asks.

"Because of the cloister." I stand tall in my boots. "Lead-lined walls. Eight hours every day where students don't have to worry about what's happening online. Where they can hang out with their real-life, in-person friends and focus on education."

I look at Jeremy's face and see that it is softening.

"Lots of things are messed up," I say, "but Vestals remind humanity that the people in front of you are what matter the most."

Jeremy's eyes cloud with fury again. "If people matter so much to Vestals, why do they cut kids down like grass to cull the class to ten graduates? That's sick."

"I agree. That—" But I don't have the chance to finish my sentence.

"Why not eleven graduates. Or twelve?" Jeremy spits out his questions like nails.

"Because …" I stare into the crowd and scramble for an answer. The truth is that Barbelo was obsessed with purity. He whittled down the class to ten graduates so they would be of the highest intelligence, beauty, and marketability. But surely there were a lot of borderline cases. Rejects who could have been Vestals—or Vestals who could have become Rejects. "If there are too many graduates, then there might not be enough contracts."

Jeremy snorts. "Then they shouldn't start off with two hundred kids to begin with. Do you know what that does to the graduation rate?"

I nod my head, trying to block away the numbers.

"Five percent," somebody shouts. "Only five percent of Tabula Rasa students graduate."

"That needs to change," I answer. "And maybe the Defectos can play a part in that. Offer suggestions for how to make it better."

Jeremy squares his shoulders. "We don't want anything to do with Tabula Rasa."

"Then why are you organizing?" I ask.

"For lots of reasons, Blanca. To show that we have a voice. To help each other find jobs and build lives. And for healing."

The Rejects clap, and I hear a few cheers.

"That's great." I look around the Reject audience. Scruffy beards, tattoos, fists clenched together; I see pain in their eyes.

"Okay, guys," Jeremy says to our group of onlookers. "Show's over. We film again in five minutes." He steps closer to me as the perilous crowd disperses. "You have a voice too, Blanca. A powerful one."

"I'm not sure about that."

"People listen to you. All the time on *The Lighthouse* and a few moments ago, in that spontaneous soapbox speech or whatever."

"Maybe." I'm not sure where Jeremy is going with this. I thought I had ticked him off.

"But you need healing too. Your impact will be even stronger when you get the past sorted out."

"What are you talking about? Did Cal put you up to this?"

"Cal? You mean Mr. McNeal? No." Jeremy pulls a card out of his back pocket. "I was thinking you should come to our support group."

"What?"

"Of Defectos. We meet every week to talk about stuff and figure things out."

"Why would I want to share the private details of my life with perfect strangers?"

"Because they're not perfect strangers, Blanca. They're people you knew. Some of them are your former classmates. Others are older and knew your parents."

"I didn't have parents."

"Neither did we," says Jeremy. "That's why we need each other. Together we can become stronger and rebuild our lives." He reaches for my hand and places the card on my palm. "Here's my contact info. Call me any time. We'd love to have you at our next meeting." He hurries away to the shoot.

"No, thank you," I answer, a bitter taste in my mouth.

But Jeremy is already gone.

Chapter Fifteen

I cannot possibly stand in these stilettos one more second, which is fine, because I don't have to. Filming is finally over, so I slip into fluffy white boots and a cashmere pullover. The halter still cinches, cutting off my breath. But at least I'm warm. When I see Cal enter through the security gate, I smile. It's time to go back home to the manor.

Cal lightly pecks me on the cheek. "Blanca, we've got a situation."

"What situation?" Pilar asks. She stands next to me with Fatima.

"Oh! Hello." Cal's voice suddenly becomes deep.

Is it my imagination, or did he stand up straighter?

"What's going on?" I ask. "I thought Seth was coming with you."

"Change of plans." Cal wrinkles his forehead. "Headmaster Russell's remains have been found. Somebody has broken the news that the Guardians are being called in for questioning."

"Seth?" I ask, panic in my voice. "Was Seth responsible for the leak?" *Never trust a Virus. Never.*

"I don't know." Cal clears his throat. "I haven't been able to reach him all day."

"Where is he?" Fatima frowns.

But there isn't time for Cal to explain because we hear what sounds like thunder from outside.

"Is it raining?" Pilar pats her hairstyle protectively.

"No," Cal answers. "A mob of reporters. I was barely able to make it through."

"We need to warn Jeremy," I say. "Immediately. How will the Vestals get out?"

"Mami!" Fatima grabs her baby bump.

"Don't worry," I tell her. "I'll figure something out."

"Blanca, wait," Cal says, as we rush across the stage. "There's one more thing I didn't explain."

"What?"

"You," Cal says. "Your name is being mentioned too. That's why I don't think—why I *know*—Seth didn't leak the information."

"No." The small hairs on the back of my neck lift up. "Of course not."

When we reach Jeremy, he and Alberto are talking to the security guards. "You've heard?" Jeremy asks us.

Cal and I nod.

My voice quakes. "How will the Vestals escape?" I have chills beneath my cashmere sweater.

"My crew can help hold back a crowd," says Jeremy, "but we can't keep them from taking pictures. We don't have that type of manpower. Our security detail isn't set up for mob control."

"But Pilar," Alberto protests, "Fatima. They can't have their pictures taken by strangers."

"They won't," I say. "I'll protect them."

"You?" Alberto asks. "How?"

"Yeah, how?" Jeremy wants to know.

"I don't mind having my picture taken." I stick my chin up. "I'll be a decoy."

"Blanca, I'm not sure this is a good idea," Cal cautions.

But Jeremy nods his head. "It could work. Blanca could create a diversion up front while the rest of the Vestals slip out the back door."

Cal shakes his head. "That sounds dangerous."

"Nobody will hurt me with the whole world watching."

"You don't understand crowds," Cal says. "They can be deadly."

"I know all about danger," I say. "I'm a survivor, remember? I've got good instincts."

"For goodness sake, Blanca! I never should have taught you to think for yourself." Cal scowls, but a half second later, he puts his arm around my shoulder for a hug. "Well, you won't have to go alone. I'll come with you."

"Me too," offers Jeremy. "Give me a few minutes to arrange things." He darts off.

"I'll come as well," Alberto offers.

"No," says Cal. "You should stay with Pilar and Fatima."

The two men stare at each other. Alberto towers over Cal, who is only of average height. But after a moment, Alberto nods at Cal with respect. "We go with our daughters." Alberto holds his hand out to shake.

"Blanca," Cal whispers when Alberto is gone, "you need to be careful when you're in front of those cameras not to inadvertently make a statement that would incriminate you."

I search Cal's face. "Do you think I have something to hide?"

"I know you." Cal's eyes flash back at me. "You always have something to hide."

"Well then you should also realize that I know how to keep a secret."

●●●●●●●●●

My eyes are blinded by the flashing lights of hundreds of thumb-cameras. The crowd is hungry, their mood ravenous. Viral bloggers or random curiosity seekers; it's difficult to tell who I'm dealing with. I wish Seth was here to help identify my audience. But instead I have to settle for Cal, Jeremy, and a small flank of Reject security guards.

"Blanca," someone calls out, "what do you know about the death of Headmaster Russell?"

I make strong eye contact with the audience. "I am as anxious to find out the details as you. Next?"

"Were you involved in his disappearance?"

I erase all signs of emotion from my expression. "I make it a point to stay as far away from Headmaster Russell as possible."

"Can you tell us about the Guardians?" someone asks. "Do you think they're responsible for Russell's death?"

"I try not to form conclusions until I know all the facts," I say. "I eagerly await the results of the FBI's investigation into this matter."

Jeremy stands next to me with his finger-chips cupped around his ears. Then he leans down and whispers, "You're good to go. It's all clear."

"Thank you." My muscles feel weak with relief.

"You're welcome any time." Jeremy pushes up his sleeves.

I look back at my impromptu press conference. "That's all the questions I have time for tonight." I link my arm with Cal's and follow the security guards to our car. They muscle onlookers out of the way, but we're trapped. The crowd presses in deeper. Strange hands claw at me and pull threads from my sweater. I cling to Cal for support, but he is jostled too. Someone grabs the knot of my halter top and pulls the tie. My neck snaps back as I choke.

"Blanca!" Cal lashes out at the people around us, shoving them away.

"Defectos!" Jeremy shouts. "She needs help!"

Vestal-rejects stream into the fracas. The noise of the mob ratchets up ten decibels.

"That's my camera!" someone yells.

"My nose!" a guy shouts.

I hear screaming and cursing.

I hug myself and tuck my head down. Cal steps closer, a shield of protection. A minute later, the crowd ripples back ever so slightly. As the Rejects take control, an escape route opens.

"Run, Blanca!" Cal tugs on my arm, and we break for the parking lot. He clicks open the doors to his yellow sports car, and we leap into the front seat.

By the time the ignition growls, the mob has followed. Cal inches the car along for several yards, trying not to hurt anyone, until we reach the street and can pick up speed.

We don't say anything until the last Virus is out of sight.

"You did great, sweetheart. You were excellent." Cal's voice shakes.

I am trembling too. "Where do you think Seth is?" I activate my chip-watch to see if there are any messages.

"He said he had to meet with someone."

"Who?"

Cal adjusts his collar. "His lawyer," he answers.

"Oh." *Tiffany.*

"We should probably get you to another lawyer too. Nancy's excellent, but she's not a defense attorney."

"Neither is Tiffany."

"No," Cal admits, "but she's an expert in Internet law. And Seth takes care of himself. Him I'm not worried about. But you, Blanca— this is all new to you."

"No it's not. It's the same old garbage over and over again. Viruses out to get me. And why do I need a defense attorney if I'm not guilty?"

Cal presses his lips together in a tight line. "The law defines guilt in strange ways." He pauses for a moment and adjusts his grip on the steering wheel. "Is there anything you want to tell me? I might not understand, but I'll listen. There's nothing you could ever do or say that would make me stop loving you."

"That sounds too good to be true."

"No," Cal says. "That's what it means to be a father." The bright lights of the road reflect through the windshield, lighting up his face.

I lean back into the seat and wipe my nose. "I can't tell you about yesterday. It's safer that you don't know. But the important thing is that Seth and I didn't see anything. His eyes were messed up, and I didn't look. That's exactly what I told Agent Plunkett. That I have no idea what happened."

"What do you think occurred?"

I look down at my hands. "Probably Keung made things right for a lot of people, including me."

Cal grimaces. "Okay, then. That's all I need to know."

We spend the twenty-minute drive in silence. At some point, I drift off to sleep, knowing I'm safe with Cal. When he flicks on the blinker and turns the car onto the long private road of McNeal Manor, I awaken. Cal waves his chip-watch at the guard station and opens up the gate.

As soon as we roll onto the grounds, I feel at home. I'm still new to that force on my soul. *I have a home with people who love me.* A place where I am wanted. All the madness of the day fades away.

Cal pulls into the garage and parks the car next to the spot where Alan's limo should be. "Everything will be okay." Cal reaches out and squeezes my hand before unfastening his seat belt.

"Cal, wait. I have one more thing to tell you." I reach into the slim pocket of my pants and pull out the silver key. "I think this belonged to Ms. Lydia."

Cal takes the offered key and examines it closely. "When did you find it?"

I explain about the loose cobblestone in the courtyard. I also tell him how I tried to ask Pilar for ideas, but she wouldn't tell me anything. "What do you think? Could it be the key to Ms. Lydia's house?"

"That's a definite possibility." Cal places the key on my palm. "This means there's something I need to show you too. I was waiting until you had more appointments with Dr. Meredith and I was sure you could handle it, but after the courage you showed tonight in a very difficult situation, I feel remiss for holding it back."

"What?" I ask, my curiosity piqued. "What haven't you told me?"

"Your mother," Cal answers. "When Lydia was still alive, I hired a private investigator to follow her, to reveal information about the Vestals she tried to hide."

My hand claps tight around the key, and my whole arm quivers.

●●●●●●●●●

Cal switches on the lights and illuminates his extensive collection of old-fashioned books that line the library on mahogany shelves. The one row of windows is walled off by closed shutters.

"I'm sorry." I say. "I forgot to open the shutters in my courtyard so you could get some light in here."

Cal walks over to his desk. "That's okay. It doesn't matter much at this hour." He unlocks a drawer with the swipe of his chip-watch and pulls out a large folio. "I didn't trust these files to be electronic. Not when I was trying to convince Lydia that my intentions were sincere." Cal hands the bundle over to me. The weight feels heavy in my hands.

I stumble to the green leather couch. "I don't understand. Wouldn't Ms. Lydia have known she was being followed? I always know when people are watching me."

"She wasn't in the public eye like the rest of you," says Cal. "Sure, she had her usual Vestal paranoia, but for the most part, she was off the grid. She had no reason to suspect anyone knew who she was or what she looked like. The only two signs that she was a Vestal were her white clothes and platinum cuff. Apparently, most days she'd throw on a brown coat or green jacket to avoid detection. Look," Cal points to the files, "you'll see that in the notes."

I take a deep breath and open the pages, but they only serve to confuse me further. "I don't get it. This is a bunch of dates and locations."

"Flip to the back page," Cal says. "You'll find the summary."

My fingers fumble with nerves, until they finally land on the right page.

```
Case Summary: Lydia XXXX. Subject's last
name unknown at this time.
```

Observation Period: Four weeks, late fall.
Behaviors: Subject is constantly on the move.
During the course of the investigation, the
subject made frequent trips to downtown
Silicon Valley in her role as the liaison
between Vestal graduates and the companies
they work for. Subject also coordinated with
the production crew of former Tabula Rasa
students who shoot commercials. Subject
frequently seen in public wearing a brown
coat or a green jacket.

Transportation: Subject drives a nondescript
Japanese make sedan with sophisticated tech
upgrades. Unable to trail the car through
normal electronic means. On November 1,
2062, attempt was made to put a tracker on
the undercarriage of the car, but something,
perhaps lead, blocked transmission. The only
recourse was to physically trail subject,
which added considerable cost as documented
in the expense report.

Locations: McNeal Manor, Tabula Rasa,
cottage in Gilroy, Mountain View soundstage,
Vestal suites of eleven different companies,
and private terminal at Mineta San Jose
International Airport.

I let the papers fall to my lap. One word has jumped out at me in neon letters. "Gilroy? But that's where Headmaster Russell tried to take us yesterday."

"I wondered about that too. It could be a coincidence or it could be meaningful." Cal sits next to me on the couch, his hand clasped over his knees.

"But I don't understand. If you knew where Ms. Lydia lived, why didn't you tell me before now? Why hide this from me?"

"I wasn't hiding it from you, sweetheart. I didn't know if you were ready to deal with it yet. I wanted you to have more sessions with Dr. Meredith before we laid this on you."

"Dr. Meredith knows too?" I can't keep the smack of betrayal from my voice.

"Yes, and the plan was Dr. Meredith would inform me when you were further along in the grieving process for your mother. We wanted to make sure you were capable of handling your mother's death before you had to deal with her house too."

"Ms. Lydia wasn't my mother."

"Blanca." Cal touches my shoulder, but I pull away.

"She gave birth to me. There's a difference."

Cal's eyes looked pained. "Lydia had a lot of issues, but deep down—"

"No! I don't want to hear it. Ms. Lydia didn't love me like you love Seth. She wouldn't fight for me. She—" Unbidden tears spring up on my cheeks, and my whole body tenses as I try to stop them.

"I love *you* too." Cal sits there, helpless, his forehead wrinkled with worry.

A second later, I throw my head on his shoulders and cry into his scratchy tweed blazer. Cal wraps his arms around me and hugs me tight. "You're my daughter now every bit as much as Seth is my son, and I would fight for you too." Cal offers me a handkerchief, and I blow my nose hard.

A few minutes later, when all my tears are all gone, Cal says, "About this key ..."

"Yes?"

"We could drive to Gilroy tomorrow if you want. There's an address in the report."

"Do you think I'm up to it?"

"Yes. I do. But it's not important what I think. We're talking about your life, Blanca. Do *you* think you're up to it?"

"Absolutely." I nod. "And, Cal, so you know, I'm never seeing Dr. Meredith again."

"What? Why?"

"For starters, she kept this from me, and I think that was wrong. And also because the last time I saw her I was abducted."

"Blanca," Cal protests, "that wasn't Dr. Meredith's fault."

"We can't know that for certain. And it doesn't matter anyway. My instincts tell me not to trust her. You taught me to listen to my own intuition."

"Yes, but in this case—"

"In this case I'm right. Dr. Meredith will never understand what it's like to be me. She has no idea how Vestals think or what's important to them."

Cal sighs, and then pauses a moment, like he's choosing his words with care. "Blanca, there are a very small handful of people in this world who will ever understand what it's like to be you. But that doesn't mean you need to stop seeking help. You have nineteen years of turmoil to process."

"I know, but don't worry." I reach into my pocket and pull out Jeremy's card. "I've found somebody else to talk to."

"Whom?"

"A whole support group of people who get it."

Cal raises his eyebrows as understanding hits him. "You don't mean …"

"Yes. I'm talking about the Defectos."

Chapter Sixteen

I thought there would be flowers, but I was wrong. There's nothing here, not even un-mown grass or a lawn full of dandelions. Bare dirt surrounds the small house with shingle sides. There's no front porch. The only color is the grayness of the wood and the fine mist of grit that covers the doorstep.

I squeeze the key in my hand. "Are you sure this is the house?" I ask Cal.

He stares at the piece of paper he holds with the address. "I'm afraid so. I thought it would be different. Your mother was lovely and alive. I pictured—" Cal takes a deep breath.

I've waited all morning to come here. First, I attended tutoring with Irene. Then I had to wait for Cal to come home from work on his lunch break. I called Seth over and over again, but he didn't answer. Finally, on the drive here, Seth texted me.

`Seth: Still working a case. Leave without me.`

What a jerk. He's probably off with Tiffany. Or else he's trying to make me feel guilty about Keung, which is totally unfair. *Never trust a Virus.*

"Well, shall we?" Cal extends his hand to the door. "After you, sweetheart."

The small doorstep creaks under my weight. I brush cobwebs off the handle, and the sleeve of my white blouse turns gray.

I gaze up at Cal. "What if it's horrible?"

He smiles encouragingly. "It won't be."

I put the key in the lock.

And it won't go in.

"What!" I start to sweat. "Why won't it work? I thought—I was sure! How is this possible?" My voice is frantic. It's all I can do not to chuck the key out into the dirt.

Cal tries the lock too. "Wow. I was as hopeful as you were, Blanca. I was positive this would work." Cal takes off his blazer and hands it to me.

"What are you doing?"

"We didn't come all this way for you not to find answers." Cal rolls up the sleeves of his dress shirt. "We'll have to find another way in, that's all." He reaches for his jacket and wraps it around his fist. Then he steps off the doorstep and walks around to the side of the house.

"Are you going to break in?" My heartbeat races.

"Just one window."

"But what if the neighbors see?"

"What neighbors? This place is deserted." Cal sizes up the glass with dark curtains on the inside. "It's only three feet off the ground. Besides, Nancy tells me you probably own this house. The only holdup is probate court." Cal pulls back his fist like he's going to smash it.

"Wait!" I grab his elbow and stop him in time. "I won't let you get in trouble over me. What if there's a security system?"

"Not a problem," says a familiar voice. "I already deactivated it." Seth stands in the side yard, his hands hooked to the pockets of his jeans. "But why don't you jiggle the window first before you destroy anything?"

"Oh." Cal grins at his son. "Good idea. Breaking and entering isn't my strong suit."

"It's a good thing your son is a Virus then." Seth winks at me and steps up to the window. "Not this one." He runs his fingers along the sill. "Too tight." He walks farther along the perimeter of the house until he finds a kitchen window that appeals to him. "This one's perfect."

A few minutes later, I stand in the yellow kitchen of Ms. Lydia's house. Dish towels hang neatly next to the faucet. A drying rack holds a bowl, mug, and a solitary spoon. My knees feel weak when I look at it, and I sink into the only kitchen chair.

"Are you okay?" Cal asks me.

"Yes," I answer. "I'm taking it all in."

Seth rubs my shoulders. "We don't have much time, Blanca. We need to search fast."

"I thought you cut the security system?"

"I did, but pretty soon somebody will notice."

"Oh." I spring up and sprint to the next room. It's a sitting area with a floral couch and a strange looking screen.

"What is this thing?" Seth knocks his hand on the contraption.

"It's a television," says Cal. "I haven't seen one of these in years. I wonder if Lydia was able to get it to work."

I leave the guys to investigate Ms. Lydia's tech indiscretion and head into the next room. It's set up like an exercise studio, with wood floors, a treadmill, and a yoga mat. The walls have framed pictures of the most famous Vestal campaigns of all time. I see Pilar and Alberto, looking young and in love. Then there's a poster of the original Lilith, my aunt, advertising cleaning products. Her salt-and-pepper hair is tied back with a white headband. I step up to the wall and put my fingertips on the picture. Lilith's smile reminds me of my own.

"Blanca," Seth calls, "in here."

I walk to the sound of his voice and find Seth and Cal in Ms. Lydia's bedroom. As soon as I enter, I feel her presence. The gracefulness of the lace afghan. The elegance of the dressing table in the corner. Even the fan on the nightstand is reminiscent of her. I never saw Ms. Lydia perspire, no matter how high the temperature soared. There's also a twin bed, a small dresser, and a rocking chair. Seth and Cal stand in front of the closet.

"Half of the clothes are white," says Seth. "The other half is colored."

I face the rows of neatly hung garments. Then I take a step closer and bury my nose in the fabric. I hope to smell a familiar fragrance, but all I find is the lingering whiff of detergent.

"Your mother wore color." Cal holds out the sleeve of a blue blouse. "That's an example to think about for the future."

"Not now, Dad." Seth scowls. "Let Blanca have her moment."

I look down at the floor of the closet to a row of Ms. Lydia's shoes. There, in the corner, I spy a strange square book. I reach down to pick it up for closer inspection.

"It's a photo album," explains Cal. "Maybe we'll find clues in here about Lydia's private life."

I command my heart to stop hoping. The three of us rush back to the living room and sit on the couch.

I carefully turn the first page and find it yellow and sticky, covered with clouded plastic film. But underneath is a picture of a girl and a baby. The girl has a heart-shaped face.

"Your mother and Lilith." Cal smiles at the picture. "I'd recognize her anywhere."

I turn the page and find a picture of Ms. Lydia again, this time as a four-year-old standing next to my father. Barbelo Nemo stares out at me with green eyes flecked with gold, exactly like mine. "It was sick," I say. "They were twenty-three years apart."

Cal swallows. "Lydia didn't have an easy life," he says. "We need to remember that about her."

I flip through the next few pages but find them all empty, the photographs removed. "There's nothing else here." My voice is wracked with disappointment.

"Keep looking," says Seth. "You might still find something."

Thankfully, I do. On the very last page, I find a picture of three people. Ms. Lydia, tired but smiling, her sister Lilith, her hair starting to gray, and a tiny baby, wrapped in a pink blanket.

I pull the picture from the album with trembling hands. Two thick tears roll down my cheeks. I trace the image of Ms. Lydia with my fingertips.

"My mother," I whisper.

"My word," says Cal, leaning down to get a closer look at the picture. "Is that you?"

But I don't get the chance to answer.

The front door swings open, and half a dozen people invade the living room.

"Hold it!" says a gravelly voice. Agent Plunkett points her gun straight at me.

I feel no dread, only anger. I narrow my eyes at Agent Plunkett, whose boyish haircut looks freshly shorn. After nineteen years, I've finally seen a picture of my mother and me together, and now they want to rob me of this happiness.

"Secure the premises," Agent Marlow growls to one of the officers.

I sense Seth stiffen next to me.

"What's the meaning of this?" demands Cal.

"Dad," Seth says with warning tone.

"It's all clear," barks an officer, returning from the kitchen.

"Stand down," calls Agent Plunkett, and everyone lowers their guns. "What are you doing here, Blanca?"

"This is my mother's house. I wanted to see it." From the corner of my eye, I see Seth type with his finger-chips, his hands a frenetic blur.

"We've had this house under surveillance for months," says Agent Marlow. "You're guilty of tampering with evidence."

Now Cal types on his chip-watch too.

But I'm ready to bite! "You knew my mother's address and you didn't tell me? I'm her daughter. I have a legal right to her estate."

"Then why did you break in?" asks Agent Marlow. "We could have you all arrested."

"Not 'could,'" says Agent Plunkett. "Will." She takes out handcuffs and reads our Miranda rights.

●●●●●●●●●

When we pull into the parking lot of the FBI building, Tiffany waits for us in a sleek green suit and dark brown heels. Unfortunately for me, Nancy is nowhere to be seen, and there's a crowd of Viruses with thumb-cameras.

"Officers," one of the paparazzi begins as soon as we step out of the car, "did you actually arrest Blanca for breaking into her own home?"

"I don't discuss ongoing criminal investigations with the media," snaps Agent Plunkett.

"Yes, they did." Tiffany's voice is low and sultry. She shakes her finger-chips and emits a document. "Here's the official deed of the property in question which is now in Blanca's name. The writ went through this morning."

"Step aside!" Agent Marlow shoves paparazzi out of the way.

"And furthermore," says Tiffany with a flip of her hair, "my colleague, Nancy Robinson, called me a few moments ago from the office of the U.S. Attorney in charge of the case against Barbelo Nemo to report that all Lydia Xavier's property has been excluded from the warrant."

"What?" Agent Plunkett jerks her head and stares at Tiffany.

"Check your messages." Tiffany smiles a feline grin.

Agents Plunkett and Marlow hurriedly type their finger-chips. Color drains from Agent Marlow's face, but Agent Plunkett turns beet red with rage. "Let's discuss this inside," she says.

"As you wish," says Tiffany. "*After* you release my client and his friends and apologize." She looks back over her shoulder and beams for the cameras. Then she passes that smile to Seth and Cal. But when she reaches me, Tiffany's face freezes to stone.

Chapter Seventeen

"You told Tiffany about me?" It's impossible not to screech. I pace around my room like a caged animal. I glimpse myself in the mirror and only see wild. I want to kick something, or claw somebody to shreds. I know the perfect person too. "I had to ride home in her car! Do you have any idea how horrible that was?"

"Well, yes, actually, I do. *Angel.*" Seth sprawls out in my desk chair, his feet up and his arms crossed.

"Is that where you were today? And yesterday? With your skanky ex-girlfriend?"

"Whoa! That was totally uncalled for. Just because Tiffany doesn't pretend to be all holy and pure doesn't mean she's a skank."

"Holy and pure? What's that supposed to mean? And you didn't answer my question. Where were you?"

"I thought Vestals didn't pry into other people's business."

"I thought you didn't want me to be a Vestal." I stop pacing and hold my ground, my feet solidly planted on the floor.

"Look, Blanca, I did some *Veritas Rex* business. Can we leave it at that? Not everything is about you all the time."

"But I needed you. And you let me down!"

"Did I?" Seth asks. "Who disabled the security system?"

"And alerted the FBI!"

"That wasn't my fault. You and my dad would have tipped them off anyway. At least I bought you some time."

"Answer me this," I say. "Were you with Tiffany?"

Seth shakes his head. "I'm not answering that because it's entirely irrelevant."

"It's not irrelevant. You're holding something back."

"*I'm* holding something back? Well that's rich. You hold things back all the time."

"That's not true! I tell you everything, and you still don't trust me."

"Then why didn't you tell me about finding the key?"

"Because you weren't here!" I plop down on my bed. I'm so angry I shake.

Seth climbs out of the chair, then kneels on the floor in front of me. "Blanca, I can't tell you where I was today. Not yet anyway, but it wasn't anything bad. I promise. And for what it's worth, you don't have the best track record when it comes to sharing pertinent information."

"What do you mean? I tell you everything now."

"You didn't tell me you'd slept with Keung."

"You didn't ask!"

Seth hops on the bed next to me. "What! I'm supposed to say, 'Hey, Blanca, have you ever slept with some random foreign exchange student?'"

"It wasn't like that." My irritation boils.

"Well, what was it like?"

I wrinkle my face. "Details? You want details? Okay, let's start with *you*. How was sex with Tiffany?"

"Whoa." Seth springs up from the bed. "Maybe we should cool off and talk about this later."

"Do you *still* sleep with her? Is that where you were today? Sleeping with your old girlfriend because I haven't put out?"

"I can't believe you'd even suggest that!" Seth shouts.

"And I can't believe you're such an ass." I stomp to the corner of the room and grab my motorcycle helmet. "You know the way out. I've got someplace to go." I pull the card Jeremy gave me out of my pocket and throw it onto the bed.

"Blanca!" Seth cries. "Wait!"

But I'm already running full speed down the hall.

●●●●●●●●●

The soundstage is eerily quiet. A lone spotlight shines down on the linoleum where a circle of aluminum chairs waits. I sit in one of them, my feet locked at the ankles, and smooth out the denim of my white jeans.

"It'll be okay, Blanca," whispers Jeremy. "Everyone is nervous their first time here."

I look around the room and try to act causal. Some of the people I recognize as former classmates. A girl who was kicked out of Tabula Rasa in ninth grade for having too many freckles gives me a nod. I wave back. I think her name is Stella. The woman next to Stella was in Trevor's class. Ash blond hair frames her face like a cloud, and her skin is ghostly pale. But she offers me a faint smile.

The other Defectos are a lot less friendly. An older guy with a bald head and gray handlebar mustache narrows his eyes at me and frowns, and a woman with a pinched expression glares at me over the rim of her tortoise-shell glasses.

"Shall we begin?" Jeremy smiles hard at the audience, transmitting enthusiasm. From my vantage point, I get a better view of the tattoos on Jeremy's neck. They look like Chinese characters, but I can't decipher them.

"Can I lead the blessing?" asks Stella.

Jeremy nods. "That would be great."

"Brothers and sisters," Stella begins, "you have a hard road. In so many ways, it's difficult being you. *But I know that you can do it.* You have everything you need to achieve happiness."

"The Vestal blessing?" I blurt out. "You're not supposed to say the blessing anymore. You got rejected."

"We were released," Jeremy says. "It was for our own good. That doesn't mean we can't partake in the blessing."

"Yes, it does." I push back my sleeves. "I don't give the blessing anymore. Not since my cuff is gone. It's a bunch of garbage anyway."

"No, Blanca," says Stella. "It's not garbage. Every word is true. You have a hard road. It's very difficult being you."

I roll my eyes and look away. It was stupid to think these people could help. As soon as it's polite to leave, I'm out of here.

"Okay, friends," says Jeremy, "let's give Blanca her space and move on to new business. Who would like to share what they experienced this week?"

The burly man with the handlebar mustache raises his hand.

"Gregor," Jeremy says, "thank you for sharing."

"Well, uh, I want to say that like the rest of you I've followed the news about Headmaster Russell." Gregor rubs the back of his thick neck. "It brought back a lot of memories. Some of you know this, but Russ and I were in the same class. Only he made it and I got the axe when I was thirteen." Gregor pauses for a moment and looks at the audience with a twinkle in his eye. "After I discovered girls." A smattering of laughter rises from the group. "Anyhow, I know all you young people saw Russell as an evil guy who beat you and made you go through Discipline Hour, but to me, he was a friend. And a lot of what Russ became probably had to do with how he was raised."

At this Gregor looks straight at me. I automatically clench my fists.

"When I was at Tabula Rasa, Barbelo Nemo was still running the place. If you'll excuse me for saying, Blanca, your father was a sick piece of work. For some reason, he always took a special interest in

Russ and tapped him to be his apprentice."

"Did you know my mother?" The words leak like water.

"Generally we don't interrupt," Jeremy says. "But you're new here, Blanca, so it's okay."

"Oh," I say. "Sorry."

"No, it's fine," Gregor says. "Yes, I did know your mother. Ms. Lydia was a few years older than Russ and me. We didn't see her much after her Harvest."

I look at my white nail beds and slowly uncurl my fingertips.

"So I guess what I'm saying," Gregor continues, "is that there are multiple sides to every story. And a lot of things about a person— even somebody you hate—you have no idea about."

"Bullshit," says a Defecto a few chairs over. He's a pudgy guy with tattooed kittens on each arm.

"Victor." Jeremy speaks with a warning tone. "Please. No judgment in this room."

"I'm sorry, Gregor, but that's bullshit. No way do I feel sympathy for that sadistic bastard. Russell made my life hell. I don't care about his sob story."

Gregor leans forward and rests both elbows on his knees, his hands clasped. He looks at Victor and nods. "You don't need to feel anything you don't want to feel, buddy."

"Would anyone else like to share?" Jeremy asks.

"I would," says Stella. She colors and her freckles stick out like dot to dots. "I've got this nephew—some of you have met him. Anyhow, I love him to pieces. But the other day I was at my sister's house babysitting and all the kid wanted to do was sit in his room and play his new finger-chip game. I was like, 'You're eight years old, kid! You don't need to be staring at your palm all the time. Go outside. Get some sunshine. Let's throw the ball around.'"

I look around the circle and see nods of understanding.

"And it made me think about my life when *I* was eight years old." At this, Stella nods in my direction. I look behind me, but I don't see anything. "When Blanca and I were eight, we were stuck indoors too. We never had the privilege of playing outside. But at least we had books to read and friends to talk with, you know? I tried to explain my concerns to my sister when she got home, and she didn't get it. She said, 'You're still so messed up from that place you can hardly see it.' And maybe that's true. But part of me still thinks that not all of Tabula Rasa was bad."

Some people nod at this, but most people don't. Victor practically bounces up and down in his chair as he waves his arm around.

"Victor," says Jeremy, "go for it. I think you'll probably share what I would say too."

"Thanks," Victor mumbles. He holds his hands up, and I get a better view of his cat tattoos. One of the kittens is playing with a ball of yarn. Its innocence is a sharp contrast to the vitriol in Victor's voice. "I'm sorry, Stella. I don't mean to disrespect you or your story, but your sister's spot-on. You *are* messed up. There's a whole lot of ways to have a happy childhood without being ripped away from your family and tortured. That's why stopping the Harvest isn't enough." Victor looks in my direction. "Tabula Rasa must be shut down by any means it takes."

"No," Gregor says. "That's not what this meeting is about. We're here to support each other, not plot revenge."

"Gregor's right," says the woman with ash blond hair. Her voice is as pallid as her face. "I want to talk about other things, like jobs."

"Go ahead, Kate," says Jeremy.

Kate pushes a strand of wispy hair behind her ear and continues. "I left Tabula Rasa in tenth grade, and I've struggled ever since." When she looks around the circle and sees nods of understanding, her cheeks turn a faint shade of pink. "At first, I tried to finish my diploma at a normal high school, but I was hopelessly lost. It wasn't only the math and science. I didn't know how to talk to other kids my age or find people to sit with at the cafeteria." Kate looks at her feet. "And I had no idea how to handle boys. I'd spent my whole life being told a boyfriend would be chosen for me when I became a Vestal."

I think about my mother saying Trevor and I would be the perfect match.

And then I think about Cal doing everything he can to prepare me for college. How he's hired me a special tutor and making me see Dr. Meredith for help. If not for Cal, I'd probably be exactly like this Defecto.

Kate looks back up at the audience. "I never got my official diploma. And working for Jeremy's soundstage crew isn't my thing. So I babysit and clean houses. I can't scrape enough money together to move out of my parents' apartment. And it's awful because I know they don't want me there."

"You can live with me," interjects Victor. "Maybe?"

Kate's face freezes. "Uh, thanks for the offer, Victor, but I'm allergic to cats."

"Anyone else?" Jeremy asks. "Blanca? Do you want to share?"

For some reason, Kate's story makes me brave. I think about Fatima, fearful for her family. "Tabula Rasa could do a better job at teaching career skills," I concede. "Harvested Tabula Rasa students aren't prepared to live independently either."

"Exactly," says Victor. "Vestals are totally useless."

"No. They aren't!" I cut a glance at Jeremy to see if he'll chastise Victor for interrupting, but Jeremy doesn't move a muscle. "All of us—Vestals *and* Defectos—have skills that aren't being taught in the outside world that *are* really useful."

"Like what?" asks Kate.

I search my brain for answers. "We know how to memorize," I say, grateful that I thought of something. "We can sit still and not fidget. And we have beautiful handwriting."

At this, Jeremy chuckles. "Well, there you have it people. Thank you, Tabula Rasa, for my fine penmanship."

I didn't try to be funny. I am dead serious. But merriment overtakes the room like wildfire. It's so infectious, and this day has been so horrible, that I can't fight it.

For half a second, I smile.

●●●● ● ●●●●

The meeting ends, and the chairs are put away. I slip into my jacket and reach for my helmet when Jeremy stops me.

"Wait, Blanca. There's one more Reject I want you to hear from."

"I thought you called yourself Defectos?"

"We do, but this guy isn't one of us."

I hear a loud *bang* as the door to the soundstage closes. I look and see that the last support group member has left. Jeremy and I stand alone in the cavernous silence.

"Okay." My muscles twitch. "Who do you want me to meet?"

Jeremy points off to the side of the building lined with dressing rooms. "He's waiting for you in there."

Chapter Eighteen

"Hello, *tiānshǐ*. Did you receive my messages?" Keung sits in front of the dressing-room mirror and stares back at me through the reflection. His tailored suit makes him look ten years older, but when I look into his eyes, I see the teenager I kissed a few years ago. Beside him on the table is a book of old-fashioned stationery and a ballpoint pen.

"*You* sent the messages?" I take a small step into the dressing room, but leave the door wide open. "I thought they were from Ms. Corina or maybe Headmaster Russell."

Keung smiles and turns to face me. "No, they were from me."

I fidget with my chip-watch. It won't work in the cloistered building. "Why try to scare me?"

Keung's smile fades immediately. "I didn't! Oh, Blanca. I'm sorry.

163

That wasn't my intention at all." He points to the chair next to him. "Here. Take a seat, and I'll explain."

I sit down on the edge of the pleather.

"I've known the FBI was watching you for a while," Keung begins.

"Watching me? What?"

"Agents Plunkett and Marlow. They've been taking your pictures."

I think back to the image Agent Marlow showed me of Seth and me kissing in front of his apartment building. Where did it come from? Why didn't I wonder about it before now? "Go on."

"You're definitely a person of interest to them," Keung says quietly. "Have they asked you questions about me?"

I nod. "But I didn't say anything, of course."

Keung reaches out and takes both of my hands. "I know you would never."

We stare at each other a moment. All of a sudden I'm not nineteen anymore. I'm sixteen and sitting in the supply closet of Tabula Rasa. Keung is my tutor and the only person who's ever taken any interest in me personally. I feel special—noticed—I'm not just Fatima's sidekick but my own human being, worthy of attention.

But I'm not that girl at Tabula Rasa anymore. I'm Blanca McNeal with a parent who cares about me and a future that includes college and endless possibilities. Plus there's Seth, who might be confusing as hell, but still means everything.

I pull my wrists away.

At my movement, Keung removes his hands too. "I tried to warn you. But I didn't want anyone to figure out it was me."

"Warn me about what?"

"About how insane the world's become. I'm the delegate to the Silicon Valley Tech Council, you know."

"That's wonderful, Keung."

"No. It's horrible. You wouldn't believe how fast things are changing. Have you heard of invisi-chips?"

"Yes. My friend Ethan had prototypes implanted last year." I think back to that night, hidden at the Vestal corporate banquet where Ethan first showed me he was connected. A few days later, my mother cut his hand off as punishment.

The smallness of the dressing room makes me dizzy.

"Invisi-chips are rolling out to the general public soon." Keung grins at his flexed fingers. "Everyone will want them."

"What does that have to do with me?"

"Not you, tiānshǐ. Your boyfriend."

"Seth? What about him?"

"You need to convince him to get his finger-chips removed."

My quick laugh spews out air. "I try all the time without any luck. But maybe with invisi-chips he'll want to upgrade."

"That's not what I mean."

"Then what? I don't get it."

Keung stares into my green eyes. "Seth should respect what's important to you."

I smile slyly. "You sound jealous."

Keung tilts his head to the side. "Do you want me to be jealous?"

"Maybe a little bit."

Keung leans closer. "*Tiānshǐ*, I want you to be happy."

I lean in too. "I *am* happy."

Our faces are mere inches apart. For the first time since we met, Keung and I have complete privacy. Nobody working on the soundstage, no Tabula Rasa teacher patrolling the aisles, and nobody watching us here together.

Keung cups my face with his hands. "Are you really happy or pretending?"

For a moment, I don't know. So I pull back. "I'm *trying* to be happy. But it's not as easy as it sounds."

Keung grimaces. "Try harder then."

"What?"

"The McNeals are decent people—I've watched them. That Virus of yours is a legitimate good guy. If you stick with them, you'll have a normal life."

"I know." I sit up straight and feel my spine crack.

"So be careful," Keung says. "Don't mess it up."

"I won't!"

"That video in front of Tabula Rasa? Tonight hanging out with the Defectos?" Keung's voice is fiery. "Avoid all of it. Don't let the Vestals suck you back into their vortex."

"But I have friends who are Vestals. Fatima and Beau and—"

"Be their friends," Keung says. "But don't get wrapped up in their problems."

I think of Fatima about to pop out a baby in a few months. "I don't know if that's possible."

Keung takes both of my hands in his. "Then try harder," he says. "Maybe focus more on *The Lighthouse*."

"But I use that to write about the Vestals."

"Move on, Blanca. You have lots to say. But now, when the world looks at you, all they see is a former Vestal." Keung slowly kisses both of my hands. "But I see so much more."

I leave my hands in Keung's. "Seth and I. We haven't ... you know ..."

Keung holds both of my hands together tight. "Why not?"

I shrug.

"*Tiānshĭ*, not every guy you sleep with will get tortured."

"I know. But I still feel guilty. I should have said something— stopped Headmaster Russell from hurting you." Tears roll down my cheeks.

Keung wipes them away. "It wasn't your fault."

"Maybe it was." I cry harder. All the things I've felt for months pour out. "Barbelo was my father. My mother *helped* him. And they ruined so many lives." My head is on Keung's shoulder before I know it, his strong arms around me.

"It's not your fault," Keung murmurs into my hair. "None of it was your fault."

"But don't you see?" I say, wrenching myself away. "I have to fix it! I can't stay away from the Vestals. I have to make things right for everyone."

"No!" Keung's eyes flash. "You only have to solve problems in your own life. That's it."

"I *have* fixed my life. Now I need to help other people."

Keung shakes his head. "No, my angel. You're not well yet. You still need healing."

"How?" I ask. "How am I supposed to get better?"

Keung smiles. "I already told you. *Keep yourself private, and everything will be all right. Avenge all wrongs, especially when your honor is at stake.* And what do you deserve?"

"*Relationships and a feeling of importance,*" I answer. "I'm not sure Cal would agree with the revenge part."

Keung's voice holds a sharp edge. "That part's taken care of."

I nod. Then I ask the question I need to ask. "If you're so wise about all this, then why are you still a Guardian? Why not drop out like me?"

Keung's face is perfectly still. "Who says I haven't?" Then he leans forward and kisses me on the cheek. "It's time for you to go home before I screw everything up."

Chapter Nineteen

I don't go home. Instead, I go to the place that makes me feel terrified, relaxed, and exhilarated all at the same time.

I have security codes to Seth's apartment, so I don't need to wait for the doorman to buzz me up. When I knock on Seth's front door and nobody answers, I let myself in and deactivate the alarm.

It's almost midnight. Too late, I realize I should have texted Cal to let him know where I am. I click my chip-watch and hurriedly leave Cal a message.

Seth's apartment is full of shadows. Silvery light from downtown filters in through the windows. Seth's couch and coffee table loom like monsters. The touch screens are down but on sleep mode. A faint buzzing sound resonates from the kitchen.

Waking Seth up isn't part of my plan. Actually, I have no plan.

I run my fingers through my hair and feel snarls. I don't smell that great either. My day started with a tutoring session and went downhill from there. But maybe it can end well.

I slip into Seth's bathroom and turn on the shower. But I also lock the door, just in case.

The water is hot, not scalding like I prefer, so I adjust the faucet as high as it goes. Pretty soon the stress of the day singes away. The photograph of myself as a baby. Tiffany defending me to Agent Plunkett. The Defecto support group. Keung ordering me to be happy. The pounding water brings relief.

Unfortunately, Seth's soap options are abysmal. Hopefully his dandruff shampoo doesn't make my hair fall out. There's no conditioner or decent cleanser. I wash my face with the same bar of soap that probably cleans Seth's feet. I rinse the suds off extra-well and try not to think about fungus.

But when I step out of the shower and look in the mirror, none of it matters. My brown hair streams down my back and my clear skin glows. I'm as fresh and pure as I always was.

"Blanca Nemo," I whisper at my reflection. "The girl who could sell soap."

The mirror fogs up with my breath.

I wipe away the condensation and try again. "Blanca McNeal," I say a bit louder. "The girl who can be whatever she wants."

I pull on my shirt and lace panties but fold the rest of my clothes into a neat pile on the bathroom shelf. Then I unlock the bathroom door and tiptoe into Seth's bedroom.

The room is pitch-black. It takes a minute for my eyes to dilate so I can see where I am. But the sound of Seth's soft breathing leads me straight to his bed.

His big, warm, inviting bed.

This was a horrible idea.

My worst decision yet!

I root myself to the carpet, too nervous to move. The stupidest thing of all was leaving my pants in the bathroom.

Right when I'm about to hightail it out of there, Seth rouses himself awake. I see him stretched out with one leg outside of the covers.

He must see me too because he yelps.

Suddenly, lights turn on all around me.

"Whoa!" I cross my arms over my T-shirt. "It's me!"

"Blanca?" Seth exclaims. He springs up to his knees. Seth's dark hair is wildly disheveled. Plaid boxers hang on his hips. I get a nice view of his naked torso, each muscle defined by a different tattoo.

"I should go." I spin around at top speed only to feel Seth grab my fingertips and pull me toward him.

"Not so fast." Seth kisses me tenderly, his hands at my waist. But soon a rising heat engulfs us both. Seth's hands move down to the bare skin of my ass, his thumbs grazing under my panty line.

"I came here to sleep," I declare, tearing myself away from his kisses.

"Uh-huh." Seth grins. He takes a deep whiff of my wet hair. "Is that my shampoo?"

"Yes," I answer. "I borrowed it." I de-wedgie myself. "Scoot over and make room for me in the bed."

Seth leans back on his heels. "What is this? A slumber party?"

"What's that?" I ask, confused.

"Um. Never mind." Seth pulls away the covers and fluffs up a pillow for me. "I'll take what I can get."

I lie down next to him and pull the blankets up to my chin. The glare from a dozen lights assaults my vision.

Seth flicks his finger-chips, and most of the lights turn off except a soft bulb up above. "So you came here to sleep, did you?"

I bite my lip and nod. "And to say I'm sorry. For earlier. I should have trusted you. It doesn't matter who your lawyer is or how well you know her."

"I wasn't trying to hurt you, Blanca." Seth leans his head on his elbow, and I see the McNeal Family tattoo, a brilliantly inked sun, next to the angel for his mom. "You said you wanted details, and I can't give you any of those, but you do deserve an explanation."

"No, it's okay. I don't really want to hear it."

"You *need* to hear it." Seth sits up and leans against the headboard. I rise too, only I take the covers with me.

"I was so angry with my dad after my mom died that I created *Veritas Rex* and posted that awful video about him. I thought it showed Dad sleeping with a redheaded woman, but really it was my mom in a wig."

I grimace at the memory of the first time I saw that video. Cal's eyes filled with shame when he showed me. "Sophia would have been mortified," Cal had said. "I protected her reputation by sacrificing my own, but I didn't know it would cost me my son's respect."

Seth's shoulders rise and fall. "The video didn't get much traffic for a few days, but by day five—boom. The founder of McNeal Solar cheating on his dead wife was big news. Some other sites picked it up, and it went viral. I moved out of the manor before Dad could stop me."

"Before he could explain."

Seth nods.

"Where did you go?" I've never heard the full story before.

"Tiffany's house. Her parents were really cool about it and let me stay in their spare bedroom. I was seventeen."

"Is that how you finished high school?"

"Yeah. Luckily it was only a few months until graduation. Then over the summer I turned eighteen and my trust fund kicked in." Seth looks around his room. "I've been in this apartment ever since, blogging away."

"You didn't want to go to college?"

Seth looks down at his finger-chips. "I did. That was always the plan before my mom became sick. I got into a bunch of places too. But success with *Veritas Rex* happened overnight. I decided to stick with viral blogging for a while, to see where it went. I had no idea how famous I'd become."

I take a deep breath. "So where does Tiffany fit in?"

"She helped me through all of it when my mom died, especially during that summer. Then Tiffany went off to Berkeley, and we broke up over winter break—six years ago. But we're still friends. So when she graduated from law school, I put her on retainer as the lawyer for *Veritas Rex*."

"Why did you tell Tiffany about me?" I bite the inside of my lip.

"Why wouldn't I tell her about you? If I never mentioned you at all, that would be weird. Plus I had to tell Tiffany when I deactivated the security system to Lydia's house. I knew it was potentially illegal, and I didn't want to risk getting you or my dad in trouble."

What Seth says makes perfect sense, but lying here with his glowing blue finger-chips puts my senses on high alert.

"I take risks to be with you all the time," I say. "I've begged and begged you to get your finger-chips removed and you won't consider it."

"Because that's nuts!" Seth's voice gets louder.

"It's not!" I pull my knees up and hug them tight. "I've given up everything to be with you, and you won't even switch to a chip-watch."

"I've given up things for you too."

"Yes?" I snap. "Like what?"

"Stories," he grumbles. "Leads. The best headlines around. Being with you makes me a shitty Virus."

"All Viruses are shitty," I say before I can stop myself.

"What the hell? Why would you say that?"

A scumbag Virus like him. Headmaster Russell's words echo in my head.

"You were so wrapped up in *Veritas Rex*, you got us both kidnapped."

"By your crazy Vestal stalker!" Seth counters.

"Not all Vestals are crazy! If you can't see that, then what type of future do we have together?"

"Blanca," Seth says darkly.

"No," I say. "You're addicted to tech, and I'm old-fashioned. How will this work?"

"It'll work," Seth says. "It's got to."

I hold out my wrist and show him my chip-watch. "How can it if you won't meet me half way?"

"I do!" Seth declares. "Who the hell wore those freaking lead-lined gloves the other night? You're the one who won't budge."

"What's that supposed to mean?"

"The white wardrobe. The antique chip-watch. The blank skin. Tiffany has ten tattoos, and you don't have a single one."

"You *did not* just compare me to Tiffany!" I throw the covers back exposing my two perfectly shaped legs. Then I jab my finger into Seth's side where Tiffany's name is written in elaborate cursive. "Maybe you and *Tiffany* would be better off together."

"Maybe we would." Seth's face blotches red with rage. "At least Tiffany knows how to have fun."

"Fun?"

"Yeah! Fun. You won't even leave the house."

If I stay one moment longer I'll burst into tears. Only my years of Vestal training keep me together.

"You're my brother now. *Not* my boyfriend." I run to the bathroom and pull on my pants. Then I grab my shoes and dash out of the apartment barefoot.

"Blanca!" Seth calls after me. "If you don't come back, I'm not chasing after you!"

I don't bother turning around.

●●●●●●●●●

I have the whole ride home on my motorcycle to think. By the time I arrive at the manor, it's almost two a.m., but I don't let fatigue stop me now. I wave my chip-watch against the great hall hearth, and a fire springs to life. It casts an eerie glow against the darkness. Then I curl on the ground in front of one of the sofas and open up *The Lighthouse*, which I have sorely neglected these past few weeks.

Keung said that I had lots of things to say. He said I should use *The Lighthouse* to talk about more than what it's like being an ex-Vestal. So I decide to take him up on his suggestion. I stare at the fire a moment, and then type.

```
Loyal Lighthouse Friends,
I am more than my present. I am more than
my past. I am more than whatever name the
world wants to call me this week. My name
is Blanca, and my future is as limitless as
yours.
A friend reminded me tonight that human
beings want two things: relationships and
```

a feeling of importance. You, my friends,
deserve both.
Choose the person in front of you, not your
finger-chips.
Online connections are powerful tools that
you must respect, not fear.
But a stronger force is love. We must never
allow technology into the middle of our
relationships.
I pity everyone who can't see that.

Right when I click Publish, an awkward thing happens. The door opens, and I hear delicate heels click on marble, then a flirtatious giggle.

"A fire!" Pilar exclaims. "How romantic."

I scoot down lower behind the couch.

"It must have been the servants," Cal says. "Blanca isn't here tonight."

"Lucky us," Pilar murmurs.

I hear the sound of bodies pressed together and heavy breathing. How can this day get any worse? Should I sneak away? Announce my presence? I wish Seth were here. He would know exactly what to do.

The thought of Seth stabs me in the heart. I can't think about him right now.

From the echo of Pilar's heels on the floor, she and Cal are headed my way fast. I look at my chip-watch and receive a bolt of inspiration.

With a quick wave of my wrist, I turn off the gas fire in the hearth, and the room shrouds in darkness.

Then I flee for my life.

"That's odd," I hear Cal say to Pilar. "I better have this fireplace checked out tomorrow."

By the time the flames turn back on, I reach the safety of upstairs.

Chapter Twenty

I don't venture from McNeal Manor all week, and Cal doesn't notice. He's too busy with work and Pilar. But to be fair, it's not like I locked myself in my room like I did last year when I was upset. My insides are in turmoil, but my outsides look fine. Yesterday, I wandered the halls of McNeal Manor until I came to Seth's childhood bedroom. I couldn't bear to enter. I just pressed my forehead against the door and tried not to hurt.

I'm a walking heartbreak, dressed up like myself.

Every morning Irene tutors me, and then I study some more outside on the grounds. I stretch out on a quilt under the orange trees, and the sunshine offers a pittance of solace.

A couple of days ago I showed up at breakfast with a sunburned nose, and Cal lectured me about sunscreen. A maid delivered a bottle of SPF100 a few hours later.

I'm not sure if Cal knows that Seth and I broke up.

I have said nothing.

In the evenings, I float on my back in the indoor pool and stare up at the skylights. It's my personal sensory deprivation unit—only gigantic. Before my first swim, I climbed up on a chair and blacked out all of the security cameras with electrical tape, just in case. Cal said they were deactivated, but you can never be too sure. Alan is still on paid vacation, and I don't know who mans the guard station now. I won't give the new guy a peep show.

Today I sit outside on my blanket focused on my engineering notes when Jeremy calls on my chip-watch. Luckily, he calls on audio because I haven't brushed my hair all day. Or my teeth.

"Are you coming to tonight's meeting?" Jeremy asks.

"Sorry," I answer. "I'm busy."

I wonder if he'll pry. A Vestal wouldn't press for private information but a Defecto might.

"What you posted on *The Lighthouse* moved me," Jeremy says. "It's getting a lot of attention."

"That's nice, but it's not why I wrote it." I think about Keung and the little pep talk he gave me before I went to Seth's house and accidentally dumped him. I did exactly what Keung told me *not* to do. How did that happen?

"Why did you write the post if you didn't care if people read it?" Jeremy asks.

"Because it was true," I answer. "That was enough."

"Oh. Are you sure you won't come to the support group tonight? You sound a little down."

"I'm fine," I say briskly. "Sorry, but I have plans." I click off the watch.

At least I told the truth. Tonight I have company. Fatima and Pilar invited themselves over for a swim before dinner.

● ● ● ● ● ● ● ● ●

"My back's killing me." Fatima slowly treads water. "The doctor said swimming might help. Thanks for this, Blanca."

I tread water too, but Pilar lounges poolside in a white bikini, waiting for Cal to come home. I'm pretty sure this is an excuse for Pilar to show him her supermodel attributes.

"When's your mom's contract up?" I whisper to Fatima over the water.

"What?" Fatima asks. "I have water in my ears."

Pilar glances over the book she reads and looks our way.

I sink into the pool and swim closer to Fatima. Maybe I should ask my question in a different way. "How old is your mom?"

Fatima glances at Pilar and back to me, like she's scared to get caught revealing such private information. "She's forty-two," Fatima says. "One more year to go on her contract and she'll be free."

"Does she want to return to Tabula Rasa and become a teacher?"

Fatima shrugs. "I don't think school's her thing. Probably she'll just retire."

And wouldn't it be nice to end up as the lady of McNeal Manor? I tread water angrily. "Oh," I say, to Fatima. "That's great. But honestly, your mom doesn't look a day over thirty-five."

"That's because she has no stretch marks." Fatima leans back to float, her gigantic stomach protruding like a basketball from her slim frame.

"You won't get stretch marks," I say. "Don't be ridiculous."

Fatima rubs her stomach, her face contorted with worry. "Sarah gave me some special cream that's supposed to help but …"

I give Fatima a playful splash. "You're gorgeous, and after the baby, you'll have even bigger boobs."

"Great. Just what I need. Double Gs." Fatima splashes me back and smiles. "So what's new with you and Seth? Where is he?"

"Doing *Veritas Rex* stuff," I offer. Which is probably true.

Underneath the water, my chip-watch buzzes. I feel butterflies at the thought that it might be Seth, messaging me after a week of silence.

But it's only a text from my lawyer.

Nancy Gilbertson: Good news! Your mother's estate releases to you shortly. Expect delivery in the next 24 hours.

"What is it?" Fatima asks.

"Nothing," I say. "My lawyer's dropping off some boxes. That's all."

I glide through the water at top speed, and the chlorine stings my eyes.

•••••●•••••

At least I have Irene. She comes to tutor me every morning in the library. Most days, I wait for her, immersed in calculus. Something comforts me about studying the math of change while I attempt to reboot my life. It's been over a week now since Seth and I broke up, and I've never felt better.

I don't need Seth. I don't need the Vestals. I don't need a support group, and I certainly don't need Dr. Meredith.

The only thing I need is a plan to take care of myself. I won't be like Pilar and wait for someone to rescue me. I want to be independent.

College is the first step.

The problem is that Irene still doesn't think I can do it.

I only score eighty-five percent on a quiz today, and she spouts her irritation. "You started off too far behind to make meaningful progress." Irene pushes a chunk of dark black hair behind her ear.

"Then I need to study harder. The interview is still six weeks away."

"And you're going to embarrass yourself," Irene says. "Mr. McNeal will blame me."

Her words hurt, but Irene has always been a tough teacher. It's hard to argue with brutal honestly.

Still, some small thing inside me speaks up. A little voice begs to be heard.

"I won't embarrass myself. I always say the right thing in difficult situations. I might not have the best math and science background, but I can discuss history, literature, or languages with any professor in that room. That gives me an advantage."

Irene sniffs. "Maybe."

"And Cal won't blame you. No matter how I do."

Irene shakes her head. "You don't know that for sure."

"If you thought I'd fail, why did you take the job?"

"I'm a McNeal Solar intern! It's not like I get to choose!"

"Cal said you volunteered."

Irene stares at her cuticles.

Something clicks in my brain. I zero in on what she's already said. *It's not like I get to choose.*

My hands curl into tight fists. "Who do you really work for, Irene? Did Keung put you up to this?"

Irene colors but doesn't answer.

"I know it's not the Vestals. I would have recognized you."

Irene hastily gathers her tablets. "I told you. I work for Mr. McNeal. It's time I head back to the office."

I watch her closely and notice her eyes glance toward the windows of my walled-in courtyard.

"It was you." I stand up tall. "You put the last message from Keung on my pillow."

"I don't know what you mean. Who's Keung?" Irene grabs her coat.

"How many other Guardians did Keung plant at McNeal Solar?" I demand. "Tell me or I call the FBI."

Irene whips her head and glares at me. "You wouldn't dare! Keung said we could trust you."

"*How many?*"

"Only me," Irene answers. "And I quit." She stalks out of the room but turns and sneers at me from the doorway. "Good luck getting into Stanford, Vestal."

The door slamming rattles my nerves. My chest contracts with stress. I stare at the notes Irene left behind. The entrance interview is the least of my worries now. I can't allow spies in McNeal Solar.

The horrible thing is I don't know if Irene is telling the truth. If not, who should I tell? If I mention this to Cal, I'll have to explain about Keung. "Oh, by the way, Cal. I know you trust me and think I'm worthy of being your daughter, but I secretly met with a Chinese diplomat who I slept with when I was sixteen. I think he planted people in your company to spy on me." Lovely conversation that would be.

If I tell Agents Plunkett and Marlow, they'll ask why I'm suspicious. How can I do that without getting myself in trouble?

If I told Fatima or Beau, they would understand, but they couldn't help.

Jeremy would probably lecture me about how evil Vestals and Guardians are to begin with.

No. Only two people can really help: Seth and Nancy. I take a deep breath and brace myself for what I need to do.

I text Seth on *Veritas Rex* so he'll know this is business, not personal.

Me: McNeal Solar might have Guardian spies
in their midst. Start with Irene Page first.
She is no longer my tutor.

Then I load up my physics tablet and get back to work. My chip-watch buzzes immediately.

Veritas Rex: What do you mean?

Me: I don't know for sure. Only a hunch.

Please look into it and broadcast at will.

Veritas Rex: On it.

I stare at my wrist a full two minutes before I put my hand back down, hoping the conversation will continue.

But it doesn't.

I knew I could count on Seth. So why did I screw things up? Over finger-chips?

I try so hard not to let technology get in the way of relationships, yet here I go doing exactly that.

I click on my chip-watch again, only this time I text Seth on his personal account.

Me: Do you have a minute? Could we talk?

I wait, breathlessly, staring at the silvery gray screen.

Seth: Not right now. I'm with Tiffany.

A sucker punch in the stomach.

I click off all my electronics and stack the tablets neatly on the desk. It's time to leave the manor.

•••• ● ••••

I put on my mother's blue coat. The wool feels scratchy but warm. I've never worn color before, except that one time my mother shared her red scarf when she kidnapped me. I paw through the clothing, hoping to find it, but the scarf must be lost in Nevada.

When the courier delivered the boxes this morning, I knew exactly what they were. Nancy had warned me. "I'm sending over Lydia's wardrobe," she said. "I thought you might like to have her things."

Two of the boxes are filled with white. My mother's long silk initiation robes, her traveling cloak, the fluttery dress she wore the night she went to the Vestal banquet with Cal and me. But the other box holds a kaleidoscope of colors I never imagined my mother wearing. Reds, blues, yellows, and greens. A purple swimsuit. Where did she wear that?

She owned jewelry too. Costume items that sparkle in the light and a tiny silver chain that twinkles delicately. I see a turquoise bracelet with an ornate silver clasp. I inspect it closely and smile. The gemstones wink at me. My mother had many secrets.

Exactly like me.

I wear a short white dress. When I button up the blue coat, I don't look like a former Vestal. I slip the turquoise bracelet on my wrist above my chip-watch. Then I bury my hands deep in the coat pockets. It's like my mother and I hold hands.

I can do this. I'm a big girl now.

It's time to stick up for myself and protect my family.

●●●●●●●●●

The new white limo glows like lightening in the bright sun. When Alan holds the door open for me, he looks tanned and refreshed.

The backseat has butter-yellow seats, soft as velvet. I click on my chip-watch to see if it will work, and only get static.

"Lead-lined walls," Alan says through the divider. "Especially for you."

Or Pilar, I can't help think. It's only been two weeks, but Cal is definitely infatuated.

"I'm glad to have you back," I say to Alan. "How was your vacation?"

"Not long enough," Alan answers. "But wonderful. I told Mr. McNeal that your family deserves a vacation too."

"Wouldn't that be nice? I'm sorry your trip was a consolation for being carjacked."

"Don't worry about it. I'm only sorry I didn't see it coming. Where to now?"

"Downtown Silicon Valley," I say. "The Chinese consulate."

Alan looks at me through the rearview mirror. "Are you sure about that, Miss Blanca?"

I lean back and tighten my seat belt. "Yes. I'm positive."

Chapter Twenty-One

· · · · · · · ● ● ● ● · ● · ● ● ● · · · · ·

I feel invincible in this blue coat. It makes me invisible, and for me, that's the same thing. When I walk into the foyer of the consulate, nobody stares. The security guard who conducts my full-body scan doesn't blink. Without my cuff or my glaring white outfit, I'm nobody. At least on the outside.

The women at the counter have sleek pageboy haircuts. They work the lines efficiently, scanning people with their finger-chips and entering data on another screen.

"Visas in lines one and two," says an announcement in Mandarin. "Travelers in line three. For all other business please wait in line four."

I pause for the instructions to repeat in English before I walk to the fourth line. While I wait my turn, I surreptitiously scan the room for cameras. Above the life-size mural of the Boxer Rebellion, I see a circular lens that blends into the molding. I check the corners of the room and find four more cameras. But the spies I don't notice worry me the most. The man who stands to my left looks at me over and over again. Does he recognize me from the news, or is he one of Keung's men?

When it's my turn at the counter, I smile in a friendly manner.

"Good afternoon." The receptionist speaks perfect English. "How may I help you today?"

"I would like to speak with Mr. Timothy Wu," I answer.

"Mr. Wu is a busy man," she says. "Do you have an appointment?"

"Not at this moment."

The woman wrinkles her nose. "I'm sorry, but Mr. Wu does not have time to see every person who wants to meet him. Are you a reporter?"

I shake my head.

"Then I apologize, but the best I can do is take a message for him with your contact information."

"I understand." I lean forward slightly. "Thank you for your help." Then I switch from English to Mandarin. "Instead of a message for Mr. Wu," I say, hoping she can understand my horrible accent, "could I please leave a message for Keung?"

The receptionist's eyes pop when I mention Keung's name. "Who should I tell him is calling?" She speaks so fast in Mandarin that I barely understand.

"Blanca McNeal." I stand up straight.

"Please wait a moment." The woman types rapid fire with her

finger-chips. She eyes the man standing next to me nervously. But he's already moved up in aisle three, as if he has a burning traveler's question for the consulate to answer.

With nineteen years of uneasiness, I sense myself being watched. I look up at the camera above the mural and see it zoom in on my face.

I shake back my hair a little and keep my face relaxed.

A minute later, a gentleman in a dark suit comes out from behind the counter. "Ms. Blanca," he says graciously. "Would you please follow me?"

I give him the full force of my smile. "Absolutely. Thank you for your help."

When I follow him back into the consulate's inner rooms, I feel the movement of heads.

People are watching.

• • • • ● • • • •

Keung's first words to me when I enter his office are, "Blanca, you shouldn't have come." He stands in front of a tall window that frames the skyscrapers of Silicon Valley. His designer suit accents every sculpted line. Keung could model for Fatima's company.

I unbutton my coat and lay it casually on the back of a chair. "I had to come."

"No." Keung walks toward me and puts his hands on my bare shoulders. "This was dangerous. For both of us. You have no idea how closely your government watches me. Agents Plunkett and Marlow have interviewed me half a dozen times."

I smile up at him. "I thought you had diplomatic immunity." I let my eyes go dreamy. "I had to see you again." *If you want to control somebody, instead of be controlled, tell that person what they want to hear.*

Keung's expression softens too, and he rubs both of my shoulders. Then he pulls me in for an embrace and strokes my hair. "You should have reached out through Jeremy. He would have arranged for us to meet." He leads me to a couch where we sit down knee to knee. The hemline of my dress rises up.

I lay my hands neatly on my lap, and my new bracelet twinkles. "I know, but something happened today that disturbed me, and I knew you were the only person who could possibly fix it."

"What?" Keung places a hand on my bare knee. "Is it Seth? Is he in trouble?"

There is no hope in his voice. No question. My instincts tell me that Keung already knows.

So I say it decisively. "I broke up with Seth." I shift my legs ever so closer to Keung, causing his hand to slip down toward my thigh.

"I'm sorry about that." Keung swallows. "I want you to be happy."

"I want to be happy too. And I have it all planned out." I flick my hair behind my shoulder. "I don't need a Virus like Seth. I can take care of myself."

"Of course you can, *tiānshǐ.*"

I stare at Keung when he says that and try to gauge what he's thinking. But his hot hand on my thigh tells me all I need to know.

Now's the moment to strike. *Vestals avenge all wrongs, especially when our honor is at stake.*

"I'm going to college," I say forcefully.

"You'll be brilliant."

"That's not what my tutor says."

"Then she's stupid." Keung places a second hand on my leg.

"Then why did you plant Irene Page at McNeal Solar?" I feel Keung's fingers dig into my muscles.

"What?"

"She was my tutor. And she was horrible."

"Blanca, I—"

"It's okay." My voice is soft and delicious. "I'm fine with having your people around." I place my hands on top of his own. "It's so sweet that you want to keep an eye on me. But couldn't you have given me a better teacher? Irene was awful."

Keung shrugs. "She came highly recommended. I thought her expertise at math and science would be perfect."

I giggle. "Well you were wrong." I reach up and brush an imaginary piece of lint off Keung's shoulder. Then I let my hand linger on his chest. "Any other people I should know about?"

Keung grins. "Not at your mansion."

"So what do I have to do if I want to see you again?" I slide my hand behind his neck and play with his hair. "Go through Jeremy?"

Keung leans down and crushes his mouth on mine. He cups his hand under my dress and lifts me onto his lap. Old memories assert themselves. We kiss frantically. Passionately. Until I feel Keung's hand on the back zipper of my dress and I pull away.

"There are people outside," I whisper.

"That never stopped us before."

I comb Keung's hair with my fingers. Then I straighten out his suit with both hands, and slip back to my own seat. "Not here."

Keung reaches for my wrist and waves his fingertips over my chip-watch. "This is my private number. For later."

My eyebrows shoot up. "How'd you do that? You don't have finger-chips."

Keung holds up his palms. "Invisi-chips. By the time I'm done, everyone will want them."

I stare at his hands closely and finally see them. Faint pinpricks of glowing blue.

Just like Ethan had.

My insides quake, but hopefully my body doesn't betray me.

"I'll be in touch," I say. "Count on it." Then I stand up, cross the room, and slither into my coat.

"Oh, Blanca," Keung says before I leave.

I turn to look at him. "Yes?"

"You look beautiful in blue."

I blush.

I bet that's the first honest thing Keung has said.

Alan takes me directly to McNeal Solar. As soon as I walk into Nancy's office, I hold out my wrist. "Here," I say. "You need this." I slip off my mother's bracelet and place it in her hand.

"A bracelet?" Nancy straightens out her plum colored suit. "I'm not sure if turquoise is the best color for this outfit."

"No. That's not what I mean." I slide open one of the stones and reveal a tiny camera. "A recording and video. I made them for you. As McNeal Solar's chief counsel, I think you should investigate. Or maybe we need to share this with Agents Plunkett and Marlow. You tell me."

Nancy snatches up the bracelet "What?"

I fill Nancy in on my meeting with Keung, even the part about me crawling all over his lap.

Nancy grins like the Cheshire Cat. "Well, Blanca McNeal, you are full of surprises!

"Always," I answer.

Ten minutes later, while Nancy and I analyze every nuance of Keung's voice on that recording, my chip-watch goes off with a call from Cal. "Great news, sweetheart!" His silvery image stands outside of Pilar and Fatima's building.

My heart drops to my stomach over what Cal might say next. First my mother and now Pilar. How can Cal be so gullible? If he's calling to tell me that he's proposed, I'll have to break it to him that Pilar's using him for his money.

But Cal mercifully interrupts my train of crazy thoughts. "We're going on vacation," he says. "You, Pilar, Seth, Fatima, Beau—everyone's coming. We leave in two days."

"What?"

"An island retreat!" Cal gushes. "In the Pacific. The private investigator recommended the place. The resort sits in a satellite shadow with no tech reception. It'll be perfect!"

"What?" I gasp. "How's that possible?"

"I don't know," says Cal. "Ask Nancy. She says you might own it."

"*What?*"

"Wait," says Cal. "Where are you? Is that Nancy's office?"

I turn around so that Nancy appears in the frame. "Hi, Cal," she waves.

Cal's face blanches. "Oh! I didn't realize you weren't alone. Uh, Nancy? This trip is confidential. The Vestals don't want the news to get out."

"Attorney-client privilege," Nancy says. "I won't say anything." She locks her lips with an imaginary key.

"We'll talk more when you get home. Be safe, Blanca."

"I will." I click off my watch and stare at Nancy. "An island?" My voice raises an octave. "My mother owned an island?"

When Nancy nods, I suddenly remember the purple swimsuit.

Chapter Twenty-Two

Seth's white T-shirt hugs his skin, showing off every last tattoo. I spot a new one. Under his elbow snarls an ancient face with a gaping mouth. It looks puffy, like it was freshly inked a few days ago. My own skin feels clammy.

The tight quarters of the airplane cabin activates my latent claustrophobia. The low hum of the environmental systems has me on edge. One moment I'm freezing; the next minute I suffocate. But mainly, I'm terrified. This is the first time I've flown. Cal promised me the McNeal Solar private jet is perfectly safe, but that doesn't calm my nerves.

I look at Seth's head bent low over his finger-chip screen, engrossed in whatever he's reading, and wish that I could bury my head in his shoulders and have him tell me it will all be all right.

I would tell him I was a fool for giving him an ultimatum. That I don't care if he has finger-chips so long as he stays true to me. And I would kiss his beautiful mouth and feel the scratch of stubble against my lips.

"Are you okay?" Seth jerks his head away from his screen and looks at me.

"What?" I ask.

"You were staring." He waves his finger-chips and the image jiggles. "Did you want to read this?"

"No. I was ... What's your new tattoo supposed to be?"

Seth twists his arm for inspection. "It's the Mouth of Truth from ancient Italy. I saw it online and thought it was cool."

I struggle to think of something honest to say. "Oh. It's very fitting." I turn back toward the physics book I brought with me from Cal's library.

"Here we are!" Fatima announces with delight. Her spaghetti-strap tank top and maternity shorts make her look like a beach ball. I never thought it would happen, but Fatima's curves have melded together into one huge lump.

Beau comes two steps behind her in an ivory silk shirt and linen shorts. The two of them scoot down the aisle of the McNeal Solar private jet and take a seat across from me and Seth.

Pilar and Cal have the seats in front of us. Pilar looks especially svelte in a white strapless dress and gladiator sandals. Alberto's a few rows behind, his shoulder-length hair a mane of silver.

"Richard," Cal says as Trevor's family comes on board, "I'm so glad you could make it."

"The soap family's invited?" Seth narrows his eyes. "Why?"

"I don't know," I whisper. But when I see Richard make a beeline for Alberto, I have my suspicions.

Trevor and Sarah board the plane next, holding hands. Sarah's prematurely gray hair looks especially surreal next to her T-shirt, flip-flops, and shorts.

"What's up?" Trevor asks as he escorts Sarah past us. The corner of his carry-on bumps Seth in the head.

Seth frowns. "Why did I agree to this again?"

"I don't know." I point to the seats in front of us. "Didn't you tell your dad we broke up?"

Seth shakes his head. "Didn't you?"

My face gives away my answer.

"Well, shit," Seth mumbles. "No wonder our seats are together."

Suddenly the whole plane feels tiny.

Then it shrinks smaller when Beau's brothers board.

"Dude!" the big one yells. By big, I mean six feet six. "Let the party begin!"

"That's Ryan," I say. Then I nod at the blond guy behind him. "And the one holding the Hacky Sack is Zach." Both brothers grin when they spot me staring.

"Hey, Blanca." Ryan winks while he walks to his seat.

But Zach pauses, right in front of Seth. He rolls the Hacky Sack down his forearm, shoots it back up with his biceps, and catches it with a smack. "If this Virus gives you any trouble, princess, you come tell me."

"Dude," Seth says, "I can hear you."

Zach grins. "People can always hear me, Rex. And I inspire my lady friends to be even louder."

"Ladies and gentleman," the pilot announces, "this is Captain Milo Lin from the cockpit. Please take your seats and prepare for takeoff."

A pretty lady in a red pantsuit walks up and herds Zach to the rear of the plane. She gets rewarded with a full dose of Zach's charm.

"Who's the woman in red?" I ask Seth.

"I don't know. Probably the flight attendant."

The lady spins on her heels when she hears Seth's voice. "I'm not a flight attendant. I'm the copilot. And, sir, you need to turn your finger-chips off now."

"But we haven't left the gate!"

The copilot shrugs her shoulders. "I don't make the rules. But I do enforce them."

"Bloody hell." Seth slouches down in his seat and closes his eyes for a nap.

I do my best to ignore him.

That is until about ten minutes later when the plane taxies down the runway for takeoff. I didn't know an engine could roar so loud. Then the plane rattles, and I really get nervous. I look across the aisle to Beau and Fatima, who hold on to each other for dear life.

None of us have flown before except Beau's brothers.

"Seth!" I jab him in the arm with my finger to wake him up. "What's going on? Are we crashing?"

He opens one eye to look at me. "This is perfectly normal, and it's going to get louder here in a sec."

"Louder?" I grip the armrest so tight my knuckles turn white.

The whole plane jerks and throws me backward. Momentum presses me into my seat. The plane moves faster and faster. Then it lifts off the ground and clatters. Equipment squeals like something is breaking.

"Those are the wheels retracting," Seth offers.

"What?" Beau shouts across the aisle.

"The wheels retracting," Seth says louder, so everyone can hear. "It's normal, people."

A few seconds later, the captain's voice overtakes the cabin.

"Ladies and gentlemen, I understand that for many of you this is your first flight. Please let me reassure you that all that noise and turbulence is common. Once we reach our cruising altitude, things will calm down, and you'll be free to move about the cabin."

Up in front of me, I hear Pilar let out a loud sigh of relief.

"Vestals," Seth mumbles under his breath. "You guys are nuts."

●●●●⬤●●●●

I peer down the window at water as clear as glass. It's the same turquoise color as my mother's bracelet. The plane circles lower and lower. Amid the palm trees and thatched huts, I see a tiny strip of land that must be the tarmac.

Cal leans back over the seat to talk to us. "We're not that far from

Tahiti," he says. "Prepare yourselves for the best snorkeling of your life."

"How did you find this place again?" Seth asks his dad.

Cal looks at me. "Blanca owns it."

"What?"

I shrug. "It's more like the sham company my mother created owns it. I'm still not sure of the details."

The plane quakes from the descent. I reach absentmindedly for my cuff that is no longer there. I feel my chip-watch instead and spin it around and around my wrist.

I don't know why I bothered to bring it. Cal said that this entire island was off the grid in a dead-zone of satellite reception. When my mother was here, Barbelo couldn't bother her.

Unless he came too.

I never thought to ask Nancy the specifics.

"Stop it," Seth says.

"Stop what?"

"That thing you do with your wrist. It's really annoying."

I look down at my chip-watch. "Oh. Sorry." I blink my eyes rapidly and look away.

When the plane touches ground, it makes so much noise that I'm positive we're crashing. But pretty soon things quiet down, and we roll across the runway. Islanders wait for us in flowered shirts and shell necklaces.

"Look. There's a welcoming committee." I turn to Seth and smile.

He doesn't return my expression. "Damn. My finger-chips won't work." Seth shakes his hands, trying to activate the batteries.

My face clenches. Does Seth not know?

"Ladies and gentlemen," the pilot announces, "this is Captain Lin again. Paradise awaits. You may now unfasten your seat belts."

At this, Fatima rises to her feet. "Hi, everyone. I want to say thank you for coming, and a special thank-you to my mom and dad and Cal for organizing all this." Fatima blows Pilar and Alberto a kiss. Then she gives me an air kiss too. "And to my best friend, Blanca, for hosting us on her island."

"Um, you're welcome." I wave.

Fatima's smile is wide. "But what most of you don't know—and especially not Beau—"

"What?" Beau interrupts. "What's going on?"

"—is that these three days aren't just a vacation," Fatima continues. "It's Beau and my top-secret wedding!"

"Really?" Beau jumps to his feet.

"With no photographers," Fatima adds. "No companies! No public relations game plan. It's our own private celebration."

"Babe." Beau looks at Fatima with a face full of love. He leans Fatima as far back as she can go with her pregnant belly and kisses her.

Trevor claps, and pretty soon everyone joins in.

Up in front, I see Pilar bounce up and down excitedly on her chair. Then she grabs Cal by the shoulders and plants one on him.

Seth witnesses this too. "Gross!" he mumbles, looking away. He jiggles his finger-chips one more time.

"Uh, Seth." I hesitate before delivering the facts. "Those things won't work here."

"What do you mean 'won't work'?"

"This island? Um, the reason my mother liked it so much is the whole resort is cloistered." I explain about the satellite shadow.

Seth slams his head back against his seat. "Enough with the Vestal shit!"

I turn my head and look back out the window so he won't see my glee.

•••••⬤•••••

The hand-stitched quilt on the bed reminds me of my mother. Ms. Lydia never did any sort of sewing or crafts as far as I know, but the white background, gentle stitching, and purple flowers echo her gracefulness.

Was this the room my mother stayed in when she came? I look around the bungalow excitedly and search for clues. But all I find is simple bamboo furniture. A table and chair along with a small dresser. There is nothing of my mother's here. At least that I can see.

It was stupid of me to hope.

I lift my small suitcase onto the table and unpack. There's a gigantic bottle of sunscreen Cal insisted I bring and several outfits, but the only thing of real importance is the small velvet bag with the mysterious key. Maybe I'll find the lock it goes with this weekend. The sooner I explore the island, the better.

I search through the garments and select the white bikini. But then I drop it back on the pile. Who would I be showing skin for? Seth? Beau's brothers? I stuff the spandex away and pull out the purple one-piece.

I try it on in front of the mirror, delighted that it's a perfect fit. The suit scoops down the back, revealing my naked skin, and pushes me up in the front, which makes my modest cleavage look a little more inviting.

And purple is definitely my color.

Chapter Twenty-Three

• • • • • • • • • ● • • • • • • • • •

The black sand burns my feet when I take off my flip-flops, but I run down to the shoreline fast enough that the heat doesn't stick. The water hits the beach with a sharp impact. No gentle slope leads into the waves, only a steep shelf. My white cotton maxi dress billows around me, and sunglasses shade everything pink.

"Over here, sweetheart!" Cal calls to me from a collection of lounge chairs up the beach. "I ordered you a punch." He holds up a gigantic coconut with a straw and umbrella sticking out. Seth and Pilar lie on chaises next to him.

Cal's torso appears diminished next to his son's. I wish Cal would put his shirt on. Actually, I wish both of them would put their shirts on. Seth looks like he's spent every last minute of our thirteen-day breakup lifting weights at the gym. He wears dark sunglasses, so I can't see his expression when I walk up. But he probably notices my inadvertent glance at the Tiffany tattoo scribbled on his side.

"Isn't this nice?" says Cal when I'm settled in my chair. "All of us together on vacation."

"Mmm," Pilar murmurs. "Wonderful."

I take a sip of punch. Chunks of coconut float in ice, and the taste is pure heaven.

"Blanca," Cal asks, "are you wearing sunscreen?"

"On my face."

"Not good enough." He hands Seth the bottle. "Make sure to get her back."

Seth mouths, *You still haven't told him we broke up?*

You do it.

"Blanca," Cal shields his face from the sun and stares out at the ocean, "sunscreen isn't optional."

"I thought you said I was old enough to make my own decisions."

"Of course you are, sweetheart. But we couldn't have the face of McNeal Solar be sunburned, now could we?"

"Fine," I grumble. I pull the dress over my head and throw it down next to me.

"Oh, my God!" Seth gasps.

"What?" Pilar startles. "Is somebody hurt?"

"No." Seth lifts up his sunglasses.

"Blanca!" Cal's voice is full of emotion. "You're wearing color."

"Yes. So?" I turn around so they won't see me blush. My face gets even hotter when I feel Seth's hands rub against my back. I close my eyes and focus on images that will make the blush go away. Steamed tilapia. Gluten free porridge. Ms. Corina. Alan driving the limo. Latin conjugates.

Seth's hands are on my arms now, rubbing down my perfect skin. My spine tingles with pleasure. It takes all my resolve to pull my arm away. "Hey," I say, "I can do that part myself."

"Fine," Seth mutters and hands me the sunscreen.

"Is that my former girlfriend in color?" I hear someone call. I look over to see Trevor and Sarah walk up the beach, hand in hand. Sarah's gray hair is pulled into a high ponytail that looks cute with her white tankini.

Beau's brothers, Ryan and Zach, bound up the beach behind them. "Check out Blanca," says Ryan. "Damn, girl."

"I'm going to swim." Seth throws his sunglasses down and stalks off into the waves.

"Too bad you're dating a Virus," Zach says as he motions at Seth's backside with his thumb.

"I'm not," I announce. "Seth and I broke up last week."

"What?" Cal sits up straight. "Why didn't anyone tell me?"

"I don't know," I mumble. "Maybe because saying it out loud makes it real."

"Trevor's taken," Sarah snaps.

"I know." I wrinkle my nose.

"We're not." Zach flexes his muscles.

"And we're a whole lot of fun," adds Ryan.

Butterflies overtake my stomach. The type that make me want to throw up.

"Get the flippers, Zach," says Ryan. "We're teaching this woman how to snorkel."

Zach reaches down and pulls me off the lounge chair. "I hope you know how to blow."

●●●●●●●●●

After dinner, Cal, Alberto, Beau, and the rest of the men take off with cigars for another part of the island. I can't say I'm sorry to see Ryan and Zach go with them. I've spent all day smothered by attention. But I'm surprised Seth chooses to follow. "I didn't know you smoked," I tell him.

"Blch. No way. I'm just succumbing to peer pressure." He winks before he leaves.

I don't think it's very funny. Especially when the only two people left are me and Sarah because Pilar has already rushed Fatima off to bed for her last night of beauty sleep before becoming a married woman.

Sarah takes one look at me and screws up her face. "Um, I better go wash my hair."

I hum the "Citrus Sunshine" jingle from her last commercial as she leaves. That probably won't help our relationship any.

But there are worse places to be alone than on a Polynesian beach. The breeze is warm against my face. Plumeria tucked behind my ear gives everything a sweet, soft fragrance. The moonlight sparkles on the water. I spin around on the sand and my dress twirls around me. I reach my hands out wide like they could stretch out across the whole island.

"Lovely, isn't it?" A deep voice interrupts my revelry.

I come to a halt and immediately feel foolish.

In front of me stands Captain Lin, the pilot of our private jet. His dark black hair falls forward, slightly askew. The legs of his uniform are cuffed, his feet ankle deep in the ocean. "Your mother loved this island too."

"My mother? You knew her?" I peek for the workers behind me, clearing off the tables. But everything is gone. I'm completely alone with a strange man.

"Yes." Captain Lin nods. "For years."

I dig my feet deeper into the sand. "But I thought you flew the McNeal Solar jet."

"I do. At the moment."

The McNeal Solar HR department needs a seriously better screening protocol. But that's not particularly helpful now.

"This afternoon, you looked like a younger version of your mother in that bathing suit," Captain Lin says.

I feel goose bumps. Every instinct I have tells me to escape, but the buildings are too far away. I'd never outrun him.

Maybe I could throw sand in his eyes. I could stay and fight!

Or maybe, something whispers from deep inside my soul, *you could play this straight by the book. Controlling people is easier than you'd think*, I hear Barbelo say. *Speak their name softly, melodically.*

I adjust the flower behind my ear. "Captain Lin, it's so nice of you to mention my mother. I cherish every bit of information people share about her." *A little appreciation goes a long way.*

"I could talk about Lydia all day." Captain Lin traces the sand with his toe.

"I'd also like to hear about you." I coil my shell necklace around my fingers. *People love to talk about themselves.*

"Me?" Captain Lin answers. "There's nothing much to tell."

I beam my most friendly smile. "I highly doubt that. Were you a Vestal?"

Captain Lin laughs. "No, not me." He holds out his hands and shows me his finger-chips. "The only bad thing about this island is that these don't work."

Neither does my chip-watch. There's no way I can call for help.

"Are you a Guardian?" My words are slow and measured.

"What's that? Oh, you mean the Chinese Vestals. No. I was born and raised in San Jose."

Is he telling the truth? I can't tell for sure. Keung all but said he had other people working for McNeal Solar. Captain Lin might be under orders to keep mum.

If Keung planned this, maybe this situation isn't as dangerous as it seems. Maybe Captain Lin isn't a psycho killer. Maybe he's here to keep me safe.

Still, I'm taking no chances.

"How did you meet my mother?" *Clarifying questions are your friends.*

"She flew all over the world. But of course you probably knew that."

I nod. My mother was Barbelo's representative when he sold or acquired important secrets for the Vestal archives. She was second-in-command.

"I worked at a company that offered jet-for-hire services. Lydia brought important clients here several times a year. She always requested me because we were friends." Captain Lin sighs deeply. "But sometimes she'd come on vacation too. I taught your mother to copilot."

"Really?" I try to picture my mother in the cockpit, aviator sunglasses on her heart-shaped face. "Was she a good student?"

"The best." Captain Lin looks at me sideways. "I didn't see her much after she began dating Mr. McNeal. She's the one who suggested I work for McNeal Solar."

I swallow hard. "I'm sure she valued your loyalty."

"I like to think so." His voice is as soft as the Polynesian breeze.

Holy crap! I got this all wrong. I don't need flight *or* fight. Captain Lin isn't a threat to me. He misses my mother because they were friends.

I pull the plumeria from my ear and toss it into the waves. "When's the last time you saw her?"

"I flew her to DC and back about a month before she moved in with Mr. McNeal." Captain Lin looks out at the water as the flower floats away. "After that I never saw her again."

"But you decided to come work for McNeal Solar anyway? After she died?"

Captain Lin shrugs. "You got to pay the bills, right?"

"Yes," I say on the outside.

On the inside, a little voice whispers, *something doesn't add up.*

But what?

●●●●⬤●●●●

I've been awake for hours, listening to the sound of the ocean, and second guessing everything I ever knew.

Vestals are the only people you can trust, they told me at Tabula Rasa.

Never listen to anything Headmaster Russell says ever again, Cal told me. *You've got good instincts. You can think for yourself.*

I'm sorry if I frightened you, said Keung. *That wasn't my intention at all.*

We need each other, insisted Jeremy. *Together we can rebuild our lives.*

I wasn't trying to hurt you, said Seth before he broke my heart.

The sick part is all of those voices in my head that confuse me—they're all male. There aren't any female voices giving me wisdom.

What did my supposed mother teach me? *Nothing.*

What did Ms. Corina teach me? *How to smile.*

I don't know how Cal could possibly think I'm ready for college. I can't even have a normal conversation with someone on the beach without assuming he's a psychopath stalker.

But what if Captain Lin is a spy? What if he really works for Keung and has orders to keep tabs on me?

I squeeze my eyes shut and will sleep to come. All I hear is the static of my brain on high alert.

Then I hear shuffling at my door.

"Blanca," a low voice moans. "Blanca, it's me." The person outside fumbles with the handle.

I spring out of the covers and rush to the door, my white cotton nightgown flowing behind me. I'd recognize that voice anywhere.

"Blanca?" Seth mumbles through the lock. "Are you there?

My hand hovers over the doorknob while I unlock the dead bolt. "I'm here." I throw the door open wide.

"Great." Seth's breath stinks of alcohol. "Because I can't find my room." He stumbles a few steps toward me, and then crashes down face first on my bed.

By the time I shut the door, Seth's snoring.

● ● ● ● ● ● ● ● ●

The sheets are cool and silky, but Seth's body emanates heat like a furnace. When I wake up at dawn, hot and sticky, I turn the air-conditioning on high. By the time I climb back in bed, Seth has claimed the entire thing. For the past few hours I at least had a pillow and a narrow place to stretch out straight. Now I'd have to be a contortionist to lie on the bed.

Seth reeks like the bottom of a garbage can. Cigar smoke and rum make a nasty combination.

I'd be better off sleeping on the ladder-back chair in the corner.

Except ... the way Seth's hair sticks up every which way around his head makes me think of our first conversation, while he was stuck in jail for sneaking my picture. He had the dirty gleam of sweat on him then too. I thought Seth was horrible. Disgusting and cruel. But after I got to know him, I realized he was smart, brave, and fiercely loyal. And so much fun. *Unlike me.*

Seth gave me my first taste of pure happiness.

Now, I don't know what to believe.

I climb into the bamboo chair and wrap my arms around my knees. In the small light of dawn I can decipher the McNeal family sun tattoo, next to the angel for Sophia inked on Seth's arm.

Cal and Sophia, the two good parents. I never got the chance to meet Sophia, but Cal has changed my whole life.

There's nothing you could ever do or say that would make me stop loving you, Cal said to me. *That's what it means to be a father.*

That's the only message running around in my brain that I know for sure is the truth.

I want to be able to love like that. Unconditionally and with total trust.

I watch Seth sleep, his face completely at peace. His five o'clock shadow makes him look like a pirate.

Could Seth love unconditionally like his father? Could he love me no matter what crazy Vestal situation I brought down on him next?

Or could I love Seth, finger-chips and all?

If he took my picture while I was brushing my teeth, would I still love him? No matter what?

Or what if it was altogether worse? If Seth took a video of us making love and uploaded it straight to *Veritas Rex*, what would I do? Could I forgive him?

I'm messed up to think that. Seth would never do something so deplorable. He wouldn't betray me in such a horrible way. What's wrong with me that my mind always jumps to the worst?

It's like I'm playing Questions with myself. But there's no Dr. Meredith or support group of Defectos to offer the answers.

What do I really want?

Seth, my heart whispers. *I want Seth.*

But my head tells me a stronger message. *Healing*, it shouts. *I want to be whole.*

And in the glimmering stillness of morning, I see opportunity.

Maybe my heart and head both want the same things.

I lightly step over to the bed and push Seth's sleeping form to the side. Then I climb under the covers next to him.

"Blanca," Seth murmurs sleepily. His arm wraps around me and pulls me in tight. "I love you," he says with a voice half drunk.

"I love you too," I whisper. Then I snuggle up close to his side and fall asleep.

Chapter Twenty-Four

· · · · · · · · · ● ● ● ● ● ● ● ● · · · ·

When I wake up, Seth is gone. I pat the bed wildly and reach for him before I'm fully awake. But once I open my eyes, I see that his side is empty. The air conditioner clicks on and the coolness turns frigid.

I lie back into the pillows and stare up at the ceiling fan, collecting my thoughts. But Fatima interrupts my meditation when she bounds into the room and piles into bed next to me.

"Why wasn't your door locked?" Fatima's wet hair drips over her fluffy white bathrobe. "And why are you still in bed? It's almost ten!"

"What?" I rub my eyes. "I had a hard time falling asleep last night."

"Well, get your butt into the shower, missy. It's time to get ready for my wedding."

"I haven't had breakfast," I object.

"I'll have the kitchen send over some sushi."

"Aren't there any croissants?"

"Pastries! Are you crazy? Vestals don't eat—" Fatima closes her mouth with her hand. "Oh. Never mind."

"Sushi will be fine," I grumble. "I'll see you in your room in twenty minutes."

I pad over to the bathroom and shut the door behind me with a sharp *click*. With my pale skin and long cotton nightgown, I look like a ghost from an ancient era. But my brown hair is soft and wavy, and the slight pink of my cheeks is a pretty color. At least when Seth woke up and left me, I didn't look like a hideous hag.

I turn the faucet on in the shower to warm the water up and then come back to the sink for a fresh bar of soap. There, underneath the complimentary tray of toiletries, I find a note in Seth's slashing scrawl. "Sorry for last night," it says. "I must have been rude."

Instead of signing his name, Seth left the initials VR.

I crumple up the paper and toss it into the trash.

● ● ● ● ◉ ● ● ● ●

It's an all-white wedding. I stare out the window of the bridal room and watch the men gather on the sand in front of the flowered altar. When I see Seth barefoot in the sand, freshly shaved and with his hair slicked back, I feel my heart lurch. It's like looking at Seth transformed into a Vestal. The living, breathing flesh of a dream come true. The side of Seth's face with the lion-headed cobra is turned away. All I see is his profile, the un-inked skin of a gorgeous man in white. Then Seth turns his face toward me, and I read his discomfort. He tugs on his collar and shifts positions.

I don't know who convinced Seth to wear that suit, but it mustn't have been easy.

Cal, tanned and smiling, was probably a cinch for Pilar. Cal looks handsome in white and completely at ease. I watch him shake Alberto's hand and chat with Richard and Beau.

"Are they ready?" Fatima whispers.

I pull my head away from the window. "They're all set. Let me take one more look at you."

Fatima wears a silk dress with a crêpe sash tied around the empire waist. The fabric across the top of the gown is gathered to show off her impressive *décolletage*.

"Stunning." Pilar adjusts the tiara of orchids that are pinned into Fatima's elaborate updo. "*Aye, mijiha.* I can't believe this day is here so soon." Pilar's face melts, and she rapidly fans away tears with her hands.

"Mami," Fatima cautions, "your makeup!"

"I don't care!"

I hurriedly hand Pilar a tissue.

"Thank you." Pilar blots away tears under her eyes and looks at Fatima. "First it's your wedding; next it'll be your baby. I don't think I can do this."

"What do you mean, Mami?"

Pilar clasps Fatima's hands tightly. "I don't think I can leave you. When my contract is up next year, I'll find a way to extend it."

"Mami! You can't."

"I've waited my whole life to have a daughter," Pilar says. "And now I get to have a grandbaby too. I can't give either of you up."

"You shouldn't have to," I offer. "I mean, I'm not a Vestal anymore, and I still get to see Fatima."

Pilar sniffs hard and then looks at me. "It'll be different when the baby comes. You'll see."

"But the baby won't have a contract," I protest.

"Not yet," Fatima says. She looks down at her abdomen and then darts her eyes away.

"What's that supposed to mean?" I ask.

"Nothing." Fatima turns to her mom. "Do you really mean it? You'll stay with me?"

Pilar nods with her supermodel pout. Then she throws her arms around Fatima lightly and air kisses her a dozen times.

"What about Cal?" I ask. Here I had been so worried that Pilar would use him as her escape route, but now all I can think is how crushed he'll be when she leaves him. "You can't date Cal and still pretend to be married to Alberto. That's not fair to anyone."

Pilar stands up straight and adjusts her strapless dress. "No, it's not. But Cal's a good man. He'll understand why I need to put my daughter and grandbaby first. Besides, we've only dated for a few weeks."

There's a light rap on the door. Alberto opens it a crack and sticks his head in. "Showtime, ladies."

Fatima squeals with delight. "Papi!"

Alberto's handsome face appears even more regal when he smiles at Fatima in her wedding dress. Then seconds later, he gets tears in his eyes.

"Not you too." Pilar hands him a tissue, and Alberto blows his nose. He runs his hand through his silver hair and whispers, "Gorgeous. Both of you." Then he looks at me and adds "All *three* of you."

Fatima jumps up and down a few times with excitement and then clutches her belly like that hurt. "Ow!" She looks at me. "Where's my bouquet?"

I hand over the large cluster of fuchsia orchids and collect my own small bouquet of pink. The flowers look pretty next to my dress of crocheted lace. The fabric skims my body and stops a few inches above the knee. Pilar tied up my hair in an elegant knot, which exposes my naked back. The overall effect is sweet and sexy all at the same time.

"See you out there," Pilar says before she heads out the door.

I watch Fatima link her arm with Alberto.

I wait a minute before I say, "I guess it's my turn."

Then I step outside into the sunshine.

A musician softly plays the ukulele. Our small group of travelers lines up in a semicircle in front of the beachside alter. I clutch my flowers tight and take small steps in the hot sand, grateful to be wearing sandals.

When I walk past Cal, standing next to Pilar, he smiles brightly at me. Is that pride on his face? But with the corner of my eye, I see Seth look away.

I look straight toward the altar and take the last few steps to my place at the front, pretending my heart doesn't hurt.

Then the music changes, and all eyes are on Fatima as she walks down the aisle with Alberto.

When they reach Beau, he smiles so hard I think he might burst.

His joy is contagious. A few months ago, Beau and I were trapped in Nevada with Barbelo. Now we're on the beach in paradise surrounded by family and friends. I have a reason to smile too, no matter if Seth stands by my side or not.

Richard steps behind Fatima and Beau and folds his hands. Trevor told me last night at dinner that his dad was really nervous about serving as the officiant since he had never married anyone before.

When the music stops, Richard clears his throat. "In this strange experience we call life, we don't always get to choose the people we love." Richard looks out into the small audience and smiles at his friends. "Friends come and they go at the whims of fate. One moment they are with you, by your side, your best friends and constant companions; the next day they could be gone, never to be seen again." Richard looks down into the sand and pauses before he looks back up. "So when you find love, when it comes to you with the full force of glory, you need to embrace love and hold onto it with all your might. Fatima and Beau, I am honored to officiate at your marriage. Everyone who loves you—"

But I don't hear what Richard says next. My mind is stuck on what he's already said.

How could I be so stupid?

How could I have never thought to ask?

Before Sarah, Richard was married to Lilith.

The real Lilith.

My aunt.

●●●●●●●●●

Between the two of Beau's brothers, I don't get the chance to sit down. It's one dance after another underneath the stars. Ryan is so tall that I can't reach his shoulders. My arms come to a stop at mammoth biceps. He steers me around the dance floor like a ship, and my feet hardly touch the ground. Zach likes the fast songs and twirls me around so rapidly I can barely catch my breath. He throws me into a surprise flip, and my sandal flies off.

Seth, who's dancing with the pretty copilot from the plane, slides by next to us and says, "Be careful where you aim that thing."

"Oh, I always aim it in the right direction," says Zach.

I can't believe how desperate I've become, but I find myself eyeing Trevor and Sarah gliding across the floor. Sure, he was a horrible boyfriend, but Trevor was always an expert dancer. I'm formulating my excuse to sit the next song out with Ryan when mercifully, Cal cuts in.

"May I have this next dance?" he asks, politely.

"Of course," I reply before Ryan can say no. I extend my arms in the perfect frame and Cal leads us into the box step.

He nods his head toward the old-fashioned stereo on the table. "Sinatra," Cal says. "I brought it especially from home."

"It's beautiful. I have never heard his music before."

Cal leads me out into a gentle spin. "Someday we'll dance like this at your wedding."

"Maybe," I say. "If I marry."

Cal laughs. "Of course you'll get married. And it could be the father-daughter dance." Cal smiles. "If you wanted to make it official."

"What do you mean?"

"Since you and Seth are done with—" Cal hesitates "—whatever it was you were doing. I could adopt you. You could legally become my daughter."

"Oh, Cal."

"What Alberto said, earlier during the service ..." Cal pauses midsentence, and I see his eyes fill with tears. "It made me think of Sophia and how she left me too soon. If it weren't for her, I wouldn't have you in my life. So I want to make that permanent. I want the whole world to know you are my daughter."

"I don't know how to answer."

"You don't?"

"No," I admit.

Cal looks away.

"Don't get me wrong, Cal. I want to be your daughter more than anything in the world, but ... I think I'm in love with Seth."

Cal looks right back at me and chuckles. "Oh, sweetheart. Good luck with that." He twirls me into a spin and pulls me back in. Our steps match up perfectly.

I lean my head on Cal's shoulder, and he shelters me around the dance floor.

Chapter Twenty-Five

· · · · · · · · · ● · · · · · · · · ·

We're lined up on the tarmac about to board the plane. I sidle up to Seth and hiss in his ear. "Who do you want to sit next to: me, Ryan, or Zach?"

He grins roguishly. "Who do *you* want to sit next to?"

Now's the time to be brave.

And honest.

"You, Seth. I will always want to sit next to you."

Seth wipes his smirk away. He eyes Beau's brothers lumbering in my direction and grabs my hand, lacing our fingers together. "Only for the plane ride."

I feel Seth's pulse through my palm.

"So," I say, once we sit down, "are you in tech-withdrawal yet?"

Seth clenches his fingers. "As soon as we're in satellite range, I'm checking my stats. Who knows what's happened to *Veritas Rex* these past few days?"

"It's probably gone down in smoke," I tease.

"Are you sure you want make jokes like that on a plane?"

My stomach drops. "No," I say. "That was bad."

"Ladies and gentlemen," a voice announces in the cabin, "this is Captain Milo Lin speaking. I hope you enjoyed your vacation. We'll depart in a few minutes as soon as my copilot gets the all clear."

"Your second flight is never as scary as your first," Seth offers.

"I'll be fine." More than fine. I've got things to do.

I lean across the aisle to where Alberto and Richard sit. "Richard, I never felt like I got the chance to talk with you this weekend."

Richard raises his expertly groomed eyebrows at me. "Oh?"

This is it. My last best chance. "I want to ask you about my aunt Lilith."

Richard settles back in his chair and sighs. "I see. You're not the only one."

"I'm not?"

Next to me, Seth snorts.

"First Cal, then the FBI, then Seth," Richard begins. "But I told them nothing."

"Oh." My face falls.

Richard smiles. "Because you deserve to hear it first."

Hope stirs me up. "Really? Do you know where my aunt is?"

Richard's expression clouds and he shakes his head. "I wish I did. But I can tell you other things. What would you like to know?"

"What was she like? Did she ever talk about me?" It's hard to keep the yearning from my voice.

Richard gazes at Alberto, who gives him a small smile of encouragement.

"Yes," Richard says. "When you were born, our company let Lilith take time off to stay with your mother."

"They did?"

Richard nods. "Lilith helped your mother care for you for almost six months."

"What?" My voice trembles.

"Your mother wanted you," Richard affirms. "But she was afraid. Both Lilith and Lydia were terrified."

"Afraid of what?" But I know the answer. "Barbelo Nemo. They were afraid of my father, weren't they?"

"No." Richard grimaces. "They feared technology. Lydia and Lilith dreaded that what happened to your grandparents might happen to you."

"My grandparents?" I've never thought that far up my family tree.

Richard's expression is somber. Instead of a razor model, he looks like he could sell columbarium plots. "Your grandparents died during the Brain Cancer Epidemic. They became infected early on. That part of Vestal history is true."

A lump in my throat threatens to choke me.

"'Barbelo began the order with the children of his friends who had died,'" Alberto quotes. "'He vowed to protect them. He vowed to keep them safe from all the things that had consumed his loved ones.'"

Richard picks up with the second part of the paragraph from our long-ago textbook. "'His brilliance let him realize that technology and cancer were one in the same. Some people died of brain cancer and some people didn't, but everyone suffered the same fate in the end.'"

"'Technology drove people apart and tore them away from the physical presence of the people they loved,'" the three of us say together.

"So my mother worried that I'd get cancer?"

Richard nods. "Your grandparents worked as newspaper publishers. Did you know that?"

I shake my head.

"Really, it was more of a newsletter," Richard says. "They called it the *Homestead Economist*, and it had a strong readership of people committed to living a self-reliant life apart from government intervention."

I think of Barbelo and his three-hundred-gallon tank of tilapia. Plemora was its own self-sustaining compound in the middle of the Nevada desert.

"My parents worked at *Homestead Economist* too," Alberto adds.

"Alberto's quite a bit older than me, you see," Richard says with a smile. But then his face turns somber again. "*Homestead Economist* was conducted through websites, blogs, and cell phones. A great tragedy. Their poor gray matter never had a chance. That's why Lydia and Lilith were so terrified. They truly believed you would be safer at Tabula Rasa, away from all technology."

"But Barbelo," I start to say. "My father. He—"

"Gave Lydia his blessing," Richard says. "Not at first, of course. When Lydia initially told him she was pregnant, he was furious. I think he sent her away for a time, but I don't know the specifics. Later though, they established a peace. And I believe Lilith had a big part in that. She brokered a truce between your parents."

Richard blew his nose on a handkerchief. "Lilith was very clever, you see. She *is* very clever." It takes a few moments for him to continue. "But we thought—planned—that you would be Harvested as our daughter."

"Everyone said you had a face that could sell soap," Alberto offers.

"It seemed foolproof," Richard says. "Lilith, Lydia, and I. Your father didn't object. Even after Lilith disappeared I was still going to honor our plan. Then that Virus of yours stole your picture and ruined everything."

To my left, Seth squirms.

"And you don't know where Lilith is now?" I ask. "Or if she's still alive?"

Richard slowly shakes his head. He tries to speak, but emotions choke his voice.

Alberto answers for him. "One day Lilith received a summons from Barbelo. And the next day, she vanished."

"Ladies and gentlemen," Captain Lin says from the cockpit, "please fasten your seat belts for takeoff."

"Thank you." I reach out and touch the side of Richard's face. He grabs my hand and squeezes it. Then I sink back down in my seat.

"That's where I was," Seth mumbles.

"What?"

"When you thought I was with Tiffany. I tried to investigate what might have happened to Lilith."

I click my seat belt. "Why didn't you tell me?"

"I didn't want to get your hopes up. And I found nothing." Seth leans on his armrest. "You just found out more about Lilith than I was able to discover in months."

"Sometimes it helps to be a Vestal." I try not to sound smug. Then I open up my physics book to study.

●●●●●●●●●●

I stare at the same page for hours. It's not that it doesn't make sense. If I concentrate hard enough, I can figure out the equations. Or I'm sure Cal would explain them to me if I asked.

No, my real problem is my proximity to Seth. Questions about my grandparents swirl through my head. I wish I could talk to him about them. Really, I wish I could talk to Seth about anything.

Seth's hand sits on the armrest, inches from mine. His head leans low over a book he borrowed from Cal, and he bends the pages back like an animal. Doesn't Seth know that book is an antique?

I should be horribly annoyed, but instead, all I can think of is how good Seth smells, like ocean and soap. I search my brain for some way to start a conversation.

It used to be so easy, talking to Seth. In the beginning, I always had a plan prepared for what I would say. Then as we got closer, the words came naturally. But now my words jumble together. "Seth?"

"What?" is his gruff answer.

"Nothing. I was hoping for a turn with the armrest."

"Oh. Sorry." He slides his arm away.

I didn't mean to say that at all! *If you want to control someone, instead of be controlled* ... the old voice whispers.

I push Barbelo's words away and try to think for myself.

"Seth?" I try again.

"Yeah?" He doesn't look up from his book.

"I want you to know—"

"Hey, look!" Seth flicks his finger-chips, and they glow blue. "We're back in satellite range!"

"I'm sorry I pushed you away, and I wish we could get back together." My words rush out at top speed.

"What?" Seth jerks his head to look at me.

"Ladies and gentlemen," Captain Lin's voice says loud and clear above the hum of the cabin noise, "we have now begun our descent. We'll be landing in about thirty—"

The announcement cuts off abruptly.

And Seth screams.

"What's the matter?" Cal jumps from his seat and hurries over.

"Seth!" I shout.

"Make it stop!" Seth cries. "Make it stop!" He waves his arms around like they're on fire.

"What's going on?" Beau leaps out of his seat to help. "Are you okay?"

"No, I'm—" Seth's words are cut off by a lurch of the plane.

Sarah howls like a banshee.

"Mami!" Fatima calls. "The airplane!"

The plane rolls again, and I look at Cal. "Is that normal? Is this the descent?"

"No," Cal blurts. "It's not normal."

Alberto rushes to the cockpit. "I'll see what's going on!"

Richard follows.

"Seth, please. Talk to me," I plead. "What's wrong?"

Seth's arms shake as he tries to hold up his fingers. "*Get. Them. Out.*" His teeth chatter so violently that it's hard to understand him.

"Bring me a first-aid kit!" Cal shouts. He grips Seth's wrists, and we all see the truth.

The finger-chips have come alive.

Chapter Twenty-Six

· · · · · · · · · ● ● ● ● ● · · · · · · ·

E lectric blue and humming, the chips crawl up Seth's hand. They bore through veins and leave a splotchy purple trail of broken blood vessels in their wake.

"Good God," Cal says. "Where are they going? An artery to his heart?"

"No. Never!" I brush Seth's hair out of his eyes and put my cold hand on his forehead.

"The captains!" Richard rushes from the cockpit. "Their finger-chips have gone crazy."

"Who's flying the plane?" Pilar screeches.

"Alberto," Richard answers. "But barely. Captain Lin is trying to give instructions, but he's really messed up."

"Don't worry, comrades," announces Ryan. "We've got this." He and Zach stomp down the aisle.

"A couple of Boeing commercials do not make you experts!" Beau streams forward in pursuit of his brothers.

"Take the chips out," moans Seth.

"Hold tight. We'll land in San Jose soon." I cradle Seth's head.

"No," Seth whispers. "Now." His face whitens with pain, like he's about to pass out.

"Richard? Do you have any razors?" Cal paws through the first-aid kit.

"Razors!" I cry. "No!"

"Blanca," Cal's voice is stern, "we don't have time to argue. We need to take care of Seth."

"I'll help." Sarah pulls her ponytail back tight. "Tie him down with seat belts so he doesn't struggle."

Fatima holds out her arms. "You're a soap model. Not an expert on antiseptic."

"So what?" Sarah snaps. "That doesn't mean I couldn't be a nurse." She reaches for hand sanitizer and slathers it on.

"Blanca," Seth whimpers. The chips are crawling toward his elbow now. Seth's beautiful tattoos are ripped to shreds. Any second the angel for Sophia will be destroyed.

"I'm here." I stroke his hair. "I'm not going anywhere."

I keep my eyes on Seth and ignore the commotion coming from up front as Trevor and Beau carry Captain Lin and the copilot's writhing bodies back to the cabin.

"There." Cal holds up an impromptu scalpel. "I think this will work." It's a spoon taped to a one of Richard's razors. "Let's get these out of you, my boy." But when Cal looks down at his son, his face turns ashen.

"It'll take two of us." Richard's voice is deep and low. "One on each arm before it's too late." He rolls up his sleeves and rubs his hands together with antiseptic while Sarah fashions an extra scalpel. "Give him some gin."

Fatima raids the beverage cart for anything that might help.

I open a tiny bottle and pour it down Seth's mouth, but he sputters.

"Enough," Seth gasps. "Do it."

I don't watch what happens next. I focus my green eyes on Seth's brown ones. I hold his face in my hands, and I put our noses close together.

He screams in pain. Terrible cries of agony rip the air in two.

But I keep my tone calm and steady. "I love you, Seth. No matter what I will always love you. I'm here for you. I'll do whatever it takes to make this okay. I promise."

I don't know if Seth hears me. I keep saying the words over and over anyway. "I love you. No matter what I love you."

"There," Cal says with a voice dry as dust. "It's done."

I look and find Sarah madly wrapping bandages around Seth's arms. Richard helps control the bleeding. Cal's shirt is smeared in blood, and he drops the improvised scalpel like it's on fire.

"Now people!" Zach yells from the cockpit. "Hang tight 'cause we're landing this thing."

"Woo-hoo!" Ryan's voice echoes.

"Everyone," Cal orders, "fasten your seat belts."

I take the first seat I can find and buckle up. Then I brace for impact.

"Blanca," Seth's small voice whispers in front of me, "do you have your chip-watch?"

"My chip-watch? You're talking about tech now? We're about to crash!"

"Turn it on." Seth struggles to speak. "Don't you see? What happens when we land? This could be the work of terrorists."

Keung, my brain shouts.

In the last few seconds of our descent, I somehow manage to turn on my chip-watch.

And hear a partial sentence in Mandarin.

Only after winter comes ...

The McNeal Solar jet is battered. But Beau's brothers activate the escape hatch moments after landing the plane. We all manage to slide down the emergency chute with only minor scrapes and bruises.

Except for Seth and our two captains.

Trevor carries the copilot, her limp arms smoking at the shoulders. I smell the aroma of roasted flesh.

But Captain Lin holds tight to coherence. "Blanca," he whispers as Alberto rests him on the asphalt, "I lied to you." I reach down and hold his hand. "I *was* a Guardian, but I became loyal to your mother, not to Beijing. That's why they did this to me."

"Who did this to you?" My heart palpitates. "Keung?"

"No," Captain Lin whispers. "Bigger than Keung. Our boss, Wu Park." Then his eyes roll back in his head.

Wu Park? The woman who founded the Guardians? *She's like the Chinese version of Barbelo.*

"Blanca," Call hollers, "we must take Seth to a hospital."

"No," I say, "not a hospital."

"What?" Cal asks.

"Don't you see?" I cry. "This is a terrorist attack."

"Only one place will be safe," Pilar answers.

I know exactly where she's talking about.

"Tabula Rasa!" Fatima exclaims. She places her hands protectively over her baby bump.

I look out into the parking lot and see Vestal limos pull up.

Cal whips his head from the limos to me. "No," he shouts.

"Yes! Tabula Rasa has lead-lined walls. Whatever the terrorists do won't be able to penetrate them." I look to my friends, and the Vestals nod their heads in unison.

"Absolutely not." Cal tightens his grip on Seth, who leans heavily against his father.

"Come with us, Blanca," Richard says. "We'll keep you safe."

Fatima and Beau nod their heads in agreement.

"Please, Cal?" Pilar pleads. "Come with us too."

"I'm sorry, Pilar, but no." Cal gives Pilar a wistful look and then shakes his head.

With the corner of my eye, I see Alan's limo pull up.

"It's time to decide," Seth gasps. "Once and for all. Are you a Vestal or are you a McNeal?"

"Do you really have to ask?" I run over to my family and wrap my arms around Seth's other side.

Pilar follows me, and for a moment, I think she'll come with us. But then she bends down and kisses Cal farewell.

A mass of Vestals file forward and carry my friends away into the waiting cars, corporate logos on every one. When I watch the limos leave without me, I feel abandoned.

And I know that it's my own fault.

●●●●●●●●●

"I'm sorry, Mr. McNeal. But I don't dare step out of this car." Alan sticks his head out of the window of the limo and inches the vehicle up closer.

"That's okay. Fill us in on the ride to the hospital." Cal gently places Seth in the back seat and then looks back toward the airplane. "We've got to get the pilots."

"Agreed." I buckle Seth's seat belt and then race back to help Cal. He carries the copilot to the front seat of the limo with ease, but it takes the two of us together to drag Captain Lin back to the limo.

The ride to the freeway is laborious. There are car crashes everywhere, as if everyone's chips activated at the same time. I hear a helicopter buzz above me and spot countless fires along the road. Alan drives on sidewalks and around smashed-up cars, forging a path.

"Thank goodness for this cloistered limo," Alan says to Cal in the front seat. "It probably saved my life."

Cal looks at all the wrecks. "We'll never make it to the hospital this way."

"You're sure that's the place to go?" I ask.

Cal glances back at Seth and the pilots. "What choice to do we have? These guys need care."

I hold my hands out wide. "And so does all of Silicon Valley."

A streetlight bursts overhead, its solar box buzzing.

"McNeal Solar," Cal exclaims. "How could I be so stupid? It's probably chaos in the control room. I need to help stabilize the grid." Cal rolls down the window and leans outside with his chip-watch, trying to get a connection. Then he pulls back inside the car. "Dammit! All I can hear is blathering in Mandarin."

"Ask Blanca what they say," Seth mumbles.

"What?"

"She's fluent." The color slowly returns to Seth's cheeks.

"Well, I'm not fluent exactly, more like—"

"Blanca," Cal says, "save it."

I take a deep breath. "Sorry." The limo grinds to a halt, boxed in by cars, so I open the door, step out, and turn on my chip-watch. It's always harder to understand a foreign tongue when you can't see the mouth move. So it takes me a moment for my brain to adjust to the different language.

Only after winter comes, the voice says with a thick Beijing accent. *Do we know that the pine and the cypress are the last to fade.*

My heart beats so fast it feels like my chest will explode.

Only after winter comes, the announcement begins again. *Do we know that the pine and the cypress are the last to fade.*

"What?" Cal calls from inside the limo. "What is it saying?"

I climb back into the car, my limbs shaking. "It's from Confucius." I say before translating it for them. "I need to tell the FBI. I think the Guardians might be behind this all!"

"How will you do that, Miss Blanca?" Alan asks. "I can barely move this car."

"You need a motorcycle," Seth suggests, his voice weak.

Cal looks out his window. "So we'll take one."

"What?" I ask. "You mean steal one?"

"Not steal," Cal says. "Borrow."

I stare through the glass. There are fatalities everywhere. Up ahead I see a group of riders thrown to the ground. "I don't want to leave Seth."

"You won't have to," Seth slurs. "I'll come with you."

"No," Cal cautions. "Stay in the car with Alan. Let him take you to the hospital."

"I'll be better off with Blanca," Seth argues. "And I don't want her going alone."

"She won't be alone," says Cal. "I'll come with her."

I look at the both of them, the two men I love. My life wouldn't be complete without either of them. "No, Cal. You need to go to

McNeal Solar and deal with the power grid. This whole state is counting on you. Seth will be safe with me."

"But!" Cal protests but then stops himself. "Let's not waste time arguing. All three of us are too stubborn."

So after commissioning Alan to take care of the injured pilots, we set off on the road on foot. Seth stumbles at first; soon his steps grow steadier. Fifty yards ahead of us, we reach the fallen motorcycle gang.

I look down at one of them, a big guy with a handlebar mustache who reminds me of Gregor from the Defecto support group. "Excuse me, sir. Could I please borrow your bike?" But he's passed out and doesn't answer. I see singe marks on his shoulders where his finger-chips burned out. His leather kutte exposes long bloody trains of gore. I carefully remove the rider's helmet and examine his bike. It's banged up but still functional.

Seth attempts to pick up a bike too. "No way." I glare at his shredded arms. "You ride with me."

"Good idea." Cal puts on a leather jacket. He lifts up a bike that's only slightly damaged.

"Can you ride a motorcycle?" I ask Cal.

He shoves a helmet on. "Who do you think taught Seth?"

"Be careful, Dad." Seth's voice is full of emotion.

"You too, kids." Cal turns on the ignition. Before he takes off, he looks at us over his shoulder. "In case I haven't said it before, you two make me proud every day."

I put Seth's helmet on him since his hands are wounded. Then I find one for myself: red with a lightning bolt.

Seth gives me a once over. "Looks like you've become a pro at wearing color."

"Looks like you got rid of your finger-chips like I asked," I retort.

I take it as a good sign that Seth can make jokes. But as we pull away from the wreckage, Seth can barely hold on behind me. I take it slow, for Seth's sake, which is agony because every fiber of me twitches for speed.

Another helicopter flies overhead, but I can't figure out where it's going.

Or who might be watching.

Chapter Twenty-Seven

· · · · · · · · ●●● ● ●●● · · · · · · ·

Everywhere I see destruction. The people who operated vehicles had it the worst. I steer our motorcycle around twisted fiberglass and shattered windshields. Some drivers died on impact, but others, trapped in their cars, scream in agony.

"How are you doing?" I call back to Seth, my voice muffled by my helmet and the wind.

"My arms are on fire, but I'm feeling better."

"Good."

"Turn on the radio and let's look for news."

I briefly take my eyes off the road and glance at the bike's tech system. It's ten times more complicated than mine. "I don't know how!"

Seth reaches forward and flicks a switch.

Only after winter comes, says the voice in Mandarin. *Do we know*

244

that the pine and the cypress are the last to fade.

Seth switches the channel and the same message plays on repeat, but in English. He flicks the channels again and again. We hear Confucius in Spanish, Farsi, Arabic, and German. "They're not messing around." Seth paws the radio off in anger.

I pull off the Interstate through an exit clogged with debris. The city streets aren't much better. My heart breaks when I see a school bus smashed into an RV. I veer our motorcycle onto the sidewalk and then back into the road, along whatever path I find.

Sometimes we pass clusters of people, their shoulders burned, fallen in front of stores or stacked up on balconies of apartment buildings. Some walk around like zombies, their singed shoulders smoking. In the distance, I hear an ambulance and feel sad knowing there's no way for it to get through the maze of destruction.

We ride underneath a traffic signal and the lights sizzle out.

"Will your dad be okay?" I shout to Seth.

"He'll be fine," Seth yells from behind me. "He'll get the power grid secured in no time."

But I'm not sure that's possible. Not if Keung planted Guardians at McNeal Solar ...

I halt my brain from thinking. I don't have time for worry now.

The FBI building in front of us is protected by a perimeter of officers in SWAT gear. I pull as close as I dare, and they aim their semiautomatic rifles at our hearts. I see the target lines on our chests.

"Halt!" somebody shouts. I can't tell if it's a man or woman because of the protective padding.

"Careful, Blanca," Seth murmurs through his helmet. He holds up his hands and freezes.

"I'm taking off my helmet so you can see my face," I shout. Then slowly, ever so slowly, I remove the headgear, and my long brown hair tumbles out, hot and sticky against my neck.

"Don't move!" the officer calls again.

I hold up my hands and become still as ice. "I'm Blanca McNeal, a former Vestal, and I need to speak with Agents Plunkett and Marlow immediately."

"Stay where we can see you!" The officer pulls out a small rectangular box with some sort of antennae and holds it against his mouth.

"What's that?" I ask Seth.

His voice sounds odd as he keeps his face stiff. "I think it's an old-fashioned walkie-talkie. I've only seen them in movies when I was a little kid. What I don't understand is how these guys are still okay."

I look at the officer's thick protection equipment. "Lead-lined gloves. They blocked the transmission signal that activated the chips. The first time they brought me here and took my chip-watch away, the guy in processing told me—"

But I don't get the chance to finish my sentence. The front doors to the building open and Agent Plunkett stalks out.

Her right hand wears a solitary glove, but her left arm is bandaged and bloodied, the sleeve ripped off at the elbow. It looks like she cut out her own finger-chips with a penknife. She cradles her damaged arm with her gloved hand. "Blanca Nemo? Why are you here?"

My body trembles but my voice is steady. "I'm here to tell you everything. I don't know if it will help. But I have to try."

Agent Plunkett turns to the officer with the walkie-talkie. "Let her through. She's the best hope we've got."

●●●●●●●●●

Seth and I follow Agent Plunkett through the first floor of the FBI building past major triage. Not everyone had lead-lined gloves apparently. Impromptu surgeries take place on desks and conference tables. People moan on the floor, their shoulders singed. A generator hums in the background and provides barely adequate light.

Agent Plunkett opens a door and takes us up a stairwell, guiding our way by flashlight. I shield Seth against the wall so he doesn't get hit by men and women rushing down the stairs.

"Marlow is up here," Agent Plunkett says. "He didn't get his chips removed in time. I'm not sure which is worse—cutting the damn things out or letting their batteries run out of juice and trying to recover from that."

"You mean I could have left them in?" Seth contemplates his mangled arms.

Agent Plunkett slams open the door to the fourth floor and leads us through darkened halls. "They don't seem to kill people, but they definitely do a number on you."

"You can never be too careful," I say darkly.

We pause at the door of a small room, Agent Plunkett turns to look at me. "Bingo."

Inside I see Agent Marlow's office. His desk sits close to the window, and he slumps in his chair, grimly pale. Burn marks circle each shoulder like pocks.

"How's the morphine, Marlow?" Agent Plunkett asks brusquely.

"I didn't take it. Gotta focus." His eyes move slowly between Seth and me. "A Vestal and a Virus." Agent Marlow takes deep, regular breaths like it's hard for him to speak.

"Burns are the worst," Seth murmurs with empathy.

"You know where to find me when you feel better," Agent Plunkett says. Then she stalks down the hall to what appears to be a major command center. Plunkett nods her head and alerts a tall African American woman in a dark sheath dress. Like Seth, her arms are bandaged at the elbow where her chips must have been removed. "Blanca and Seth, this is Elizabeth Lister, the Executive Assistant Director for Criminal Cyber Response."

"So?" Director Lister looks me up and down. "What have you got? Unless it's critical, I'm busy."

I gulp. Critical? A half hour ago, I thought my news was paramount. But under scrutiny, I wonder whether I've once again fallen victim to my overinflated sense of importance as a Vestal. Maybe this was a bad idea.

"Tell them, Blanca." Seth's voice is clear.

The directions help. As if on autopilot, I follow orders and spill. "I believe that Keung and the Guardians did this."

"Keung?" Director Lister raises her eyebrows. Her hair pulls back into a slick ponytail.

"You know him as Timothy Wu," I continue. "A Chinese diplomat and representative to the Silicon Valley Tech Council."

Director Lister scowls at Agent Plunkett. "You tracked Wu for months and never discovered his true name?"

Agent Plunkett grits her teeth.

For some reason I defend Agent Plunkett. "She tried," I say. "But when Agents Plunkett and Marlow questioned me about the Guardians, I didn't feel comfortable sharing."

"And now you do?" Director Lister holds out her bandaged arms. "What else?" she snaps.

"A couple of weeks ago, Keung warned me that Seth should get his finger-chips removed." Seth looks at me with surprise. "But I thought Keung gave this advice for philosophical reasons. Then five days ago, he showed me his invisi-chips. He said that very soon, everyone would want them."

"That could mean anything." Director Lister looks back through the windows to the command room. "Look, we consider all possible scenarios, but at present, we have no reason to believe that Guardians are behind this. At most they're an organized crime group, but they're not international terrorists."

"But Wu Park," I stammer, "the founder of the Guardians, she might be behind this too."

"And how do you know that?" Dr. Lister's glare could cut glass.

"I don't know. It's only a hunch." I feel my confidence shatter. "I'm sorry I wasted your time."

"Wait," says Director Lister, inspecting Seth, not me. "Veritas

Rex, is it? We need more hackers. Can you help?"

Seth nods, and then looks at me, as if asking permission.

But I'm not the boss of him. "I'll be downstairs," I say.

"I'll escort Blanca out." Agent Plunkett barely looks at me. She leads me halfway down the hall with stomping footsteps. But before we reach the stairs, somebody stops us.

"Wait!" An agent in lead-lined gloves runs after us. "Come back! They need you both in the command center."

Agent Plunkett and I hustle back at top speed. Director Lister and dozens of agents wait in a room crowded with tech screens. Every display shows the same message in ten different languages.

Giant speakers fill the room with sound.

"The world watches the light that shines in the darkness," the voice says in English. *"The Vestal Harvest will begin in three hours. Now you understand our true worth. Only after winter comes do we know that the pine and the cypress are the last to fade."*

"What's that supposed to mean?" Director Lister's tone is as cold as ice.

"Lux in tenbris lucet." I repeat. "The light that shines in the darkness." I look at Agent Plunkett who nods with understanding. "It's the Tabula Rasa motto." I think about Fatima and Beau, who left the airport and drove straight to Tabula Rasa where they thought they would be safe. My voice wavers. "My friends are there."

"You!" Director Lister points her maimed fingers straight at me. "Tell me everything you know about Tabula Rasa. *Now.*"

I swallow hard. All eyes in the room are on me.

●●●● ● ●●●●

"It's worse than we expected." Agent Marlow passes handwritten notes to Director Lister. "Every terrorist organization in the world wants a piece of this Harvest. They're phoning the bids in right now." He barely gets the words out before he sways a bit.

"Sit down, Marlow," says Agent Plunkett.

"No. I'm okay," Agent Marlow claims. But he's not. His knuckles are busted open, patched haphazardly with bandages. Burn marks pock his shoulders like spots. The trashed skin makes me think about Seth and his ruined tattoos. Seth, who took off to help the cyber squad ten minutes ago.

"Tell me again," Director Lister instructs me. "Where are the entrances?"

I look down at my hand-drawn map and point them out.

"But that's not what our sources say," says Agent Marlow. "We were told there were only five exits."

I shake my head. "Your sources are wrong. There're six." I point to a small mark beside the underground parking garage. "This is the tunnel Seth used last year when he snuck in and took my picture. But entering isn't the biggest problem," I caution. "Can you get the graduates out without turning this into a hostage situation?"

"It's not just the graduates," Agent Plunkett snarls. "We need to release everyone."

I take a sharp breath. "The younger students too?"

"Absolutely." Director Lister taps her finger on the map. "Right there. That's an elevator?"

I nod my head. "For staff. I rode in it twice. You need a key to operate—" I stop myself midsentence. Then I pat my pockets for my mother's ivory bag. "I think I might have it." Did I bring it with me or is it still in my suitcase? I reach into the back pocket of my jeans and touch velvet. "Here! This might be it." I pull out the small bag and dump the key on the table.

Agent Plunkett picks it up and looks at it closely. "Could be. But the stairs would be quieter."

"Definitely." Director Lister nods her head. "But the key might work for other doors too. Bring it with you, Plunkett."

"No," I declare.

"What?" Director Lister's voice has the tone of somebody who isn't used to disobedience. I shudder because it reminds me of Headmaster Russell.

"I'll take the key. I'm coming too," I say with grit.

"Like hell you are," answers Agent Plunkett.

I seize back my key. "Even if you get inside unannounced, you won't find your way without getting caught. There are twenty stories not including the garage! You need me as your navigator."

"You can help via the wireless," suggests Agent Marlow.

"It won't work! Tabula Rasa is cloistered," I say. "We're talking about my friends' lives. I must come with you."

Agent Plunkett shakes her head.

"These are my people! Tabula Rasa is my former home. My lawyer thinks I might own the building."

"You do own the building," Agent Marlow interjects.

I glare at Agent Plunkett. "When were you going to tell me?"

She grunts. "When the investigation was complete."

"Don't you see?" I say. "This is perfect. If I own the building, if I have a key—" I hold up the silver "—then I can slip in unnoticed and leave the door open for you. I can talk to Ms. Corina and make her listen to reason."

"Officers could trail her in, dressed in white so they blend in," Agent Marlow suggests.

"No. Black would be better," Agent Plunkett says. "They would need to be black. That's what novices wear."

I can tell she's coming around.

"Pick your smallest people," I say to Director Lister. "So they look like children."

Director Lister paces the room, her tall heels clicking on the tile. Then she turns and rests both hands on the conference table. "If you volunteer for this, Blanca, I won't stop you. But you may not come out alive."

I stand up straight and smooth my face to neutral like Ms. Corina taught me. "So be it," I answer.

Somewhere, deep inside my soul, my mother's voice whispers, offering comfort. *There are many paths a Vestal can take, and they all have honor.*

Chapter Twenty-Eight

I'm back where it all started: the underground parking garage of Tabula Rasa. I even wear black spandex like I used to when I was student. That day, a year ago, when Seth snuck in and took my picture, was the first time I remember seeing my mother. Now, I hold her key in my hand and creep through the secret tunnel like a rat. What's worse, I bring a host of invaders with me.

Ahead of us is a circular metal door that I know leads into the parking garage. As I approach the lock, my insides squish like gelatin. If this key doesn't work, blasting the door away will be a noisy disaster.

Agent Plunkett aims her flashlight at the dead bolt so I can see better. Slowly, and with great trepidation, I slip the key into the lock. It turns effortlessly, and the door swings open.

FBI agents swarm past me into the underground garage, stunning the security guards into submission. Agent Plunkett signals for the rest of her men and women to follow.

I lead them straight to the stairwell next to the elevator. We're about to open the door when a sickly sweet voice stops us.

"Thank you for attending the fifty-first graduation of Tabula Rasa students. The privacy Harvest is about to begin. Bidders, please gather in the auditorium for the auction."

"That's Ms. Corina," I say. "She's cagier than I thought." But something doesn't add up. "I thought Agent Marlow said most bidders were phoning in their prices?"

Agent Plunkett furrows her eyebrows. "Let's go find out."

"The auditorium is one floor up." I look over and see an officer try to scan the building with tech. "That won't work in here. Lead-lined walls."

Agent Plunkett nods. "We do this the old-fashioned way."

The officer abandons his equipment, and we race upstairs.

The hallways are dead silent. Tabula Rasa feels eerie without the shuffle of feet walking to class. But of course on the Harvest, everyone's in the auditorium, watching the action. It's the one day of the year when younger students get to see people from the outside world. Bidders are permitted to size up next year's crop. That's how I became known as the girl who could sell soap long before my senior year.

I tiptoe to the double doors that lead into the auditorium, Agent Plunkett beside me.

"Thank you for attending the fifty-first graduation of Tabula Rasa

students. The privacy Harvest is about to begin. Bidders, please gather in the auditorium for the auction." Ms. Corina's voice sounds again.

I open the doors a crack and peer inside. The back rows of the audience are packed with black. I see hundreds of Tabula Rasa students sitting ramrod straight, their eyes fixed straight ahead.

But I don't see any bidders. The front rows are empty.

I whip around to face Agent Plunkett, my face drained of all color. "You need to let me handle this. On my own. Otherwise there'll be chaos."

Agent Plunkett pushes me aside and stares through the crack parting the double doors. Then she turns. "You've got two minutes. Then we're coming in."

●●●●●●●●●

My boots fall silently on the short pile carpet. I march down the aisle and feel eyes on my back. I don't pause to turn around until I reach the steps to the stage. When the leather soles of my shoes hit the linoleum stairs, the sound carries all the way to the rafters. I hear a child sneeze and a teacher hush him.

The quiet is nerve-racking, but I don't allow fear to take hold. I push my shoulders back like the whole room belongs to me.

In fact, it does belong to me. According to Agent Marlow, Tabula Rasa is mine.

But right when I open my mouth to speak, my words are interrupted.

"Thank you for attending the fifty-first graduation of Tabula Rasa students. The privacy Harvest is about to begin. Bidders, please gather in the auditorium for the auction."

As soon as Ms. Corina's voice fades away, I launch in with the truth. "My name is Blanca Nemo, and I am here to help you. I am the sole heir of Barbelo Nemo and the new leader of Tabula Rasa."

Murmurs ripple across the audience like waves. I search the sea of faces for students I know. A little third grade girl I used to tutor waves to me until Ms. Lara gives her a scathing look. The girl sinks back into her seat and shudders.

"There has been a change of plans," I declare. "The privacy Harvest is canceled."

The noise in the audience grows louder. A teacher in flowing white robes jumps to her feet. It's Ms. Alma, my language instructor. She opens her mouth to speak but then snaps it shut. She twists the hem of her sleeve into knots.

"Ms. Alma?" I ask. "Do you have a question?"

"Yes, Blanca. I mean, no, Ms. Blanca. I mean …" Ms. Alma looks back to other teachers for support, but they don't move. Then she turns forward again and drops her voice so quiet she almost whispers. "Where is Headmaster Corina?"

"My friends are searching for her as we speak." I look up to the doors where the FBI waits. Then I scan the audience for teens I know. "Where are grades ten and eleven? Where are the graduates?" *And more importantly, where are Fatima and Beau?*

Ms. Alma twists her sleeve so hard I'm afraid she'll tear a hole in the fabric. "We're still waiting for the older grades. Bidders will be here any minute. The privacy Harvest is about to begin."

I shake my head slowly. "No, Ms. Alma. There's been a change of plans, remember? The privacy Harvest is canceled for today."

My two minutes are up. At the top of the auditorium, the doors swing open. FBI agents clad in black stream down the aisles like invading ants.

"Remain calm!" I say at the top of my voice. "My friends are here to take care of you."

Bodies squirm all around me. Frantic shouts call out with terror. I realize my words aren't having any effect at all.

So for the sake of the children, I use my father's words instead. "Tabula Rasa students!" I shout. "You have a hard road. In so many ways it's difficult being you." At the sound of the Vestal blessing, all eyes turn to me. I hold up my wrist where the platinum cuff used to be. "But I know that you can do this. You have everything you need to achieve happiness." I pull my hand to my heart and watch hundreds of people do the same. "My friends will take care of you. I promise."

Agent Plunkett looks up at me from the aisle and nods. Then she motions me to follow her.

●●●●●●●●●

The remaining officers explore the building floor by floor but find no one. At every turn, I pray we'll see Pilar hugging Fatima or Sarah rolling her eyes at me. They should be here by now.

"Where is everyone else?" I can barely force the question out. "Where are the graduates? Where are the sophomores and juniors?" My heart is ready to explode. But then we pass Ms. Corina's office, and I remember my lessons from long ago. *Cry on cue. Stop crying. Tears are a tool.* In this case, I can't let tears be a tool for my own destruction. I need to stay strong to save my friends.

On the twentieth floor, we come to the room with a wall of windows. I remember standing here with my mother and Headmaster Russell. "There's a phone in here," I say to Agent Plunkett. "Could that be important?" I point to the wall where the old-fashioned contraption hangs.

"Maybe," Agent Plunkett says. Then she holds her finger up to her lips and cups her ears. From the corner of the room comes whimpering.

Agent Plunkett motions with her fingers and officers flood the room. "Over here!" one of them calls.

There, underneath the table, we find Ms. Corina. Her white Vestal robes are tangled around her, and someone has bound her with tight rope. A bandanna fills her mouth, making it impossible for her to speak.

"Ms. Corina!" I fall to my knees and undo the gag. "What happened?"

"Blanca, oh, Blanca," she cries, snot running down her nose. "This is your fault."

"My fault. How?"

She grimaces. "You wouldn't help me with the Harvest even after

I asked so nicely. So I had to ask him for help instead."

"Keung?"

Ms. Corina shakes her head. "Who's that? No, I asked Jeremy." For half a moment she gets a soft look in her eye. "I knew he would help. He was always my favorite student."

"Who's Jeremy?" Agent Plunkett asks. "A Guardian?"

I shake my head. "No, not a Guardian. Ms. Corina, what happened?" I release the binds on her wrists so she can push herself up.

"They came this morning for the graduates. It was only supposed to be the graduates! Jeremy said the Harvest would be more successful if it wasn't held here." She looks at me. "I believed him."

"It's okay," I lie. "What happened next?"

"It was just supposed to be the graduates. Blanca, you've got to believe me!"

"I do, Ms. Corina, I do."

She grips my arm tightly and then stares off into space. "But then they came back for the eleventh graders. And then the tenth! I tried to stop them." Ms. Corina dissolves into tears.

"Where did they go?" Agent Plunkett asks.

"I don't know." Ms. Corina rocks back and forth on the ground. She pulls her hair in front of her and stares at the split ends. "He was supposed to help me. Jeremy said he would make it all better. I was his favorite teacher."

"Who's Jeremy?" Agent Plunkett asks again. "Blanca, what is she talking about?"

I throw the gag back down on Ms. Corina, not bothering to undo her other ties. "A Vestal-reject."

"What?"

"A Defecto," I snarl.

Agent Plunkett stares at Ms. Corina and growls. "Where are they?"

Ms. Corina's head shakes like a rag doll. "Jeremy said you would ask. But I won't tell you and you can't make me." A simpering smile rests on her face.

Agent Plunkett coils back her hand as if getting ready to strike but then lets her hand drop. "Blanca? Any ideas?"

There's only one place I can think of that would shelter that many people with lead-lined walls.

"The soundstage," I say, "that's where the Harvest will happen."

From down below a small voice giggles. "This morning," says Ms. Corina. "The Harvest is already over."

Too late, I remember the sound of helicopters.

●●●●●●●●●●

We ride our cavalcade of motorcycles through the dusk. Instead of Seth and Cal, I'm surrounded by total strangers, uniformed men and women in black. Agent Plunkett breaks the trail in front of me, and I follow blindly, forced to trust. If there's any hope of rescuing my Vestal friends or saving the Tabula Rasa students, I have to cooperate.

It's a lonely road, my mother taught me. But she was wrong. All along there have been people trying to help me, but I haven't let them in.

A few hundred yards from the studio parking lot, Agent Plunkett pulls to a stop, and we gather close together. "I don't want them to hear us," she says.

"Too late for that, Plunkett." A male officer points to the air where a circle of helicopters hovers over the soundstage.

"Defectos?" I look up at the sky.

"No." Agent Plunkett scowls. "Those are ours." Her walkie-talkie buzzes.

"Breaker 1-9, this is Oscar Marlow. Do you copy?"

"Roger that, Marlow. This is Margie Plunkett."

"The cyber squad has located the source of the transmission as coming from a soundstage in Mountain View. It's believed Defectos are involved. Birds are in the air. What's your 20?"

"We're on the ground, Marlow, and you blew our cover."

"What?"

"We planned to surprise them!"

From my wrist, I hear my chip-watch crackle. It's hard to hear with my helmet on, so I hold it up close. I catch Seth's voice, small and faint. "Blanca, are you there?" I text him back.

Me: I'm here. But I can't talk.

Seth: We unjammed the signal!

Me: Congratulations.

Too late, I realize how bad that sounds. What if Seth thinks I'm being sarcastic?

Me: You're amazing, Seth. I really mean that.

Seth: You're terrific too. I'm sorry I've been such a jerk.

Me: I'm sorry I didn't trust you.

Seth: Doesn't matter. Let's go find my dad.

I gulp. The last time I saw Seth, I was headed downstairs. Seth has no idea where I am or what I've gotten myself into.

Seth: Meet you in the lobby?

Me: Can't.

Seth: Why not?

"Blanca!" Agent Plunkett barks. "Are you ready? Let's go."

One more text! I only have time for one more text.

Me: I love you. Tell your dad I love him too.

I click off my chip-watch before Seth can text back.

Chapter Twenty-Nine

• • • • • • • • • ● • • • • • • • • •

Vehicles are parked everywhere. Police, fire engines, FBI sedans, and motorcycles form a giant group. Generators hum, providing small pools of light. Then the air sizzles, and the streetlights turn back on all at once.

Cal did it! The grid is back on!

The extra light allows me to see a small fleet of parked cars that I recognize. "Agent Plunkett!" I point to the black cars. "Those are Guardian vehicles."

Her eyes get big, and she speaks into her walkie-talkie. Then she hurries me over to a large SUV where we find Director Lister in camo and a flak jacket, with three different walkie-talkies hanging off her utility belt.

"Guardians?" she asks when Agent Plunkett tells her. "But I

thought you said we were dealing with Defectos. Recon has been digging into this Jeremy fellow for the past fifteen minutes." She holds out a profile picture of Jeremy.

Agent Plunkett stands her ground. "Blanca says those are Guardian vehicles, and I believe her."

Her support warms me up. I take a step closer and look at the picture Director Lister holds. For the hundredth time I see Jeremy's neck tattoos.

Only now, when I see those Chinese characters, they make sense. I was always horrible at written Mandarin, but two of those symbols are familiar.

It's like time stops, and I'm back in the cafeteria.

"Tell me who it was," bellows Headmaster Russell, lashing Keung's back.

"Tiānshǐ," Keung whimpers, "don't say anything. I endure this for you."

The painful truth hits me. I don't want to believe it, but there is the evidence, right before my eyes. Maybe I wasn't the only person Keung called *tiānshǐ*. Maybe I wasn't his only hookup.

"Angel," I whisper, looking at the first two tattoos. Then I slowly decipher the others. I point my finger on the picture of Jeremy's neck. "*Guardian* angel. Keung and Jeremy were lovers."

"She told you," Agent Plunkett says squarely to Director Lister. "From the very beginning Blanca told you the Guardians were involved."

Director Lister grabs one of the walkie-talkies from her belt and bellows into it. "Get everything you have about the Guardians to me ten minutes ago!"

I stare back at the stage worried about everyone inside. These are my people. These are my friends. I may never bear a child, but my Vestal Brethren will always be my flesh and blood. The only sister I'll ever have is Fatima, and she might be in that box of a building, held captive by madmen!

While Agent Plunkett and Director Lister argue, I slip away. My black spandex obscures me. I sneak among shadows away from the floodlights. I duck behind a fire engine and inch my way closer and closer to the building.

By the time I'm walking, it's too late for them to stop me.

It's also too late for me to stop myself.

I don't have a plan. No brilliant strategy ruminates in my mind. Only the strong pull of the Brethren, joining their fates to mine. *Vestals are a collective power. United by secrecy and code.* I don't want to live my life knowing I didn't do everything in my power to save them.

Tears roll down my cheeks, and I can't force them back in. These tears are human. I wipe them away with my sleeve and knock on the soundstage door.

No one answers.

"Blanca Nemo!" Agent Plunkett calls on a megaphone. "Return to the federal vehicles!"

I don't turn.

"Blanca *McNeal!*" Agent Plunkett tries again. "This is a hostage situation. Please let the authorities handle it."

I turn my head and look back at the lights. I can't see anything because of the glare so I hold my arm up to protect my eyes.

Then I slip inside to total darkness.

My heels echo on the concrete. I pause a minute, trying to let my eyes adjust. In the pitch-black, I can't see anything. On my very third step, I bump into an aluminum chair, and it makes a wretched scraping sound. So much for the element of surprise. "Hello?" My voice echoes from every wall. "Jeremy? Keung? Fatima?"

I click on my chip-watch. The connectivity features won't work, but the flashlight will. I hold up my wrist and shoot a tiny arc of light around my perimeter. All I see are rows of chairs. I take a cautious step forward but then retreat.

I'm a survivor, I've got good instincts, and I can think for myself. That's what Cal taught me. Well right now, I'm terrified of the dark. I walk back to the doorway and look for a light switch. "I'm turning on some lights," I say loud and strong. Then I flick a switch.

And my greatest fears are realized.

My best friends are missing.

"Where is everyone?" I murmur. There are hundreds of chairs, some askew but most still arranged neatly. "Hello!" I call out again. "Jeremy! It's me, Blanca!" I sense movement from the dressing rooms. Then I hear a moan.

Frantically, I look around for a weapon. A broom? A wrench? But there's nothing that can help. There's only me and my bad-idea brain.

"I'm coming to the dressing rooms!" I shout. "I'm walking there now!" I will myself to step forward.

The first room I come to, the one where Fatima, Pilar, and I lounged a few weeks ago, is empty, save for some old clothes on the floor. But when I come to the next room, I see a faint light emanating from underneath the door.

I lift up my hand and knock. "Jeremy? Keung?" When nobody answers, I push the door open. My feet crunch on broken glass.

Keung stares at me with dying eyes. He lies on the pleather couch, a shard of mirror stuck through his chest. Blood pools around him.

So much blood.

But there is a fragment of life left in the look Keung gives me. He smiles weakly before his eyes flicker to the side.

I follow Keung's gaze and see Jeremy on the chair next to him, both wrists slashed.

"Jeremy," I say slowly, "what happened? Are you okay?"

"Go away, Blanca." His voice gurgles. "You shouldn't be here."

"But I want to help. Can you let me help? You told me we need to stick together."

"It's too late for that now." Jeremy heaves a great sob. "I've ruined everything."

"No. You haven't. We can fix this." I take a cautious step forward. "Why don't you tell me what happened and I'll figure out how to help?"

"It's too late for that now!" Jeremy tries to stand up and face me, but he's too weak from blood loss. He slumps down in the chair.

"Stay there! I'll be right back." I race to the next room and collect an old dress from the ground.

"No," Jeremy says when he sees me return with the fabric. "Let me die. I tried to stop him, and look what happened! I broke the mirror and stabbed him in the heart."

"Jeremy," I say, "it'll be okay." I kneel next to him and bind his right arm.

Jeremy tries to wiggle out of the way. "Don't bother." But he's too weak to fight back.

I cut a glance at Keung who groans on the couch next to us. I want to save Keung too, but if I pull out the mirror stabbed in his chest, he could die. As soon as Jeremy's stable, I'll race to get help.

"Jeremy. What happened? Where did the Vestals go?"

Jeremy cries so hard I can barely understand him. "They were supposed to return home. Keung told me we'd reunite the students with their parents. But he tricked me! We weren't sending them to their families. Keung was rounding them all up for her."

Chills prickle my spine. "For Wu Park?"

Jeremy nods. "She wants them, Blanca. She wants all of them. As soon as I realized where the kids were really going, I ended it." Jeremy looks down at my handiwork and frowns.

"Where are they now?" I can hardly hear my voice over my heartbeat.

Jeremy doesn't get the chance to answer my question.

A harsh, raspy sound comes from deep in Keung's throat. We look back at him just in time to see the final breath release from his soul.

"*Tiānshī!*" Jeremy and I both say together. But thankfully Jeremy doesn't hear me.

"No!" Jeremy cries. His sobs pound into my heart. His anguish fills the small room. As gently as possible, I bind the wounds on his left arm

I stuff my own pain down as deep as it will go. I don't think about Keung tricking me into believing I was special. I don't remember his lips, warm against mine. I don't look at his brown eyes that were once so full of life, now staring at the ceiling. I focus on right now. My mission. The words I need to say to find my friends and the lost students.

When I finally speak, I force my voice to be gentle. "Keung was your angel?"

Jeremy nods. "And he was mine. That's why I left Tabula Rasa. I had to follow him! Especially after Headmaster Russell punished him. '*Tiānshī,*' he said, 'I endure this for you.' Oh, Blanca, what have I done?" The strength of Jeremy's voice fades.

I tie the final knot. "You did your best," I offer. "I see that. But, Jeremy, where are the others? Where did the Guardians take them?"

"I don't know," Jeremy whispers. "They were supposed to go home to their parents. That's where I thought the buses would go. But then helicopters came, and I realized the truth. I was betrayed. He wanted them all, Blanca, but I stopped him ..." Jeremy's face becomes very still.

I fling my hand against Jeremy's neck to check for a pulse, which greets my fingertips with a tiny whisper. Then I put my wrist on his heart, the position for the tightest blessing.

"Jeremy, you have a hard road. In so many ways it's difficult being you. *But I know that you can do it.*" The Vestal blessing rolls off my tongue like water. "You have everything you need to achieve happiness." My last words are a whisper.

●●●●●●●●●

I didn't expect Agent Plunkett to give me a big bear hug when I came out of the sound stage alive, but she did. After we watched helicopters whisk Jeremy off to the hospital, she yelled at me for ten minutes straight. "How could you be so stupid? You could have made things a thousand times worse for your friends! Did you think of that?"

At the mention of Fatima, Beau, and everyone else, I disintegrate. Wherever they are, Jeremy didn't know.

Cal and Seth arrive to find me in hysterics and Agent Plunkett still shouting at me.

"Back off, lady!" Cal rushes up to Agent Plunkett and looks her in the eye. "No one yells at my daughter like that."

Agent Plunkett squares her shoulders and explains that I ran into a potential hostage situation. Then Cal yells at me too.

But Seth puts both arms around me in a circle of protection. "I love you, Blanca," he murmurs in my ear. Over and over again. Then he tilts my face up and kisses me so hard I feel tingles all the way down to my toes. "I love you. I love you. I love you."

Chapter Thirty

● ● ● ● ● ● ● ● ● ● ● ● ● ● ● ● ● ●

Seth, Cal, and I ride motorcycles back to the manor. The roads are still chaotic, and looters have emerged like locusts. Seth wraps both arms around me and holds on tight. I keep my vision pegged on Cal as he leads the way home. I don't think any of us breathe easy until we're past the security gate.

When I swing open the mahogany door, I swear I see heaven. There, in the great hall, are Fatima, Beau, Pilar, Alberto, Richard, Sarah, Trevor, Ryan, and Zach. They're all piled on couches eating sandwiches. Fatima has her legs up and Beau rubs her feet.

I don't stop to shut the door. I run straight to my friends and throw myself into Fatima's arms. "Where were you?" I reach across and hug Beau too.

"Stop freaking out!" Fatima's smile is enormous. "We walked all the way here."

"I thought you were headed toward Tabula Rasa?" Seth tosses his jacket down on a couch.

"We were," says Alberto. "But traffic was so bad, we couldn't reach it. Pilar suggested we come to McNeal Manor because it was closer."

Pilar runs up to Cal and snuggles. "And because of the company."

Cal cups her beautiful face in his hands. "You came to the right place." He kisses her warmly.

I discreetly look away, but Seth stares at his dad with eyes like saucers.

"I wasn't sure my bride could make it," Beau says, indicating Fatima's swollen feet.

"Hey!" Fatima protests. Then she nods her head in agreement. "I had my doubts too." She pats her baby bump. "But I was *really* hungry, and I knew there'd be food."

"Definitely," I answer. "There's always food at the manor. And I bet you're hungry enough for croissants."

"Well," admits Fatima. "Maybe this once."

●●●●●●●●●

Agent Plunkett calls me in the next day, and I answer every last question. Honestly and without reserve. Even though some of what she wants to know is none of her business, I don't hold back. Nancy isn't there, and I'm pretty sure Agent Marlow and Director Lister are spying on me through the one-way window, but I tell Agent Plunkett every last secret.

I tell her about sneaking kisses with Keung underneath Ms. Alma's watchful eyes.

I tell her I hid in the back of Keung's car with Seth and heard an explosion.

I tell her my suspicions about what happened to Headmaster Russell.

I tell her about Irene Page really working for Keung and that there might be other Guardians planted in our midst.

I tell her my heart ripped open when I saw Seth in so much pain.

And I tell her other things too. Because once I start talking, I can't stop.

I tell her that Sarah is dating Trevor and isn't actually his mother.

I tell her that the real Lilith is my aunt and that she is missing.

I tell her how I'm still not sure if I should say "Ms. Lydia" or "my mother." I tell her I'm not sure I can forgive my mother for leaving me.

I tell her that I'm sorry I told Agent Marlow about her being a home-wrecker, but that I still think she's a pretty good federal agent.

I tell her how Dr. Meredith made me feel horribly uncomfortable and that I'm still not sure if she was spying on me or not.

At this point, Agent Plunkett interjects. "Dr. Meredith checked out. I looked into her a few months ago."

"Oh." I look down at my chip-watch.

"If I see anyone tail you in the future," Agent Plunkett says, "I'll tell you. I tried to warn you about the Guardians, you know?"

I swallow hard. "It's my fault those kids are missing. If I had cooperated with you from the beginning, none of this would have happened."

Agent Plunkett shakes her head. "We can't know that for sure, Blanca. But what we do know is that what the Guardians did is not your fault. And if you hadn't helped us break into Tabula Rasa, it could have been a bloodbath. You helped keep a lot of kids safe."

"But not all of them." I clasp my hands together. "I'll do anything, whatever it takes to find the missing Tabula Rasa students."

The wrinkles around Agent Plunkett's eyes are more pronounced than ever. Her boyish haircut has several more gray hairs. "Blanca," she says with sincerity, "I believe you. Now you need to believe me too. I'm going to find them."

There is only one thing for me to say, and I force myself to believe it. I nod my head slowly and whisper those five little words.

"Agent Plunkett, I trust you."

•••• ● ••••

A couple of weeks later, when I'm ready, I write a new post for *The Lighthouse*. Seth posts it on *Veritas Rex* too.

    Dear Friends and Followers,
    Like you, my own life has been forever changed by the Finger-Chip Outbreak of two

weeks ago. I am encouraged by your messages of support and saddened by your messages of hate. But mostly, I am bereft because this great tragedy occurred.

When my birth father, Barbelo Nemo, died last year, a vacuum was created in the crime world. Secrets, spies, and political contacts were up for grabs. Wu Park, the founder of the Guardian order, saw her chance.

For years the Guardians worked to develop the technology that could corrupt finger-chips. Their ultimate weapon was finally ready. In one foul move, they attempted to wipe out their Vestal competition and seize control.

Now, three entire classes of Vestal children are missing. Fifty students are unaccounted for, and I am heartbroken.

I, Blanca Xavier Nemo McNeal, will not rest until my sisters and brothers are found.

To Wu Park, know this:

Vestals avenge all wrongs, especially when our honor is at stake.

You have been warned.

Epilogue

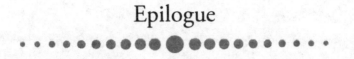

So many workers crawl around McNeal Manor that it is difficult to walk down the hall to breakfast without tripping over a caterer. Tonight is the Vestal corporate banquet and I am hosting it at the manor instead of Tabula Rasa. Cal encouraged me because he said it's important for life to go on, regardless of tragedy.

I hope things aren't too awkward for Cal with Pilar. She's decided to renew her contract with the fashion house to stay close to her family.

As for the rest of the Vestals, I hope they drink way too much wine, so that I can weasel information out of them. Somebody somewhere must know information about Wu Park and where the Guardians took the lost fifty Tabula Rasa students.

But instead of thinking about tonight, I should focus on this afternoon. My Stanford interview is a few hours away. I'll do better with a healthy breakfast. Cal is eating eggs and toast when I join him in the dining room.

"Blanca, sweetheart." Cal puts down his coffee when he sees me. "You look beautiful."

I give a little twirl to show off my new purple dress. "Thank you. Only I wish I weren't so nervous."

"You'll do fine." Cal pours me a glass of orange juice.

"Better than fine." Seth strides into the room. "You'll be brilliant. That panel of professors won't know what hit them." He takes a seat and grabs a Danish.

"I'm fine with calculus," I say matter-of-factly. "But if they ask me about linear algebra, I'm done for."

"Don't worry so much." Cal looks at me reassuringly with his brown eyes. "You have more to offer a college than any person I know. Those professors will see that."

"Yes, but what if I clam up? What if—"

Seth puts down his pastry. "You won't clam up. You'll be fine."

"What if they ask me to describe my plans?" The question weighs on me like granite. "What if they want to talk about my professional goals?"

"Tell them the truth," Cal says. "You *want* to become an engineer and join McNeal Solar as my successor."

"I still want that," I say. "Really and truly I do." Then I pull out Agent Plunkett's card from the side pocket of my dress. "But I have other goals now too."

"Yes. And so do I." Cal slides an envelope across the tablecloth. "I've waited to give this to you for a long time. I had the papers drawn up months ago."

"What is it?" My curiosity is definitely piqued. I open the brass clasp of the envelope and pull out paperwork. There on the top in big font, it says FILE FOR ADOPTION.

"Don't look too closely," Seth says. "I don't want you to sign them." Underneath the table, he runs his hand against my thigh.

"And *I* want you to know that these papers exist." Cal smiles and looks at me expectantly. "You can choose to sign them whenever you want—or not."

I look back and forth between the two. "I don't know what to say."

"I do." Seth takes both my hands in his own. "Someday, one way or another, you'll legally become a McNeal."

Cal reaches out and covers our hands with his own. "That's a promise."

"Okay," I answer with a smile. "But don't expect me to get the family tattoo."

Seth smirks. "Never say never."

THE END

ACKNOWLEDGEMENTS

The people who matter most in my life, my husband Doug and our two kids Bryce and Brenna, sacrificed a lot for me to make my dream of becoming an author come true. They put up with a messy house, frozen dinners, a spacey mom, and my tech-addiction to Facebook and Instagram. Without their love and support *Genesis Girl* and *Damaged Goods* would not exist.

My parents Bruce and Carol Williams, my sister Diane Williams, and my grandparents Gerry Stevens, Ken Williams, and Bob and Darlene Woodson, gave me a childhood that was rich in love, laughter, and learning. I wish every child could be so lucky. My inlaws Marc and Lynn Bardsley, are the best bonus parents I could wish for.

People I have never had the privilege of meeting in real life have helped me too. Bloggers, bookstagramers, and booktubers took *Genesis Girl* someplace Blanca would never want to go: all over the Internet! Search for the hashtag #GenesisGirl and you'll see what I mean. My social media friends on "The YA Gal" Facebook page as well as my Instagram account @the_ya_gal have made a huge impact. Every person who left an Amazon or Goodreads review made a difference.

A special wave goes to YA authors Joshua David Bellin, Elisa Dane, Melanie McFarlane, Laurie Elizabeth Flynn, Jeanne Ryan, and Stephanie Scott. These authors are not only terrific storytellers, but wonderful friends.

Damaged Goods owes a huge debt of gratitude to my beta readers Sharman Badgett-Young, Carol Brudnicki, Karyn Brudnicki, Sara Cessnun, Antonia Hillman, and Jack Hillman. Thank you also to my friends from the Liza Royce Agency, Month9Books, The Sweet Sixteens, and Sixteen To Read.

I live in Edmonds, Washington, and write a column called "I Brake for Moms" for *The Everett Daily Herald.* To my *Herald* readers, it is a joy spending Sunday mornings with you. Thank you to my former editor Jessi Loerch for making me a better writer, and to executive editor Neal Pattison for being the first person to ever think my words were worthy of a paycheck.

An enormous thank you goes to my agent Liza Fleissig, who is friendly, responsive, encouraging, and wise. Thank you also to my publisher Georgia McBride, who is a champion for everyone who loves books. Without these two fine women *Damaged Goods* would not be in your hands right now.

My final thank you goes to you the reader. If you enjoyed *Damaged Goods* please pop on over to Instagram or Facebook to say "hello." You can also find me on Twitter @JennBardsley, or at my website: http://JenniferBardsley.net.

JENNIFER BARDSLEY

Jennifer Bardsley writes the column "I Brake for Moms" for *The Everett Daily Herald.*. Her novel *Genesis Girl* debuted in 2016 from Month9Books. *Genesis Girl* is about a teenager who has never been on the Internet. Jennifer however, is on the web all the time as "The YA Gal" on Facebook, the @the_ya_gal on Instagram, and @JennBardsley on Twitter. Jennifer is a member of SCBWI, The Sweet Sixteens debut author group, and is founder of Sixteen To Read. An alumna of Stanford University, Jennifer lives in Edmonds, WA with her family and a poodle named Merlin.

OTHER MONTH9BOOKS TITLES YOU MIGHT LIKE

GENESIS GIRL
STATION FOSAAN
FIRE IN THE WOODS

Find more books like this at http://www.Month9Books.com

Connect with Month9Books online:
Facebook: www.Facebook.com/Month9Books
Twitter: https://twitter.com/Month9Books
You Tube: www.youtube.com/user/Month9Books
Tumblr: http://month9books.tumblr.com/
Instagram: https://instagram.com/month9books

Their new beginning
may be her end.

BLANK SLATE: BOOK 1

GENESIS GIRL

JENNIFER BARDSLEY

DEE GARRETSON

SIXTEEN-YEAR-OLD QUINN WAS GIVEN THREE RULES TO FOLLOW,
AND HE'S ABOUT TO BREAK EVERY LAST ONE OF THEM.

STATION
FOSAAN

FIRE IN THE WOODS

JENNIFER M. EATON